Twice Upon a Time

Michael Combs

TWICE UPON A TIME

Copyright © 2022 by Michael Combs
Edited by Meghan Stoll
Book layout by Evernight Designs
Front cover photo by Nevodka, via Pond5
Internal photo by Capuski, via iStock
Back cover photos by Chelsea Audibert, and Ross van der Wal, via Unsplash and Vac, via Pond5
Cover design by Michael Combs
All rights reserved.
ISBN: 978-1-7359703-8-7

ACKNOWLEDGMENTS

To my beautiful bride Gwen, may we continue to find each other time after time.

Thank you to my mom, Glenda Combs, for always encouraging me to listen to music and write. I know this was always your favorite of all my manuscripts.

A special thank you to Jim Palculict for your invaluable knowledge and insight into long-term care facilities.

Thank you to the city of New Orleans, the Birthplace of Jazz, for capturing my soul. The moment I landed in the Crescent City, this story was set in motion.

Look in the back of this book for a preview of **The Long Road Home**

"How short is the longest Life—I wish to believe in immortality—I wish to live with you for ever."
-John Keats

THE LETTER

SEATTLE, Washington, July 1993. Chloé Taylor, who has just turned twenty-two, sits on a bench at the Pike Place Public Market, staring at an unopened letter in her hand.

Spanning over nine acres of the iconic Seattle waterfront of Elliott Bay is the oldest operating farmers market in the United States. Dating back to 1907, the Pike Place Public Market is a popular location for both tourists and locals. There one can find over five hundred restaurants, shops, local vendors, and bars. Also located there is the first Starbucks, which opened in 1971 and is still satisfying coffee enthusiasts to this day. As Chloé and many locals know, there is nowhere in the city better for the art of people-watching.

Chloé's jet-black hair blows in the breeze coming off the bay. Her pale white skin is commonplace in a city with more rain than shine. She was a good kid growing up, except for the usual problems teenagers cause during those crazy years of adolescence, such as crawling out her bedroom window late at night to hang out with friends on more than one occasion.

Having just completed her bachelor of fine arts degree at the University of Washington School of Art, Chloé is now faced with the big question: Now what? Today, however, there is even more than that weighing on her mind. Chloé was told for the first time almost a year ago that she had been adopted. Her entire life, she thought these two amazing people who raised her were her birth parents. These two Volkswagen bus-driving, outdoorsy, artist hippies from Vancouver, Washington who had taught her how to love everything and everyone, think outside the norm, and truly appreciate art and beauty, are not her real parents. To her, however, they will always be Mom and Dad.

Her adoptive parents told her what little they know of her birth family. Her biological parents were killed in a car accident when she was a baby. Chloé was told there was only one surviving member of her family, and that was her great-grandmother. Being close to eighty years old when Chloé's parents died, her great-grandmother would not have been able to raise her, so she found the best possible home for Chloé instead.

Chloé is soon joined on the bench by her best friend, Teresa Martin. Teresa is also twenty-two but with sandy blonde hair. She is one of the friends for whom teenage Chloé crawled out of her window. Unlike Chloé, Teresa did not go to college. She spends her time bartending and being heavily involved in the local music scene, which recently has erupted in Seattle. Chloé expects her to jump on a band tour bus one day and ride off to musical oblivion.

By way of greeting Chloé asks Teresa, "How long do you have left on your break?"

"Ten, maybe fifteen minutes."

"Has it been busy?"

"Not too bad."

Over all the chatter around them, they sit listening to a young man who could pass as Bob Dylan on the nearby curb singing and playing his guitar. Teresa is engrossed in the music, while Chloé's mind is on one thing: the letter.

Chloé recalls receiving the letter from her great-grand-mother almost a year ago. The day it came in the mail, her parents sat her down. They told her of her adoption and handed her the unopened letter. Along with her great-grand-mother, they had agreed not to disclose the adoption unless her great-grandmother initiated the contact. They were surprised to receive the letter after so many years had passed; they thought for sure the elderly woman had passed away by now. Having so much to take in that day, Chloé placed the letter on her desk, where it sat unopened. As each day passed, she kept saying every day, "Tomorrow, I will open it."

"Teresa… Teresa!" Chloé repeats, trying to get her attention away from the street performer.

Teresa responds while still looking away, "Yes?"

"I think today is the day."

"What day?"

"The day I will finally open this letter."

A long stretch of silence occurs. Finally giving Chloé her undivided attention, Teresa turns and replies, "Oh, that day? Wow! Are you sure?"

"Yes. I can't go on wondering what it says. I have to learn to accept what I can't change. I can't go on pretending in my mind that I wasn't adopted. I've felt this entire time that as long as I don't open the letter, then it's not true. But I can't go on thinking like that."

"Don't let it affect how you feel for your parents, no matter what it says. You have the most amazing parents I've ever known."

"No. Nothing will ever change the love I have for them."

"Good. Do you want to open it now, while I'm here?"

"No. No, thank you. I want to be alone, you know what I mean? I want to open it at home tonight. I hope you understand."

"Yes. I understand completely. But please call me if you need me."

"Thank you, I will."

"What do you think it will say?"

"I don't know. Hopefully it will give me some insight into where I came from and who my parents were."

"I for one cannot imagine not knowing my parents, much less knowing they were dead." Teresa puts her head down. "Sorry if that sounded bad."

"That's okay. It was a lot to take in a year ago and just as much to take in today, but I've accepted it. So, on a brighter note, are you and—was it Bobby this time?—still dating?"

"It was Billy, and not so bright of a note."

"I'm sorry," Chloé says.

"No worries. He was not an awfully bright note himself. He dumped me, but I'm telling myself and anyone who asks that I dumped him."

"What happened?"

"He was messing around with the blonde from Starbucks around the corner."

"Wow. What a jerk. I thought you said he dumped you?"

"Yeah. Well, he was, like, calling me Felicia while we were sleeping together. I thought, Felicia, Teresa, well, they sound alike."

"No, not really. No way did you think that was an honest mistake."

Teresa shrugs. "Well, I did the first twenty or thirty times."

"Twenty or thirty times! What the hell?"

"I couldn't help it. As they say, hindsight is twenty-something-or-other. Besides, I liked him."

"You could have put a freaking Post-it note on your forehead saying, 'Hey jackass, my name is Teresa.'"

"I don't think it would have made a difference. As I said, he wasn't too bright. Okay, so we went to Starbucks, and the blonde behind the counter kept smiling at him. I looked at her name badge, and it said Felicia. So I asked him about it, and he said he has been seeing her also and said he likes her just a little more than me."

"Just a little?" Chloé repeats sarcastically.

"Yeah, just a little. So, that was it. He wasn't a hugely talented guitar player anyway. Deep Sea was his third band this year. No big loss." Teresa tilts down her sunglasses as a young man in jeans and a T-shirt walks by. "Let me just say there are other fish in the deep sea, and I just got my fishing license back."

"Gotcha. Fish all you want. I don't want any part of it. I don't miss the dating game at all."

Teresa looks at her wrist to one of the five watches she is wearing—a fashion statement she has had since high school. "Oh dammit! It is so much later than I thought."

"How is it you can have that many watches and always be running late?"

"I have no idea. I wish I could stay here all day, but I've got to get back to work. So please, please call me later."

"I will. I promise." They hug and kiss cheeks as they both stand to leave.

Once home, Chloé goes to her room, sits at her desk, and places the letter in front of her. It is addressed from Camille Laver, New Orleans, Louisiana. Chloé reaches into the desk drawer, retrieves a letter opener, and cautiously opens the envelope she has held for almost a year.

Paris, 1895

THE 1890s in Paris are a time of transition and expression. The divide between the upper and lower classes has become increasingly evident during this time of colliding thoughts, ideas, and beliefs impacting the city. There is much uncertainty in letting go of the old and welcoming a new, intensely creative period of free thinkers, writers, and artists and the beginning of a new century. Many Parisians refer to this time as the La Belle Epoque, or the Beautiful Era. In many societies, generations reflect with fondness on their past; in Paris during the La Belle Epoque, however, a few realize the significance of the times as they are transpiring.

THE WOODEN WHEEL of a covered horse-drawn carriage strikes a rut hidden by a puddle, splashing water from the recent rain in the Montmartre district. This sector of Paris has become the center of entertainment after dark, with its dance halls and bohemian lifestyles. As the coach comes to a stop, stepping out is René Nattier, a thirty-year-old, handsome, mustachioed gentleman dressed in a dashing black tuxedo, frock coat, and top hat. Greeting him instantly is Pierre, the valet.

"Bonjour, Monsieur Nattier. Welcome back to the Moulin Rouge. We have been expecting you." René traverses the red carpet before him, smiles back at Pierre, and enters the dance hall, tipping his hat as he passes the doorman.

The rich are rising fast in Paris, and René is at the top of his social class. He is a banker like his father, Charles Nattier, but that is where any comparability ends. The family is wealthy, aristocratic, strict Catholic, and ruled by its banker patriarch's philosophy: Money is success, success is power, and power is happiness. This creed has always caused René much perplexity, as it conflicts with everything he feels; for inside, he is a bohemian romantic—a true lover of romance and the arts. René frowns on the social class to which he belongs. He feels his happiness is trapped by his past, chained by his present, and stripped from his future. While Charles's happiness might well be questioned by René, however, his power and success definitely are not.

THINGS ARE PROMISING IN PARIS, but the United States is experiencing a severe two-year depression that began with the panic of 1893. It was the worst economic crisis the country had ever experienced. It all started with failed crops, drops in the silver market, the bursting of the railroad bubble, and a run on the gold supply. By 1895, the United States' gold reserve has dwindled; however, American financier JP Morgan has a plan. Backed by President Grover Cleveland, the JP Morgan Company forms an international syndicate in 1895 to sell $65 million in gold bonds as a means to buy back gold from foreign investors. On February 20, 1895, the bonds are offered for $112.25 each. They sell out within twenty-two minutes, subsequently protecting the United States Treasury. A driving force in this consortium is Charles Nattier. The plan works flawlessly. JP Morgan is highly impressed with Nattier, and a friendship grows between the two colleagues.

THE MOULIN ROUGE, a dance hall and bordello, was opened in 1889 by Harry Zidler. Looking up the building's facade, one sees Adolphe Willette's creation, a giant windmill with bright red sails. Inside, the Moulin Rouge has a large dance floor surrounded by areas where onlookers can sit and drink. A garden area features a large plaster elephant that contains a small stage and an opium den. Lights hung in the trees illuminate the outside access to the main bar. It is much nicer than the other dance halls outside the city walls. Gentlemen of all classes escape here to satisfy their guilty pleasures and see the can-can dancers lift their skirts and petticoats, losing modesty in all their gaiety.

René is seated at his regular spot next to Toulouse-Lautrec's personal table. Henri de Toulouse-Lautrec, a popular Post-Impressionist French artist who is drawn to Montmartre for its bohemian lifestyle, can usually be found at the Moulin Rouge sketching one of his commissioned posters or paintings. He often drinks with René; however, the two have an agreement to never discuss politics or religion but only art and pleasure. Mostly, though, Toulouse-Lautrec focuses on his sketches while they converse.

René is not there to sketch or smoke cigars and delve into the latest conversation regarding what many call "the new monstrosity"—the recently built Eiffel Tower—and how long it will stand before it falls. No, he is there for one thing, and that is to see Tessa Elizabeth Laver. Her stage name is Jane Pierre. Tessa is a beautiful brunette with pale skin, almost a milky white, and a beauty mark on her right cheek. Unlike the other dancers, whose natural features are buried under layers of caked-on makeup, she has a natural beauty.

Tessa was born in 1874 and raised by her gypsy family, who settled in Lower Montmartre. They struggled to survive, and as a teenager, Tessa surrendered her innocence, not for love but for money—something she has spent her life regretting.

Besides a desire for true love, Tessa has had one great passion ever since she was a child: painting. She has created many works, but no one has taken any interest in them. She wants to be the next Vuillard, Bonnard, Pissarro, or Toulouse-Lautrec, but fate can play cruel tricks on our dreams. Once she posed for Bouguereau, known as the master of nudes, but she wishes to be behind the easel, not in front of it. She knows chances are against her; however, she also knows she needs to paint, for she feels the brush is an extension of her soul—a soul yearning for life. It is her escape, her sanctuary from the empty life she has lived.

René glimpses Tessa off to the side of the stage encased by corsets, petticoats, and flowering undergarments. She blows him a kiss. After the show, he is escorted backstage, where he pulls Tessa against him and passionately kisses her. Tessa knows with this kiss, as with all the others before, that René truly loves her. She knows she should be the happiest person in the world. She has all she has ever wanted, but her heart is torn, for René has a wife and a family. This is common for the time, and René's home is no different than other upper-class households; mistresses of married aristo-crats are never discussed there. Like a puppet in a shadow play, Tessa feels like a silhouette in the background. Some might call it a comfortable denial, but she calls it her agony. She often wonders who has it harder, the wife or the mistress. She ponders that perhaps we must accept the reality of a small speck of darkness entangling each bright, brilliant, beautiful, wonderful thing that happens in our lives. She sees this with all the beautiful facets of life, from her unrecognized artistic ability to her shared love for René and her precious Camille—her three-year-old daughter who has no father.

René, with his hands around her waist, tells her, "Let us go for a picnic tomorrow at the Bois de Vincennes."

The Bois de Vincennes, located on the eastern edge of Paris, is the largest park in the city. It was created by

Emperor Louis Napoleon as a green space for the working class. Of the four lakes in the park, Tessa loves most of all the Lac Daumesnil with its two picturesque islands. One of them, the Isle de Reuilly, features the Temple of Love, a design by city architect Jean-Antoine-Gabriel Davioud. It is a round Greek temple nestled above an artificial grotto. This is her favorite place, for it is where René kissed her for the first time.

She hesitates in responding, but not because she does not want to go there with him. She loves him but knows too well the pain she will feel at the end of the day when he goes back to his wife, always back to her.

"Yes?" he asks.

She nods her head in approval.

"I will pick you up at ten o'clock tomorrow morning."

"Okay," she replies softly.

"Okay?"

She replies again, this time more confidently and with a smile, "Yes."

René looks at her and smiles back. Then he pulls a document from his coat pocket. "I have a surprise for you," he says.

"What is it? You know I love surprises."

He hands it to her, and she opens it cautiously but with the excitement of a child on Christmas morning. She begins reading it aloud. It is an announcement of art to be on display the following week inside the Palais Garnier.

She loves going to art exhibits with René. Even though this isn't an exhibit in the natural sense, it is still a chance to see and appreciate beautiful art, visit the Palais Garnier, and, most importantly, spend precious time with René.

The Palais Garnier is a nearly two thousand-seat opera house with a vast, magnificent foyer and an elegant staircase. Designed by architect Charles Garnier, it is destined to be immortalized in later years, in part as the setting of the 1910 novel by Gaston Leroux, *The Phantom of the Opera*. It features a gorgeous seven-ton bronze and crystal chandelier hanging above the audience. Tessa often remarks that it might be the most beautiful building in the world.

René prompts her, "Continue reading."

"Featuring the art of Toulouse-Lautrec, Bonnard…" She pauses. "Tessa Laver? But that is me!" she exclaims.

Smiling, he responds, "Yes, it is."

A few years earlier, this never would have happened. Women of the time were not respected in the realm of art. Dabbling work by women, such as watercolor, was applauded; it was considered disadvantageous, however, for them to attempt Realism. It was said doing so would distract them from their appointed responsibilities as wives and mothers. As the century comes to a close, however, times and beliefs are changing.

Tessa throws her arms around René with tears rolling down her cheek. "How did this happen?" she asks.

"I took some of your work there, and with a little persuading, it was done," he replies.

René will not reveal it, but even though some opinions about female artists are evolving, it actually took a lot of persuading. Sadly, the persuading to include her paintings had to take place only after it was realized a woman had created them, but he knew as well as they did that her paintings were better than those of many of her male peers.

She hugs him again, crying, "I love you, I love you, I love you!"

René interrupts her by placing his hands on her cheeks and pulling her lips to his. Following his kiss, he asks, "So are you happy?"

"Of course I am!"

"I am glad I could surprise you, beautiful."

"Yes, you did. Thank you. You have no idea what this means to me."

"I think I do. That is why I did it."

"Oh, thank you. Do you think they will like my work?"

"I know they will. The ones who have already seen it already do. That is why they choose yours. You are going to be the most famous artist in Paris."

She beams. "Do you think so?"

"I know so."

"We should celebrate."

He pauses. "Tomorrow. I promise."

Tessa looks down at the ground, and her smile fades. She knows he has to go home to his wife. "Yes, tomorrow," she responds softly. "Yes, tomorrow."

THE NEXT MORNING ARRIVES—FOLLOWED by the afternoon—and René does not call on her. Tessa tries to occupy her mind. She hopes that maybe this evening, instead, they will go to mingle at the Faubourg Saint-Germain, which is a hostel to artists and writers who share their works, or to some of the poetry recitations taking place in friends' basements across the city. It is an age of creativity for the youth of Paris, and she wants to be part of it.

This is not the first time over the last two years of their relationship when René has not come when promised. She knows Diana is the reason. As much as René romances about love, he does not love his wife. She was chosen for him, not by him. The same was true for her. Theirs is a marriage of two great banking families but not of two souls. They have kept separate bedrooms from the beginning. Anyone who knows the couple may wonder in amazement how they have managed to allow themselves to be close enough to each other to have three children. Perhaps the children, too, were manufactured along with the marriage. He feels as lonely with Diana as he does without. She is everything about society he despises. She once ridiculed him when he crossed the boulevard to give a starving child money for food. She was distressed not only because he offered the child ten francs but even more because of the fear someone they knew might see him speaking to the underclass.

As the day progresses, Tessa spends time with Camille at their flat. Together they live in the Plaine-Monceau, a new district of flats, where René pays the rent. One would assume she has everything, but inside she is yearning. She has so much love to give, if she only had René to herself.

Tessa prepares her paint and canvas as the night begins to fall, along with a light snow. In the distance, she hears the approaching carriage. Camille races to the window and wipes away the condensation from the glass with her little hand so she can see out. René is not her father, but he is the only man she has ever known, and she always becomes excited when he arrives. He often brings a small toy for her. Camille answers the door and gives him a huge hug.

"Where might your beautiful mother be?" he asks. In reply, she points to the other room. He tells her, "Now close your eyes," as he places a doll in her hands. "Okay. Open them." Camille squeals and hugs him again.

Tessa enters the room and starts to rush into his arms as usual, but this time something stops her. Such concern clouds René's face that her heart and the room fill with fear.

He tells Camille, "Go to the other room now and play with your doll."

She holds up the doll. "See, Mommy. Look what René brought me."

"Yes, I see. Did you thank him?"

She turns to René. "Thank you."

"You are welcome, Camille."

"Now go play," Tessa tells her.

Clutching the doll tightly to her chest, she quickly exits the room, skipping with a smile.

René is the first to break the silence. "I'm sorry I could not make it today."

"It is her again. I know it is." There is silence in the room. "It is always her."

She knows René has a good heart. He has always been good to her. He brings her beautiful dresses, fresh flowers, and a borrowed heart. In return, Tessa gives him pleasures many have known but a love no other has received. She is afraid to lose him, but she knows you have to have something completely before you can lose it. Even though she has his heart, another has a more legitimate claim on him.

She goes to turn, but he grabs her wrists and pulls her to him, saying, "It is not her this time. I love you more than life itself, but I have something important to tell you."

He looks as if he is losing everything. Deep down in his heart, perhaps he knows he is.

With a terrified, softly trembling voice, she asks, "What is it? What is wrong, René?" He leans in to kiss her. She stops him. "No… René, tell me what it is."

He says, as a tear forms in his eye, "I am leaving for America."

"America? When? When are you returning?"

"I will not be returning."

"What do you mean? Why?!" she cries out.

"My father has been given an opportunity there. He feels there are uncertain times ahead here in Paris and believes America is the right choice. We leave for New Orleans in a month."

"That is your father, René. Why do *you* have to go?"

"He asked me to join him. He is right. It is my responsibility as a Nattier to stand together as a family."

"Tell him you will not go."

"I must go, but I will send for you upon our arrival and find a place for you and Camille there."

Tessa knows his wife and father will not allow him to send for her. If he leaves, she will never see him again. She does not want to live in America; she loves Paris. What will happen to her home now? To Camille? They will end up on the street, and Camille will grow up living a life of desperation, struggling to survive like her mother.

"No, you will not send for me. She will not let you."

He pleads for her understanding. "I will!"

Crying, with her head buried in his chest, she begs him. "Please, René, do not go."

"I have to."

In tears, she screams out as she begins violently punching at him and screaming. "Then go! Leave! Get out!"

He grabs her wrists and pleads with her as he turns to the door. "I am sorry! I am sorry! I will send for you! I promise I will."

As the door closes behind him, she throws a vase, striking the wall, and collapses to the floor in tears.

Camille runs into the room and throws her arms around Tessa's neck. "Mommy, what is wrong?"

Tessa collects herself, hugging Camille. "It is okay, my angel. Mommy just fell. She fell really hard."

ALL NIGHT LONG, René is heartbroken by the thought of losing Tessa. What if she is right, and he cannot send for her? His father told him to tie up or cut off all loose ends before leaving. Perhaps this is precisely what he meant. Perhaps his father considers Tessa and Camille to be loose ends. He has never approved of them. After hours of deep thought, René concludes that he will tell his father he is staying here and face the economic uncertainty of the future here in Paris. He knows his happiness is with Tessa. Nothing else matters. Without her, there will be no happiness in life—no future whatsoever.

The next morning at his home, located off the Avenue des Champs-Élysées, René gets dressed. He is preparing to visit his father to inform him of his decision before returning to Tessa to let her know he will never leave her side.

Suddenly there is a knock on the door. René opens the door to find two police officers. Standing by their carriage is Camille wearing a cloak, staring at the ground. He knows why they are there before the first officer even says a word.

"I am sorry to disturb you, sir, and to be the one to tell you, but this little girl's mother took her own life last night. The neighbor was roused this morning by the girl outside her door, saying her mother wouldn't wake up. I would not have come by, but there was a letter for you."

René falls to his knees, covering his eyes. His wife peers outside but quickly walks back into the house to hide her embarrassment.

The second police officer says, "Sir, here is a letter she left for you. I took it upon myself to read it. In it, she asks that you take care of her little girl. If you prefer, however, we will take her up to the orphanage."

René takes the note from the officer as he stands and collects himself, still in tears. He reads the letter to himself. He then dismisses the officers, saying, "That is fine. I will take care of her. Also, I will be going by and collecting her things from her flat. If you could, please inform the landlord."

"We will do, sir."

"Thank you for your time, officers." He hands one of the officers some money from his wallet.

The officer responds, surprised and eager, "Thank you. Thank you, sir."

Then René motions for Camille to come to him. As she approaches, she has a tear in her eye and asks, "When will Mommy be here?"

With no reply, he hugs her tight, and tears again begin to fall.

THE NEXT DAY René enters Tessa's home. With the help of hired hands, he places her personal belongings into crates to take with them to America. On her mantle is a jar he gave her on their second anniversary together. Inside are 730 small pieces of paper, each with a handwritten reason he loves her —one for each day they had been together. All of Camille's dolls and Tessa's paintings are crated, including one he holds exceptionally dear: a self-portrait of Tessa. This would be the visual memory he and Camille would cherish of her beautiful mother.

René is taken aback when he discovers an unfinished painting concealed beneath a drop cloth on Tessa's easel. It is three-fourths completed. She was working on this the day she took her life. The painting is a family portrait of Tessa, Camille, and himself. This, he thinks, would have been her masterpiece—all she ever wanted in life, on canvas. Just as the painting will remain incomplete with her passing, so ends any possibility of Tessa's dream coming true. At that moment, René realizes his happiness and his future died with Tessa. He knows, however, that he must be strong. He has Camille to protect, and he knows the days ahead with Diana will be truly difficult.

.   .   .

THE SHIP appropriately named Paris sails out of Southampton on its way to America. René holds Camille on his shoulder as she waves goodbye to the only world she has known. The trip is long, but Camille spends every evening on deck in awe of the beautifully seeded night sky. René loves to point out the brightest star in the darkness.

He says, "See that star there?"

"The really bright one?"

"Yes, that bright one. It is called Arcturus."

"Arcturus?"

"That is your mommy watching over us. Whenever you miss her, look for her in the sky."

"What if it is daytime?"

"The stars are always there. Just because you cannot see her does not mean she cannot see you."

UPON REACHING AMERICA, René and his family settle on a large plantation right outside of New Orleans. After a few years, their new life becomes easier on both René and Camille. However, Diana never accepts Camille as part of their family. She always refers to her as the bastard child. Camille soon learns how to turn a deaf ear to her, and René is enduringly beside the girl, always reminding her how beautiful she is, just like her mother. René, for his part, learns that he did not know how much he loved Tessa until he lost her. He now knows he lost much more than a friend and lover. He lost his soul mate, but he discovers in raising Camille that Tessa lives on.

New Orleans

Sitting at her desk, Chloé begins to second-guess her decision but collects her courage. The letter opener breaks the seal, slides completely across the envelope. Taking a deep breath, she removes the letter and unfolds it slowly, feeling the texture of the paper. It has an old smell, like something you would find in an antique store.

Finally, Chloé looks at the handwritten letter in front of her. She is shocked that it is so short—in fact, not even half a page. Confusion and frustration fill her mind. As she begins to read, running through her head are countless questions about why her great-grandmother, whom she has never met and is her last living blood relative, would send a letter about her family history that does not even fill up one page.

Dear Chloé,

My dear, I am sorry it has taken this long to write you. I have struggled terribly through the years about whether to contact you. My name is Camille Laver. I am your great-grandmother. I am certain by the time you are reading this letter your parents have spoken to you. I know they are wonderful people, and I do not want you to view them negatively. They were only granting me my request of silence. I am getting quite old. I recently turned 100. I would like for you to come to see me here in New Orleans. There are things I need to show you, things I need to share with you, things you need to know about your family. I am the last one left to tell you about the happiness and tragedy that make up who we are. Please make haste. I will be waiting for you.

Love,

Camille

Chloé, stunned, stares blankly at the letter, then rereads

each word. Guilt rushes over her for waiting so long to open it. She asks herself, "Why could she not tell me what she had to show me? What is it she has to share with me that she could not have placed in the letter?" And the biggest question: "Is she still alive?"

"I must know," she says aloud. "I must know about my family. I must know who I really am. I must go to New Orleans."

Once her dad makes it home from work, Chloé goes downstairs with the letter. Her parents see it in her hand and know what is coming next. They all sit down in the living room, her mother gripping her father's hand. Chloé sits across from them and reads the letter aloud.

Her mom speaks first. "Oh Chloé, I know I've told you before, but again I want you to know, so many times we wanted to tell you."

"I know, Mom."

Her dad adds, "We love you so much. Whatever you want to do, we will back you 100 percent. If you want to go, we can go with you. I still have many friends there we can stay with."

"Yes, I want to go," Chloé responds. "I need to go, but I want to go alone."

"Are you sure, sweetheart?" her mom asks.

"Yes, I'm sure."

After talking with her parents, Chloé calls Teresa. Like her parents, Teresa offers to go with her, and Chloé considers the offer but feels this is something she has to do alone. She wastes no time packing for her trip, and Teresa comes over to help. The first things Chloé gathers are several pieces of her artwork to show Camille.

While packing, Teresa asks, "So, do you think there are any cute guys in New Orleans?"

"Honestly, I have no idea. Men are the last thing I have on my mind."

"I'm just saying, if you want me to go to distract the men away from you, I would definitely be there for you."

Chloé rolls her eyes. "I think I can handle myself."

"Seriously though, if you need me, call me."

Laughing, Chloé says, "I will. Thank you, but I think I have this."

They hear a knock on her door, and Chloé's dad enters. He tells her, "Hey sweetheart, here is my American Express card, and I have your flight and hotel reservations confirmed. All the information, including the info for our friends who live there, is in this folder."

Chloé takes the folder from her father and hugs him. "Thank you, Dad."

ALL NIGHT LONG, Chloé struggles to sleep, wondering what adventures await her in New Orleans. Both parents drive her to the airport the following morning. They worry about her going to New Orleans alone but know this is something she has to do, and they do not try to persuade her otherwise.

At the airport, her dad reminds her, "Don't forget the names and numbers for all of our friends are in the folder I gave you. Call them if you need anything in case you cannot get a hold of us. Also, call us when you get to your hotel."

"I will. Thank you. I love you both so much."

Her mom tells her, "We love you, too."

Chloé hugs them both. Her dad holds up two fingers in

his usual peace sign and she returns it, just as she has done since she was little.

CHLOÉ'S FLIGHT to New Orleans from Seattle is uneventful, with only a short layover in Denver. Upon arriving at Louis Armstrong Airport, she peruses the gift shop while waiting for a taxi. Once in the cab, the driver asks her, "So, where ya from?"

"Seattle."

"Seattle! F'true? Dat a long way away, f'sure. Welcome to New Awlans. Where ya goin'?"

"The Ambassador Hotel."

"Irite, hold on there, fren'. Here we go."

Suddenly the driver turns up the radio and begins singing with all his might, in the highest pitch possible, the song "What's Up" by the 4 Non Blondes. Chloé is trying to hold back laughter because she cannot help but notice how the song does not seem to match the look of the driver, a four-hundred-pound-plus muscular man with long dreads. He not only looks like Bob Marley, she thinks, but he looks like he ate Bob Marley. The cab's interior features the stereotypical purple fuzzy dice hanging from the rearview mirror, a green pine tree air freshener, and a felt-lined ceiling with pink fringe hanging around the edges. Also, she cannot fail to notice the Jerry Garcia bobblehead right next to the Black Jesus bobblehead on the dash.

She breaks her thoughts away from the eclectic cab experience and starts to plan for her visit to see Camille the next morning. This is her first trip to New Orleans, but already she feels truly at home here, a feeling she has never felt before anywhere. It seems to be a charming city, from what she has witnessed so far, and to have much more spice than she is used to.

. . .

CHLOÉ CHECKS in at the Ambassador Hotel and is assisted with her luggage up to her room. "What a perfect hotel," she thinks, "to begin my visit to New Orleans!"

She tells the bellhop as they enter her room, "The hotel is beautiful. The exposed brick walls take me back in time. Has this always been a hotel?"

"No, the hotel was once a coffee warehouse in the nineteenth century," he replies. "This part of the city is called the Warehouse District. I think you'll really like it here. The location is excellent, only a few blocks from the French Quarter as well as from the Mississippi River and the River Walk."

"I hope I find the time to see it all. So far, it is perfect here."

"Will you need anything else, ma'am?"

As she tips him, she says, "No. Thank you."

"Thank you, ma'am. Enjoy your stay."

Her room is breathtaking with its high ceiling, hardwood floors, exposed brick and beams, wrought iron bed, tall windows, and—her favorite part—an eighteenth-century-styled writing desk. The man at the front desk was right when he said, "The Ambassador is a blend of the old and the new, much like the city herself."

After calling her parents to let them know she arrived safely, and feeling a little tired but extremely hungry, she decides to find somewhere to eat. Not knowing the city, she stops and asks the concierge. He gives her several options, including the restaurant in the hotel. Wanting to see a little of the town, she thinks Arnaud's Restaurant sounds perfect and calls for a cab. In Seattle, she would walk, but she is not used to the city yet.

The concierge at the front desk is full of information. "Arnaud's is located just steps from Bourbon Street in the heart of the French Quarter," he informs Chloé. "It opened back in 1918 and has expanded through eleven buildings over the years. Their menu is amazing, serving classic Creole dishes. There you can find live jazz, drink at an award-winning bar, or have a romantic dinner in one of their thirteen private dining rooms."

Chloé tells him, "I am definitely not looking for romance, but the food sounds really good after only having crackers on my flight."

UPON ARRIVING at the crowded restaurant Chloé is greeted by the maître d'. Looking around, she does not miss the original ornate tile floors. She notices the tuxedoed wait staff, and she feels a little underdressed—well, perhaps a lot—in her sundress and flats. The extremely nice and polite maître d' tells her that there will be a long wait without a reservation. She is discouraged at this news and begins to leave, thinking she would go back to the Ambassador's restaurant. As her head pivots automatically at the sound of the music coming from the Jazz Room, she catches the eye of a tall, dark-haired man returning from the restroom who overhears the maître d'.

The man tells the maître d' and Chloé, "I am here alone. If she would like, I would be more than happy for her to sit with me in my private dining room."

Their eyes stay locked on one another, both feeling like they have come across an old friend but unable to place a name. At first Chloé has no thought beyond "This man has a face sculpted by the gods and the presence of a king." Then she shakes herself mentally and admits to herself, "Well, okay, maybe that's exaggerated, but he is pretty handsome."

She is not the only one impressed, for the young gentleman is also smitten with her.

Normally Chloé would decline such an offer, being reserved, but something inside her takes over. "Yes, if you don't mind."

"No, not at all. I would be honored."

"Why of course, Mr. Nattier," the maître d' says. "Excellent. Right this way, madam."

They enter the private dining room, which is gorgeous. There are antique furnishings, a crystal chandelier, plush carpet, and rich draperies in the room. The waiter greets them and seats her first. The young man stands until she sits down. At six foot four, he is tall with well-groomed dark brown hair, a broad chest, and blue eyes she cannot seem to take her eyes off of.

He tells Chloé, "I am reminded of what the founder of the restaurant, Arnaud Cazenave, once said: 'At least once a day, one should throw all care to the winds, relax completely, and dine leisurely and well.' Hello. My name is Nicholas Nattier, but you can call me Nick. And you are?"

Chloé pauses for a moment, soaking in his Southern accent. "My name is Chloé Taylor." Laughing at herself, she thinks, "If Teresa could see me now... I've only been in New Orleans two hours and already have a dinner date."

"So what brings you here, Chloé? I can tell by your lack of accent that you are not from this area."

"I am in New Orleans to see my great-grandmother— actually to meet her for the first time."

"First time? Well, I believe we should celebrate that. Please let me pour you a glass of wine. I would like to hear more about your great-grandmother," he says while reaching for the bottle of wine on the table.

Holding up her hand, she says, "No, that's all right."

"Come on. One glass on me. I insist."

He is persuasive, so she agrees, "Okay, just one glass," but thinks, "I'd better stay on my toes with this one. He's exactly what I am not looking for and the last thing I need right now."

Nick pours her glass. "So tell me about yourself and about your great-grandmother."

"Let me see. I am from Seattle."

"Wow, Seattle. Seattle is a great city. There is great music coming out of there. Pearl Jam, Nirvana, Soundgarden... Sorry, go on."

"No, that is fine. There really is. My best friend knows Chris Cornell, the lead singer of Soundgarden, personally."

"Wow, that is cool. He has an amazing voice. Again, sorry, go on."

"Well, I just turned twenty-two, and in May, I finished college with my degree from the University of Washington School of Art. So, I am here in New Orleans because I found out almost a year ago I was adopted. I have no brothers or sisters that I know of, and in fact, my great-grandmother here is more than likely the only surviving member of my birth family, if she is still alive."

"Still alive? You mean you are not sure?"

"No, I'm not. I got a letter almost a year ago saying she wants to meet me. If she is, she will be one hundred years old."

"Wow! One hundred. Seriously? I hope I live that long. Are you nervous?"

"I can't tell whether it's nervousness or I'm just anxious. Either way, I know I have to do it. My entire life, my adoptive parents have been great. They are fun-loving hippies and even drive a stereotypical 1973 Volkswagen Bus."

"Sound like my kind of people."

"Mr. Nattier, you do not take me as the hippie type, with your short hair and suit. You are noticeably clean cut."

"That's Nick, and oh, believe me. Never judge a book by its cover. Or a hippie by his hair." They both laugh.

"Well, they have been so supportive of me, and I will always consider them my real parents." She pauses. "Wow, that is probably more than you wanted to know."

While topping off her glass of wine, he says, "No, I think it's all great. So, do you have any boyfriends back in Seattle? That is, if you do not mind me asking."

She pauses, curious about his intent. "No, not at all. There's no one currently. I had a three-year relationship, but we broke it off last year. So what about you? Inside that cover, what kind of book would I find?"

"First of all, no… no boyfriends either," Nick replies, making Chloé laugh.

"You know what I mean. Tell me about you. For instance, you don't sound like someone from New Orleans."

"Oh, you mean I don't talk like this—'How da wedda, ma fren'. You gotz to hear dis joke awrite, 'bout da quarter, f'ture.'" They both laugh again.

"Yeah, now you sound like my cab driver today. You do not sound like that," she says.

"That's because I was raised and live in the Garden District here in New Orleans. That dialect you heard from your cab driver is called Yat. I have always thought it sounds a little like Brooklyn meets Boston. Different parts of town have different dialects. And for the rest, well, I'm twenty-eight years old—approaching thirty quickly. I was born and raised here in New Orleans. My family arrived here in 1895. They came over from France."

"Ah, the Nattier, a nice French name," she says.

"That's right. In fact, my family has been coming to this restaurant since it opened in 1918. So, as you can imagine, I never have to wait for a table. It changed hands in '78, but our respected name carried over." He pauses. "Let us see. What else? Oh, I'm a lawyer."

"Really?" she replies, a little surprised. "That explains the clean-cut look."

"Nothing exciting. Just a real estate attorney. Kind of boring, actually. One day…" He pauses, looking around and lowering his voice. "I want you to know only a few people know this, but I would like to open my own bar and restaurant. I just have not taken the leap. I know what I want and I have some of the money saved to do it."

"So what is stopping you? That is quite a leap, from lawyer to restaurant owner."

He just looks down at his glass, lost in thought, so she does not pry.

Then he says, "And no, no girlfriend or wife." He holds up his bare ring finger. "I was engaged for a while but realized she was not the right one."

"So, what makes a woman the right one?" Chloé asks, then pauses, embarrassed. "I'm sorry. I should not ask that. That was so forward"—her voice cracks nervously—"and I am not trying to be forward."

Nick stops her by placing his hand momentarily on hers, sending chills up her arm. "It's okay. The right one… Well, she has to be smart, independent, creative, caring, funny, and open-minded. I will not say beautiful, but there has to be a mutual attraction, and she has to want ten children…." There is another pause as they both break into laughter. "Just kidding, of course, about the creative part." Again they laugh. "Let us just say, Ms. Wrong only had the smart and mutual attraction going for her."

AFTER THEY ORDER and get their dinner, Chloé remarks, "The food here is incredible."

"Is this your first time to have Cajun food?"

"Yes, and I think I'm hooked. I'm used to a lot of sushi."

"Sushi? That is like raw fish?"

"It can sometimes be."

"Not for me. I like my food cooked."

"I thought you said you liked open-mindedness?"

"Well… hmm… So what do you think of New Orleans so far?"

"It has only been a few hours, but the people seem amazing and noticeably laid back."

"Yes. I am a big Tennessee Williams fan, and he once said he felt a freedom here. A place he could catch his breath. Many other authors described the city as the 'Greenwich Village of the South.' I have always liked that description."

As they proceed through dinner and another glass of wine, Chloé realizes Nick is harmless. But, feeling tired after the long day of travel, she eventually looks at the clock on the wall. "I cannot believe it is that late. I have really enjoyed this evening with you, and thank you for allowing me to join you for dinner."

"You are truly welcome. And do not worry about the check. Dinner's on me."

"Are you sure?"

"I insist."

"Wow. You have made my first night in New Orleans absolutely special, Mr. Nattier. Thank you."

"You are certainly welcome. I do insist, however, you let me drive you back to your hotel and that you call me Nick."

"I can get a cab, Nick."

"Nonsense. I insist. You are a pretty girl in an unfamiliar city. I will not be able to sleep unless I make sure you make it back safely."

"All right, then. If you insist," she says as they stand up.

"I do."

He has truly impressed her, which is not easy for anyone to do.

. . .

ARRIVING AT THE AMBASSADOR, Nick stops in the street, jumps out of his black Porsche 911 Carrera Convertible, and hurries to her side to open the door.

Helping her out of the car, he says, "Perhaps I can call on you while you are here and give you a local's tour of my city."

She replies, "*Your* city?"

"Yes, my city." He laughs.

"I would like that. Actually, I would really like that." She takes a piece of paper and a pen from her purse and begins writing. She jumps and laughs each time a passing car honks at them for being parked in the street. "Here is my room number. Just call the hotel and ask for my room."

"Here is my business card. I hope your visit with your great-grandmother goes well." In a humorous tone and with a bow, he adds, "Until I see you again, I bid you a goodnight, fair lady," as another car honks. Then, he takes a more serious tone and looks into her eyes. "Sweet dreams, Chloé."

She says, smiling, "Sweet dreams to you, too, good sir."

He yells at the next honking car. "I am moving! I am moving!"

The whole way back to her room, she is giggling and skipping like a schoolgirl with her first crush.

As she prepares for bed, thoughts of Nick continue to pop into her mind, but soon they are replaced by anxiety for the following morning. She wonders what she might discover. "Will I find Camille still alive?" she thinks. "If she is, will she be upset with me for waiting so long?"

Only with the rising sun will she have any answers.

THERE IS A HOUSE
IN NEW ORLEANS

THE FOLLOWING morning Chloé wakes in her hotel room, smiling immensely at memories of the previous night. She rises and walks over to the desk, the bottom of her nightgown brushing the hardwood floor as she takes a seat. Feeling an equal amount of excitement and anxiety, she begins planning her day. After writing down several questions to ask Camille, she calls her parents, followed by Teresa.

Teresa answers, "Hello."

"Well, I made it."

"So, how is New Orleans? Any cute boys there?" When Chloé does not respond, Teresa squeals, "Oh my god, there are! Did you meet someone?" Again no reply from Chloé. Squealing again—"Oh my god, you did!"

After a long pause, Chloé says, "Kinda."

"Kinda there are cute guys, or kinda you met someone?"

"Kinda both."

"Oh my god! So tell me about him. Does he have a job? Is he single?"

"Yes, he's single, and he's a lawyer."

"A lawyer! Holy wow! Does he have a brother?"

Laughing, Chloé replies, "First off, he's just someone really nice who let me join him for dinner."

"Dinner? Do you mean you already had a date? You just got there last night."

"It wasn't really a date. The restaurant was packed, and he offered me a seat with him at his table."

"Well, either way, I'm impressed. Are you sure you don't need me there to chaperone you?"

"I am sure of it, but I do miss you."

"Well, okay. I miss you too."

"Listen, I need to get ready to go see Camille. Wish me luck."

"You have it. Good luck, and keep me up to date on how that goes as well as how it goes with Mr. Lawyer."

"His name is Nick."

"Oh my god, he has a name." In a deeper voice, she says his name. "Nick... Nice, strong, sexy name."

"Good lord. Okay, I really have to go now."

"Okay, good luck. Love you."

"Love you too, bye-bye."

"Bye."

AFTER SHOWERING AND GETTING DRESSED, Chloé goes downstairs for breakfast. Arriving in the hotel restaurant, she discovers all the tables are full, so she is considering skipping breakfast when suddenly she hears a woman's voice behind her.

"You are more than welcome to sit with me, young lady."

Turning to find the source of the voice, Chloé sees a woman in perhaps her late eighties sitting alone. Making out her face is difficult due to the hat the lady is wearing. It has nine purple three-foot-long feathers rising from the left side of the large round brim. On the other side, a dark purple pom-pom flutters, larger than a basketball. But what graces the top of the hat is most shocking of all: a full-size stuffed peacock, as purple as the rest. The lady beneath it is wearing a dress of the same color with her ears, neck, and wrists covered in matching costume jewelry.

Before Chloé can get the words out to respond, a server passes by and whispers in her ear. "She is harmless."

With that bit of information, Chloé responds to the request smiling. "Thank you. If you do not mind?"

Sternly the lady responds, "If I minded, dear, I would not have asked you. Plus, I would not mind the company. When you get old, it is hard to find good company."

She sits down, a little intimidated, and introduces herself. "Hello, my name is Chloé."

"My name is Madeleine. You can call me Maddie."

"It is a pleasure to meet you, Madeleine." She corrects herself, "Maddie. Are you staying here in the hotel?"

"Oh lord, no. I live here in New Awlans. I come here for breakfast every morning. So what brings you to the Crescent City?"

Feeling more comfortable, Chloé tells Madeleine her story—from her home in Seattle, her parents, and friends to Camille and the nice gentleman she met the night before.

In turn, Madeline gives her a brief history of her life. She talks a great deal about pre-World War II New Orleans, how the city has changed, and the convoluted politics that shape the city. Also, she sadly mentions her children and grandchildren never call or come to see her. "So what is the name of this gentleman fellow?" she asks.

"Nick, Nick Nattier."

Maddie has a look of surprise on her face.

"Do you know him?"

"Child, everyone knows the Nattiers. Oh yes, he is a nice young man. Last I heard through the gossip chain was that he was engaged."

"Yes. He said he was, but he broke it off."

"Well, that's nice. Yes, the Nattiers, a highly respected family." Maddie looks down at her food and then, seconds later, back up at Chloé with surprise. "Well, hello, young lady," she says, "I didn't see you sit down. And what might your name be?"

"Chloé," replies the other, quite puzzled.

"What a nice name. My name is Madeleine, but you can call me Maddie."

As Chloé is silent, taken aback, a server walks up to their table. "Ms. Madeleine, your car is here."

"Thank you, Robert."

Chloé looks at the server's name tag. It says Steve. Then she remembers Maddie mentioning her son Robert.

Looking back at Chloé, Maddie says, "Well, Vanessa,"—her daughter's name—"I wish you all the luck in the world. Remember, if you see your great-grandmother, take good care of her. We all need that when we get old. We need to feel like we still matter."

"Thank you, Maddie. I will," Chloé replies, and watches Madeleine be escorted to a waiting limousine. The thought hits her: what if Camille is in a similar condition? What if she has difficulty remembering even sending the letter?

When the server walks up to Chloé's table again, she asks, "Can I have my check, please?"

"Ms. Madeleine has paid for your breakfast."

She says to herself, "How amazing the people here are—so much kindness. There's something really magical about this place. It feels like home... A feeling I've never experienced before, not even in Seattle. A feeling I didn't know existed."

AT THE FRONT DESK, Chloé calls for a cab. Today's cab ride is much less eventful except for, oddly, the driver having a heavy New York accent and, surprisingly, the drive being much shorter than the previous day's. On the way to the St. Charles Avenue address on the envelope, the driver says, "This here is the Garden District. Lots of money around here. Lots of expensive old homes." Chloé recalls Nick mentioning the Garden District was the district where he lived as well. Getting closer to the address, she is trying to stay calm despite the thousand thoughts racing through her head at once.

The taxi arrives at her destination as Chloé notices the streetcar line running in front of Camille's house. Her first thought is that next time, she will ride the streetcar there. If there is a next time, she reminds herself. Stepping out of the cab, she looks up at the house and simply says, "It is perfect."

The house sits in the center of what appears to be three lots, allowing privacy on both sides. It is a two-story home with a possibility for an attic or third floor, as suggested by the roof rise. Painted dark grey with white trim, and adorned with black railings and black shutters, it resembles the style of buildings she saw on the postcards at the airport gift shop. The first floor has a covered porch with two tall windows to the left and one to the right of a beautiful red door. The steps leading up to it are lined on both sides with overgrown hedges. Overhead, the second floor has a full-length balcony that serves as the roof over the downstairs porch. It has a three-foot-tall black iron balustrade ornamenting all sides and ornate black wrought iron railing columns, like downstairs. The second floor has three tall windows facing the street, but no visible way to access the balcony. Out front, the lawn is in need of maintenance; everything from the camellias to the azaleas, the crepe myrtles, Magnolia trees, and grass has grown out of control. Chloé supposes this can be expected for the home of a one-hundred-year-old person.

She asks the driver, "Can you please wait for me? I am not sure if anyone is home."

Not shying from a cliché, the driver responds, "No problem. It's your dime, lady."

The possibility continues running through her mind that Camille may have passed away. "What if I have waited too long to open the letter?" she worries for the millionth time. She quickly clears her thoughts and focuses on the task at hand: knocking on the door. Entering the rod iron gate, she walks along a stone walkway overtaken by grass. She cautiously climbs the four stairs leading to the porch, holding gingerly onto the railing that feels loose enough to fall if leaned upon. Suddenly she finds herself standing in front of the red door. As if in slow motion, her hand stretches out to lift the ornate door knocker, which is a face —part man, part lion—with fleur-de-lis on its forehead and a large ring in its mouth. Following three deep breaths, Chloé knocks and waits… with no answer. She walks to her left and looks into the first window. The house is dark inside, and the furnishings are covered with drop cloths, thus reawakening her fears that Camille might be permanently gone. At that moment, she is startled by the voice of a man coming from up the walkway, accompanied by the bark of a small dog.

"Hello, ma'am. May I be of some assistance?"

Chloé turns to see an elderly couple out walking their dog. The man has a gray beard and is wearing a light blue sweater, slacks, and a flat wool cap. The woman, also with gray hair, is wearing a red sweater unbuttoned over a flowery dress that appears to be homemade due to the bottom pattern not being straight—having been sewn in a different direction as the top—and the appearance that it might have been someone's drapes at one time. Chloé is unsure what breed the dog is under its copious hair; it may have never had a grooming in its entire life.

She replies, "This is my great-grandmother's home, and I am here to visit her."

The couple pauses and looks toward the ground. This reaction sends shocks through Chloé.

The man speaks up again. "I am sorry, miss, but Ms. Camille…" Chloé braces herself against the porch railing, preparing herself for the worst. "She was sent to the Meadowbrook Nursing Home almost a year ago when she fell and broke her hip."

Chloé is relieved and saddened all at once but still collects herself to thank the couple for letting her know. As the couple leaves, she looks down at the letter and makes her way back to the waiting taxi. She was happy Camille was still alive, but this did little to help with her feeling that she let her down by not coming sooner.

THE KING OF
NEW ORLEANS

As Chloé is leaving Camille's house in her cab, Nick is sitting behind his desk in his office, recalling the girl he met the night before. He works for the Law Firm of Jones and Thomas, one of the most successful real estate law practices in the mid-South, handling everything from estate planning, probate, and estate administration to business law. Fred Jones is the only owner remaining. Henry Thomas passed away a little over three years ago, and out of respect for his memory—and more so their reputation—Mr. Jones has carried on the name.

Nick works closely alongside three other attorneys. One is Eric Tanner. Eric is handsome in his early thirties, but with his receding hairline looks much older. He is married with two daughters and lives vicariously through Nick's single life. Originally from Mobile, Alabama, Eric is a loud and, at times, uncouth man. Many people would refer to him as simply "a typical guy." The two of them get along fine, but if they did not work together, they would more than likely not be acquainted.

Another attorney Nick works with is Lydia Jones, Mr. Jones' daughter and Nick's former fiancé. She is a tall, beautiful slender woman with long blonde hair and blue eyes, highly intelligent, a few years younger than Nick, and still deeply in love with him. While Nick has moved on, Lydia is still holding on to what they once had, and she would do anything to get back into his arms.

Nick's third associate is Sean Washington. Nick considers Sean to be his best friend. Though fresh out of law school, he is well on his way to becoming a remarkably successful lawyer. Their family's history together stretches back almost sixty years. In fact, Nick helped Sean get on with the law firm. He often jokes with Nick about how out of place he feels living in the South as a flamboyant gay Black man who performs under the name Dominique at local drag shows. They both know, however, that as far as the South goes, New Orleans is the best place for him, with its unspoken casual acceptance of diversity. It is a true melting pot of cultures, though, like many others, the city has as much darkness as light in its past. Sean demonstrates far more professionalism than Eric and can turn his loud personality on and off like a light switch. Born and raised in New Orleans, he became a lawyer because he promised his mother he would; his dream, however, is to be a hairdresser and esthetician. His mother knows he is a good lawyer and is incredibly proud of that, but "what Mama don't know," as Sean likes to phrase it, is he also attended cosmetology school and works on the side doing nails, hair, and facials. His drive to follow his passion might be why Nick respects him so much.

For his part, Nick never wanted to be an attorney. He was pushed into it by his father. When his family first came over from France, they pretty much owned Royal Street. It was once the city's financial hub, with a bank on every corner. His great-great-grandfather, great-grandfather, and grandfather were all bankers, but his father became an attorney and wanted the same for his son. Nick, however, does not want to be a banker or a lawyer. He wants to open a jazz club and to lead a lifestyle different from the rest of his family.

Those who genuinely know Nick describe him as simple, caring, creative, a free thinker, a bohemian at heart, and definitely not lawyer material. What wouldn't he give to be strong enough to take chances as Sean has!

Seeing Eric walk up to his office door, Nick calls, "Come in," and Eric enters carrying a stack of files.

Nick sees the stack. "Or don't, actually."

Placing the files on Nick's desk, Eric says, "Here you go, another stack of properties to clear, and there maybe a few wills in there to spice things up."

Nick cuts him off. "Great. Hey, I have to tell you about this incredible woman I met last night."

With a growing smile on his face, Eric sits down. "Go on."

Nick says, "Wait, we need Sean too"—then yells out his door, "Hey, come in here! You need to hear this!"

Sean walks up, rolling his eyes. "Is this another story about a girl that will just remind me how much my love life and the lack thereof sucks?"

"Well, probably," Nick says as his friend steps into the room.

"I thought you were taking a break from women." Sean comments sarcastically. "Mm-hmm…"

Eric eagerly tells Sean, "Shhh, you're interrupting him. Go on."

Sean leans back, puts his right hand on his cheek while supporting his arm at the elbow with his left hand, tilts his chin downward, and, looking Eric up and down, says, "Boy, you need to get you some, and stop always drooling every time Nick meets a woman."

Nick pauses and continues, "Well, I met an amazing woman last night. She seems incredibly smart, is extremely beautiful… She's from Seattle and is here in New Orleans for the first time."

"They always seem to fall right into your hands," Eric remarks.

Then Sean says, "And he always catches them." They both laugh as Nick modestly lowers his head.

"No, this one is different. There is something about her, something familiar," he explains.

Sean says while making a kissing sound, "Uh-oh, Nick is in love."

Nick looks at him. "What are you, nine?"

Eric asks urgently, "So you said she is beautiful, but is she hot? Does she have a nice ass? What about her rack?"

Sean interrupts, shaking his head at Eric. "How did you ever get a woman to marry you?"

Nick says, "Ouch!" as they all laugh. "Yes, she is, and as a gentleman, I plead the fifth on the rest."

"What I would not give to be you for just one day," Eric says.

"With your luck, that day would end up with you being hungover and sick in bed, a couple of STDs, and a pending paternity suit," Sean offers.

"I would hate to imagine what you would get into being me for a day," Nick responds. "I don't think I would want my body back."

Standing up, Eric says, "Yeah, you're probably right there." Looking at Sean, he says, "By the way, if it weren't for my hangover days, I never would have met my wife."

"I don't even know what that means."

Nick asks Sean, "You mean you never heard the story of how Eric met his wife?"

"Nope. Do I want to?"

"You have to," Nick replies. "It's a rite of passage of working with Eric."

Sean looks at Eric, saying, "Well, go ahead." Looking back at Nick, he adds, "Please do not make me regret this."

Eric asks Nick, "Are you sure you want to hear it again?"

"You have to tell it. Sean *must* hear it."

Eric begins, "Okay, here we go. So this is how the woman I love saved me from a life of parties, drinking, and loose women." He pauses, processing what he just said with nostalgia combined with a vigorous slap of regret and reality as he sadly adds, "And fun." He pauses again in a moment of melancholy but snaps back to excitement. "Well, in my last year of college, I met this hot chick at a party, and she took me back to her apartment."

"Is this hot chick your wife?" Sean asks.

"No," Eric replies.

"I thought this was about you meeting your wife, not another frat story."

"I'm getting to it. So we walk into her apartment, and there are photos everywhere of this guy who's a huge body-builder. I ask him who he is, thinking we might be in the wrong apartment. She tells me it's her boyfriend. I mean, this guy is huge. His lifting competition photos looked like Arnold Schwarzenegger with a seventies porn 'stache. About this time, I'm a little freaked out. She tells me not to worry, he's out of town and won't be back until tomorrow. So"—Eric gets sing-songy—"we do the wild thing."

Sean says, putting one hand in the air, "Oh Lord Jesus, help me."

Then Eric continues, "So later in the bedroom, we were lying there naked..."

"Nope! Nope! Nope!" Sean interjects. "I do not want that image of you naked. Take that back. Take it back now!"

"Wait, but you're gay."

"That does not mean I want to see your naked ass."

Nick laughs. "It's just a mental image, not his actual ass."

"Yeah, an image I don't want in my head."

Nick, still laughing, says, "Go ahead and finish, man."

"So we're laying there naked, and suddenly we hear a key turning in the front door. She whisper-screams, 'He's home early!' I start running for the closet, and she says, 'He'll find you in there!' So I drop to the floor to roll under the bed. Again she says, 'No, not under the bed, he will see you!' I'm standing there totally naked, I remind you, and she throws my clothes out the window. She says, 'Quick, go out the window!' I go out legs first. I keep reaching for the ground, but I can't find it. Damn her for not reminding me we're on the second floor…

"Longest fall ever. After an eternity, I land naked in a large row of holly bushes that are being taken over by brier. Adrenalin is keeping me from instant pain, I guess. I look up, and all my clothes are hanging on a branch outside the window. I stand up, slightly bleeding everywhere from all the thorns and branches, completely naked, when I suddenly am engulfed by the headlights of a car pulling into the parking spot six feet in front of me."

By this point, all three are crying with laughter.

Eric continues, "Stepping out of the car is Barbara, my future wife, wearing a nice dress and holding a Bible. She's returning from a church study group. She loans me a scarf to cover my man parts. Actually, I guess she was giving it to me, because when I tried later to give it back to her, she told me just to keep it. She also allowed me to use her Bible to toss into the tree to knock down my clothes. She showed me that night by her actions that she was a keeper. The rest is history."

"Wow," Sean says. "Just wow."

Nick reminds him, "I told you it was a great story."

"No, you just said I needed to hear it."

"By the way," Eric says, "when are the three of us going out together again?"

Sean raises his eyebrows. "Do you not remember the last time we did that?"

"Yeah, you almost got us killed at that biker bar," Nick puts in.

"Hey, I heard it was a cool place."

Sean says sarcastically, "Yeah, it was cool, alright."

Nick adds, "I remember it well. You were hitting on some tattooed blonde chick when her boyfriend showed up."

"What were you thinking, anyway?" Sean says. "You're a married man."

Eric defends himself, saying, "I was just talking to her."

"Her three-hundred-pound boyfriend didn't think so."

"Well, your 'just talking' was about to get our asses kicked by six bikers," Nick says, then laughs. "If it weren't for Sean's quick thinking of running to the door and distracting them by yelling, 'Excuse me. I accidentally ran over some Marleys out front...' Then I corrected him by coughing out 'Harleys' under my breath. Sean looked at me and said, 'Wait. What? Oh. Sorry, *Harleys* out front. Does anybody know who they belong to?'" Looking at Eric, Nick continues, "Then I grabbed you and all three of us ran out. So if it weren't for Sean, you probably wouldn't be here right now."

Sean grins. "We must have run at least five blocks screaming before we realized no one was chasing us."

They all laugh as Eric contradicts Sean, "You were the one doing all the screaming while we were running. No one chased us because they were too busy checking their bikes for damage. You could have heard a pin drop in that place when you yelled that. By the way, that was some fast thinking. How in the hell did you come up with that?"

"I had to come up with something to save your dumb ass, and the only thing these biker types care about are their bikes. So that's just the first thing that came to mind to get everyone's attention."

"Well," Nick concludes, "I think we can all agree that we are not ready for another night like that."

"On a different note, man," Eric says, "I still think you blew it with Lydia. I mean, you're the king of New Orleans. You can have any woman you want, and you had the perfect one. You had it made with her. She's as close to royalty as you will find in this city. Hell, she's a walking lottery ticket, and you just threw it away."

Nick shakes his head. "Are you ever going to let that go? We were and will never be again. The end. And believe me, I am the king of nothing."

Sean offers, "You know I'm gay, but if I weren't, I would definitely hit that. That girl is fine."

"Wow, between the two of you, I feel like I'm in high school again. Everything between Lydia and me is over."

"I'm glad you feel that way," Sean says. "But I don't think she's moved on as quickly as you have. Just saying... watch your back, my friend."

Nick stares at the wall in deep thought until Eric speaks up. "You have some work to do, so I'll leave you alone to close these cases. I think there are some wills in there that are a couple of weeks old."

"Joy," Nick replies. "But I'll be cutting out early today— I'm going to try and see her again tonight." As Eric is walking out, Nick clarifies, "You bring everyone so much joy when you leave the room."

Eric leans back through the door. "If you score, I want details." Then he makes a kissing sound.

Sean says to Eric, following him as their voices fade down the hall, "What are you, ten? Now one more time, how did you get a woman to marry you? I think you might need your wife's Bible again."

Nick leans back in his chair, his mind focused on one thing: Chloé.

MEADOWBROOK

LEAVING CAMILLE'S HOUSE, Chloé has the driver take her straight to the Meadowbrook Nursing Home.

Upon arrival, she reflects that this place, which resembles a cozy traditional home, would definitely be appealing to an older generation. Well-maintained landscaping across the property is lined with white picket fences. Drawing her eye is a bridge over a brook edged by wildflowers—hence the name Meadowbrook, presumably. She steps out of the cab, crosses the bridge, and walks into the entrance.

The peacefulness of the exterior is stripped away as she enters the building. The fluorescent lighting is almost blinding in the reception area, highlighting every flaw in the hideous flowered wallpaper. In fact, she wonders if they could possibly fit one more lighting fixture on the ceiling. The inside definitely feels more like a hospital than the homey impression given by the facade.

Chloé approaches the front desk and tells the receptionist, "Hello, I'm here to see Camille Laver."

"Yes, Ms. Camille. I will send for her. Are you family?"

"Yes, I am her great-granddaughter."

Surprisingly excited, the receptionist says, "Oh my. She has mentioned a lot about you. She always told us you would be coming to see her someday. Some of us here even thought maybe you didn't exist."

Laughing, Chloé replies, "No, I am definitely real."

"I know she'll be so happy. If you will please have a seat in the lobby, she will be here shortly."

"Thank you."

Chloé sees the receptionist whisper something to a

coworker as they stare at her with the excitement of children on Christmas Day. While waiting, she decides to stand. The sofa and all the chairs in the waiting area are covered in unwelcoming plastic sheets. Over to the right in the corner of the main lobby is an old piano, perhaps there for the residents to play; however, it is covered in a thick layer of dust—evidence of little use.

Several female patients walk by over the next few minutes, and one even comes up and says hello. Chloé greets each, thinking she may be Camille. She starts to wonder again, "What if Camille has lost her memory and doesn't even remember sending the letter?" At just that moment, an old lady with long beautiful white hair, in a long white nightgown, is pushed around the corner in a wheelchair. The elderly woman, in apparent shock at the sight of Chloé, takes a deep breath and places both her hands on her cheeks, smiling widely. By her expression, Chloé knows this must be Camille, but how, she wonders, does Camille recognize her?

"Oh, my Chloé!"

"Hello, Great-Grandma," Chloé replies as she hugs her.

"Call me Camille, sweetheart. Great-Grandma makes me feel old. I am only one hundred." They both smile, and she says, "Oh my dear, thank you for coming."

"How did you know it was me?" Chloé asks.

"Because you look just like my mother. Your great-great-grandmother. You even have the same birthmark on your cheek," Camille explains. "You look so much like her. How did you know where to find me, precious?"

"I went by the house first."

"How did it look?"

"It was beautiful."

"Good, good. The neighbors have been so helpful and promised me they would keep the outside presentable."

"In fact, it was your neighbors who directed me here."

"Was it a couple with a nervous little dog?"

"Yes, it was."

"The Wilsons, nice couple." Camille makes a grunting noise. "That little dog used to keep me up all night. Scared of its own shadow, that dog is." Chloé laughs, and Camille joins in. "So tell me about you, my love. Tell me about your life, growing up, boys, everything."

As CHLOÉ TELLS Camille about her life in Seattle, school, and even boys, her great-grandmother listened in delight.

In turn Camille explains, "Last year, I had a nasty fall and have been stuck in this wheelchair ever since." With a laugh and a wink, she adds, "But I kind of like being chauffeured around." She then shares with her about life at Meadowbrook and starts pointing out other residents and telling their stories.

"See that woman over there?"

"Yes."

"That is Ms. Crabtree. She is a widowed schoolteacher. And that man over there?"

"Yes."

"He is Mr. Brooks; a widower and retired New Orleans police officer. Late at night..." She lowers her voice. "He slips off to Ms. Crabtree's room. They got a thing going on." She smiles.

"Oh my."

"The woman at the table against the wall is Ms. Grant. She claims to be a descendent of Ulysses S. Grant and goes around singing the "Battle Hymn of the Republic." And the lady in the chair by the desk is Ms. Tyler. *She* says she is a descendant of Robert E. Lee. The two of them argue all the time. Then that lady over there in the wheelchair is Ms. Bellum. She is a former 'lady of the night' from the 1920s here in New Orleans. She thinks she still has it; we don't let on otherwise. It would just break her little heart. She's always pinching the male nurses' backsides." They both chuckle. "And over there by Ms. Tyler is Ms. Margaret. She's my best friend. We knew each other from my years as a nurse. An awfully long time. She's the one that encouraged me to write you." She calls out to her. "Margaret, come see my great-granddaughter I always talked about!"

As time passes, Chloé is introduced to most of the Meadowbrook residents and gets to know their stories. Camille is deeply proud to show off her great-granddaughter. Chloé feels as if she has known Camille her entire life, and Camille feels the same about her.

Finally Camille says, "So I suppose you want to know all about who you are and our family."

"Yes, I would love to hear it all," Chloé replies. She cannot help but admire how sharp Camille is mentally, for her hundred years.

Camille starts with the story of Tessa. Chloé is enthralled from the beginning with Paris, gypsies, and the Moulin Rouge—and then is shocked when Camille mentions René Nattier.

"Wait," Chloé says, "what was the last name?"

"Nattier, my dear. It is a French name."

Chloé sits there stunned. What are the chances this Nattier is related to Nick? "Must be slight," she thinks. "Paris is a big place."

Camille continues with the love story. Hearing of Tessa and René gives Chloé a feeling in her heart she has felt only one other time: the night before, when she met Nick. And as the tale of Tessa and René reaches its tragic climax, her heart begins to break like never before. She feels an unexplainable pain inside, and her tears will not stop. At the same time, her previous observation about any relation between René and Nick being unlikely becomes a strong possibility in her mind, seeing that their families came over from France around the same time. She is not sure how to process this. What are the chances she picked a restaurant that would have her run into a descendent of René Nattier? "Slight," she thinks again.

THE EVENING ARRIVED, and with it, nurses bearing Camille's medication. "Ms. Camille, I hate to interrupt you for a moment, but it is time for your medicine. You do not have to stop visiting, but I need to give you your meds."

As she takes the cup of pills and washes them down with water, Camille says, "I hate taking all these pills. I am so happy to see you, sweetheart, but I think I might need some rest."

"Too much excitement for one day?"

"Yes, it is." She asks Chloé, "Will you please come back tomorrow, my dear? We can continue the story then."

"Of course."

CHLOÉ CALLS for a cab at the front desk to take her back to her hotel. The entire ride she spends processing everything she has learned today, in particular the thought that maybe the reason Nick seems so familiar is due to some distant family connection. All in all, she feels overwhelmed and looks forward to rest and the possibility of seeing Nick again.

She is hoping for a message from him back at the hotel, and she gets her wish. He left a message and number for her to call him at his office. Not sure if he would still be there, she wastes no time.

Nick answers, "Hello, Nick Nattier speaking."

"Yes, Mr. Nattier, I was given a message that I was to call you."

Recognizing her voice, he responds, "No, you must have the wrong Mr. Nattier."

Chloé replies, knowing his voice as well and playing along, "Oh, I'm sorry. I must have the wrong number. I apologize for the inconvenience. I'll let you go."

This time Nick responds quickly, with concern in his voice. "Wait... No... I mean, yes."

"So you are then the Mr. Nattier who called on me?"

"Yes. That was absolutely me." They both laugh.

"I see you're working late this evening."

"Yes, unfortunately, I often do. I was wondering if you'd like to join me for dinner tonight."

"Yes, I would like that."

"One thing, however."

She inquires, "Yes?"

"You will need a nice dress and comfortable shoes. I could take you shopping if you didn't bring anything formal."

Chloé actually did bring a lovely dress with her, so she says, "No problem. I have the perfect dress and shoes. What time?"

"I will pick you up at seven."

"I'll be waiting."

"See you then. Goodbye, Chloé."

"Bye-bye, Nick."

BELLE REVE

SEVEN O'CLOCK ARRIVES, and so does Nick at Chloé's hotel. He waits for her in the lobby. He is dressed in grey slacks, a white dress shirt, and a navy blue blazer. Chloé steps off the elevator in a beautiful revealing black dress that stops right at the knees, low cut in the front and barely covering her shoulders.

Nick speaks first. "Wow! You look amazing."

She blushes. "Thank you. And you look handsome as well." As he offers his left arm to escort her, she asks, "Are we taking your car or a cab?"

"Neither; we are walking."

"Walking?" She looks at her feet. "Good thing I wore my flats and not my heels."

"I said the same thing to myself earlier. My heels were definitely a no-go today." They both laugh. "The restaurant is on Bourbon Street. Not far. Are you ready?" She nods yes. "Then shall we?" Nick lowers his left arm and takes Chloé's hand. "Here, let's take the banquette."

Confused, she asks, "The what?"

"The banquette… It's what we call sidewalks here."

"I have never heard them called that before."

"It came from the word for the wooden planks placed over ditches. It carried over to mean sidewalks as well." Chloé is still looking puzzled. "It's a Southern thing."

Nick walks to her right, holding her hand. Noticing that he does this purposefully, Chloé says, "My father always told me a true gentleman will always walk with you on the outside closest to the street."

"Your father is a wise man and obviously a gentleman himself."

They head towards Bourbon Street, making small talk about how their day went.

"So I bragged about you quite a bit today at work."

"Oh yeah, what did you say?" Chloé says.

"I told everyone I met this totally beautiful woman, and I cannot wait to see her again."

She blushes again as they continue to stroll. "Why, thank you."

"So tell me about your big day, meeting your great-grandmother."

"Her name is Camille, and she is the most amazing person I've ever met. I hope for one I live that long, but also I stay that sharp. It's as if she hasn't aged a bit on the inside."

"Hopefully, we all can be that lucky. If she is as amazing as you, then that says a lot."

Chloé smiles, thinking about finding the right time to ask him about René—and decides now is as good a time as any. "So your family that came over, what was their name?"

Nick chuckles and answers, "Nattier."

"No, I know that. You know what I mean. What were their first names?"

"I know what you meant."

"Brat," she says while smiling.

"My great-great-grandfather was named René and my great-great-grandmother, Diana." Upon hearing this, Nick feels Chloé's grip on his hand intensify. "Why do you ask?"

Struggling to process what has occurred, she does not tell him yet what she knows. She simply responds with, "I was just curious." She feels he is about to pry, so she quickly changes the subject. "So, what bands do you like?"

"Wow. As much as I love music, that is a tough one. I suppose a little bit of everything. Some that come to mind are, first off, my favorite, Sidney Bechet, then there is Charlie Parker, Louis Armstrong, Thelonious Monk, and John Coltrane, but I like more than just jazz. I also like Rage Against the Machine, The Beastie Boys, REM, Sinatra, Harry Connick, Jr., Radiohead, Jellyfish, Bob Dylan, and Warren Zevon, just to name a few."

"That is quite an eclectic list, but a good one. A few of those I will have to research."

"What about you?" he asks. "Being from Seattle, let me guess… Nirvana, Pearl Jam?"

"Actually, I'm not a huge grunge fan. Some of mine would be The Smiths, Janes Addiction, and The Cure, especially their album *Disintegration*. I also like a new band called 4 Non Blondes, and another new group called The Cranberries. My favorite, though, by far is INXS. Just looking at Michael Hutchence—I mean, damn!"

"Now I'm kind of jealous."

"No need to be," she tells him. "You're the one getting to walk with me and not him." Chloé pauses, processing what she just said, and blushes once more when she realizes how flirtatious it was. Recovering, she says, "I did fly to England in '91 with several friends to see them at Wembley Stadium."

"Wow. That was a huge concert. I think they released that on CD."

"Yes, some of it was released. It was a once-in-a-lifetime opportunity. So now the big question, Beatles or Stones?"

"Definitely the Stones."

"Oh wow. Really? I'm not sure we can be friends."

"So it's over. Just like that?"

"Yep. Just like that."

"Any way I can change your mind?"

"I don't know. That one may be a deal breaker."

Nick sighs. "Well, I suppose we should have a final dinner together, since you can't always get what you want."

Laughing she responds, "I see what you did there. I suppose there's nothing wrong with just one more dinner before I head alone down the long and winding road."

"Nice one. Good, because here we are. You are going to love this place."

They are standing outside Galatoire's, a world-renowned restaurant that opened in 1905. Its humble façade belies the extremely elegant dining experience found inside. There is a short line at the door, and quickly they are seated.

Nick tells her, "My family has been coming here since 1905, but this is one restaurant that even celebrities, politicians, and old families have to wait in line for. The restaurant was started by another family that came over from France like mine around the same time."

Chloé thinks, "I bet Camille came here as a little girl." The possibility sends chills through her, making the hair stand up on the back of her neck—aided slightly by the breeze from the numerous antique two-blade ceiling fans overhead.

"The line we were in tonight wasn't anything. You should have seen it this afternoon."

"You mean you already have eaten here today?"

"No. It is just that today is Friday, and Friday lunch here is a huge New Orleans tradition."

AFTER AN EXQUISITE DINNER, they exit the restaurant, still holding hands. There is a comfortable silence that Chloé soon breaks. "So, tell me about your restaurant."

"What do you want to know?"

"Tell me about what it will be like. How will you finance it? What will it be named?"

"Well, I've been saving for it since before law school. It will be a jazz club and restaurant. I will serve a Creole menu. There will be a small stage and elegant tables in the dining room with antique furnishings. I see lots of stained glass, and jazz music will always play, sometimes live."

Chloé likes how Nick glows in excitement as he speaks. "Sounds perfect," she says. "What about the name?"

"Well, are you familiar with the Tennessee Williams play *A Streetcar Named Desire?*"

"I've heard of it."

"His title was in reference to the Desire streetcar line here in New Orleans. It began in 1920 and started at Canal and ran all the way down Bourbon, making its way to Desire Street. He was inspired by hearing the trolleys pass by Desire Street. Well, the tragic character of the play is Blanche Dubois. She grew up on a plantation called Belle Reve. That's French, which means"—Chloé joins in so they both say it at the same time—"'beautiful dream.'"

Seeing the surprise on Nick's face, Chloé explains, "I took eight years of French."

"I'm impressed. Because of my family, I have taken a lifetime of it. We could have some interesting conversations. Well, that is what it will be called: Belle Reve. For it is my beautiful dream."

Chloé is almost speechless. She finally says, "That is beautiful. What keeps you from opening it, if you don't mind me asking?"

There is a long silence. "I didn't choose to be a lawyer. The choice was made for me. I lost my mom to breast cancer when I was fifteen."

"Oh, I'm sorry."

"Thank you. Well, all I had was my dad."

She asks, "No brothers or sisters?"

"None. After finishing my first year at Loyola University Law School, I was about to come home for the summer and tell him I didn't want to be a lawyer. Then I got the call that he had collapsed from a heart attack and passed away."

"Oh my gosh."

"I knew he wanted nothing more than for me to be a lawyer like him. I didn't have to go back and finish. There was no one there to push me anymore, no one to say it was what my dad wanted. But I did. I went back. I did it for him. Now, what I would not give to hear him say, 'Nick, follow your heart.' But I know that can never happen."

There is a long silence before Chloé speaks. "Sometimes, we have to let go of our pasts. We can't live our lives for others. We really do have to follow our hearts. It may lead to great happiness or great tragedy, but it's what makes us human. It's what makes life worth living."

There is silence again as Nick looks at her, reflecting. In another minute he speaks, his voice upbeat now. "Do you like surprises?"

"Yes," she says, then laughs as he begins to run, pulling her hand behind him.

"Come on then!"

Nick waves down a private horse-drawn carriage. He helps her aboard, and they lean back in their seats, looking out at a beautiful night in New Orleans. Chloé looks up to see every star shining brighter than ever, as if just for them.

Over the steady rhythm of hoofbeats, the whooshing of the evening breeze, and the blaring of a saxophone off in the distance, Chloé throws up her arms and screams aloud, "I love this city!"

Nick beams and, looking her in the eyes, leans in. "Some people come here and do not see the city's true beauty because they are not looking. But if you come here with open eyes and an open heart..." His voice gets softer. "You will fall in love." They both close their eyes as Nick places his hand gently on her cheek and, bringing his lips to hers, kisses her passionately. When their lips finally close, pulling away, he tells her, "You know now, from this moment on, our lives will never be the same."

Chloé is breathless. No one has ever kissed her like that before.

Nick places his arm around her as they pick out constellations in the night sky. He points upward. "See those two stars there? One is Altair, and the other is Vega. There is a festival in Japan called Tanabata, which means 'Evening of the Seventh.' It is normally celebrated on July 7. The stars represent two lovers, Cowherd and Weaving Girl. They are separated by circumstance, represented by the Milky Way as an imagined celestial river. They are only allowed to come together once a year. On the seventh day of the seventh month, all the world's magpies fly to the heavens and form a bridge for them to cross."

"I don't think I would like a world where I could only be kissed like you just kissed me once a year. *Mais ce serait la peine d'attendre.*"

Nick smiles and replies by translating. "But it would be well worth the wait."

Chloé softly says, "That's right. Very good, sir."

Then in French he says, "*Je ne pourrai jamais vous faire patienter.*"

Chloé now does her part to translate. "I will never make you wait."

The two lean into each other and their lips meet again.

AT JACKSON SQUARE, the two of them exit the carriage. There they see the entire area is lined with artists, musicians, and fortune tellers. They make their way around the square. Chloé is enthralled with all the beautiful street art. She looks closely at several pieces propped against the iron fence. She tells Nick, "Art is my number one passion in life. I have been painting since I was a child."

"Who is your favorite artist?"

"Gosh, I have several. Let's see; there is Picasso, Matisse, Frida Kahlo, Dali, and Warhol... Oh, and Monet, but my favorite is Pollock."

"Jackson Pollock, really?"

"Yes, I love all his paintings, especially his early work before the drip paintings."

"What do you like about it?"

"Well, I fell in love with his work when I was a child. From the moment I saw my first painting of his, I knew I wanted to be an artist."

"But what is it about his work that you like?"

"I suppose seeing his transition from Realism, his progression, and his unrealistic colors. I also love the questions that arise when searching for their meanings, like what he is symbolizing. I hope that answers your question. Some things are difficult to put into words."

"I definitely understand that. I would love to see some of your work sometime."

"I actually brought some of it with me to show my great-grandmother."

"Great, maybe you can show me when I take you back to your hotel."

"Yes, I'd like that. Just don't be too judgmental."

"No. Never. If you ever saw something I painted, you would scratch your head—or your eyes out—and say, what the hell is that. No, big ups to all you painters out there, with the utmost respect. By the way, speaking of painting, did you know a young Truman Capote once sold paintings right here in Jackson Square?"

"Wow. No, I had no idea he was an artist also. I was only familiar with him as a writer."

"Yeah, I'm really glad he didn't stick to painting."

Together they pick out several paintings they both like. Chloé says, "I wish I would have brought my camera with me tonight. There is so much to take in."

"We will just have to take mental pictures." Nick begins to snap pictures of her with an imaginary camera. Chloé poses with her hand on her hip, mimicking a model in a photo shoot. Nick starts giving her directions like a photographer. "Turn to the left. Now to the right. Give me more passion. More. Yeah, that's it. Spin. Smile. Now frown. Okay, could you give me more leg? More. Yes, that's right."

They both burst into laughter as they start taking silly pretend pictures of each other and the people around the St. Louis Cathedral. After playing awhile like two children, they go up to a fortune teller on the street corner.

Nick takes her hand. "Come on, don't trust these guys. They are just trying to get people's money. They tell you what they think you want to hear."

"I don't care," Chloé replies. "I want to try it."

"All right." He lays down twenty dollars and says sarcastically, "Oh great fortune teller, tell us our future."

Chloé looks at Nick and says, like a teacher scolding a child, "Please be quiet."

Nick turns his head away in mock shame as the man begins to read Chloé's palm.

"You have traveled a long way, my child," the fortune teller says.

Nick interjects. "He says that because he hears your accent. Anyone can tell you are not from around here."

Chloé shushes him.

"No!" the fortune teller corrects him. "Not in distance, but time. Not this life. Your soul is old. Very old. I see you were terribly hurt. Someone left you. So long ago. Too much pain for you to bear. Your heart breaks. It still breaks. The pain. The sorrow. Now your soul is searching. Wait. Your soul is searching for someone. The one you search for is here. He is here." Then the fortune teller releases her hand, leaning back as if overtaken by exhaustion.

Nick impatiently asks the fortune teller, "So who is 'he'?"

The fortune teller stares at Chloé, now with a startled look on his face, and reaches again for her hand. "She knows."

Chloé's hand trembles nervously, and she pulls back her hand. "Okay, I think that's enough." She turns quickly and walks away, visibly shaken.

The fortune teller calls out to her. "When you find him, do not let him go! You lost him once! Not again!"

Chloé picks her pace up to almost a jog.

Nick calls out, trailing behind her, "What was that all about? You shouldn't let those guys get to you. It's all just a bunch of lies. They tell people what they think they want to hear."

"Let's just go," Chloé replies.

Nick catches up to her and takes her hand.

WALKING BACK TO THE HOTEL, they keep a deafening silence between them. Nick doesn't understand what has happened, so he doesn't speak. Chloé does understand, but simply chooses not to share.

Once back at the Ambassador, Chloé tells Nick, "I am totally exhausted. I think I'll turn in for the night. I promise I will show you my art next time."

"I will hold you to that promise," Nick tells her, and adds, "Are you sure you're okay?"

"Yes, I will be fine."

"I don't know… You looked pretty rattled back there."

"No, it's okay. I just need some rest. It's been a busy day for me. I had an amazing night, though. Thank you."

Nick kisses her good night. "Sweet dreams, Chloé."

With a farewell smile, she walks toward the elevator, but her thoughts are still lost in the fortune teller's words.

Once in her room, she lies on her bed, staring up at the ceiling. She begins laying out the events of the evening. She knows her heart is falling for Nick—falling faster than her mind can process.

My First Love

THE NEXT DAY Chloé returns to Meadowbrook to see Camille. The latter is not feeling well, so Chloé goes to her room to sit by her bedside.

Camille smiles as Chloé enters, but when she speaks, she sounds much weaker than the day before. "Hello, my love. I was hoping to spend the day in the courtyard, but sometimes our bodies have different plans than our minds."

"Are you sure today is a good day for you to sit up and talk?"

"At my age, dear, there are not many good days." She laughs. "So, where did we leave off?"

"René had just moved the family here."

"Yes... Oh yes. Well, we settled in an elegant two-story plantation home with a long driveway lined with beautiful, towering pecan trees. The back of the house had a mature magnolia tree where René hung up a swing for me."

"Who lives there now?"

"Oh, that house and all the glorious trees are no longer standing. Progress, they call it. Soon there will not be a green space left on this planet. Well, my new stepmother hated me, and my new siblings would hardly speak to me out of fear of their mother."

"That is terrible."

"René was there for me, though; he was the perfect papa, always protecting me."

"He sounded like a good man."

"Oh, he was. I attended Newcomb High School, which was a prep school for the all-girls Newcomb College. There I took nursing, but my true passion was the pottery classes. I graduated in 1914, the year World War I began in Europe, but our boys did not start going over until 1917. We lost a lot of good boys, many I knew." Pausing while searching her thoughts, she asks, "Well, where was I? Oh, my pottery, I miss it so much. You should have seen some of my work. I wanted so much to be a professional artist. All these years, I never stopped working on my pottery. I was still making pieces right up until I came to Meadowbrook. Well, years after school, as an adult, my mentor was Morris Henry Hobbs. He lost his hearing in the great war, but he was an award-winning artist with an international reputation. Morris did everything so well, from etchings to paintings to wood carvings. He moved to New Orleans in 1938 and stayed. He was a good friend of mine. Morris taught me so much, but sadly he passed away in 1967."

"Did you ever have a relationship with him?"

"Oh lord, no."

"What about any other boys, then? You left them out, and you did ask me about mine," Chloé reminds her, and they both laugh.

Camille responds, "No, no boys yet; after school, I was still trying to find my place in the world. So the year I graduated, knowing his health was fading, René bought me my house on St Charles Ave. He had cancer, and I had just turned twenty-two when he finally passed away. Like René had predicted, Diana, his wife, cut off all ties with me and would not allow the other children to ever speak to me or of me again. I was dead to them. As far as they were concerned, I either died with René or never existed at all."

"I am so sorry."

"Oh, you have nothing to be sorry for." Reaching out and touching Chloé's hand, she says, "That's just life. Well, I went to work at Charity Hospital, where I worked until 1960. René left me with enough money to live on nicely, so I retired on that, but who expects to live this long? And I ended up here." The mood in the room became exceedingly somber. Then with the energy and excitement of someone popping out of a cake, she says, "Then I fell in love! A love that has lasted me all my life."

"With Great-Grandfather?"

"Oh lord, no, child! We will get to him soon enough. I fell in love with jazz."

"Jazz… as in the music?"

Laughing, Camille says, "Of course, dear. I don't know any *boys* named Jazz. Though nowadays, people are naming their kids all kinds of names, aren't they."

"So you like jazz?"

"Oh yes! I fell in love with it before it was fashionable, and it became not a luxury, but a necessity in life. It was everything. It was energy and fire, heat and spice. At my age, I may not be able to tell you what happened last week, but I can still talk all day about all the jazz greats—Buddy Bolden, Kid Ory, Jelly Roll Morton, Joe Oliver, Louis Armstrong, Charlie Parker, and the legendary Sidney Bechet." Chloé remembers Nick naming some of those artists. "I spent much of my free time in Storyville. Like the Montmartre District in Paris, where my mother worked, Storyville was our red-light district. I remember Frank Early's saloon was called My Place. Upstairs there is where Tony Jackson wrote my all-time favorite song, and to this day, I assert it was written about me: 'Pretty Baby.'" She winks at Chloé as they both laugh. "That building is still standing today. Before landing in this place, I would often take a cab there. I would stand out front with my eyes closed, trying to recapture my youth.

"My favorite place, though, was Economy Hall. It was a dance hall in the Treme section of town that just bordered Storyville. I was quite the dancer of the Turkey Trot, the Charleston, Shim Sham Shimmy, the Fox Trot, you name it."

She lowers her voice to a whisper, leaning toward Chloé. "I'll tell you a little secret that the doctor doesn't know. I was dancing the Shim Sham Shimmy at home when I fell and broke my hip." They both laugh and she puts a finger over her lips, adding, "Shhh...."

Chloé is beaming. "That is such an amazing story."

"Oh, I have lots of those. This gal has seen a lot in a hundred years."

"I bet you have."

"After I retired in 1960, I met Allan and Sandra Jaffe at Mr. Larry's Gallery. A great place at the time for local jazz performers. They were a young couple on an extended honeymoon. All three of us shared a true love for jazz. I shared my story with them, and they shared my concern about protecting and preserving New Orleans jazz. Within a year, they moved here and opened Preservation Hall. Louis Armstrong once said if you want to see the greats of jazz, just go to Preservation Hall. For a while, I helped run the cash register, which was a wicker basket. The rest, as they say, is history."

She sits up straighter. "I feel much better, dear. Help me into the wheelchair, and we can go out to the courtyard and enjoy this beautiful day."

CHLOÉ wheels her to a nice shady spot in the courtyard and sits on a bench beside her. Camille eagerly continues her tale.

"I attended the very first Jazz Festival here in 1970. It was held back then at Beauregard Square, later renamed Louis Armstrong Park. It did not move to the fairgrounds until a couple of years later. There were only a little over three hundred of us there. I paid three dollars to get in. I saw Duke Ellington, Mahalia Jackson, Al Hurt, and so many more great performers. There were four stages and no microphones. It was magical..." She reflects and then excitedly adds, "You know, jazz actually saved my life."

"I know what you mean. My art has been that way for me."

"No, I mean it in a literal way. In all likelihood, it saved my life. You want to know how?"

Chloé laughs at her. "Tell me."

"It was May of 1918 when a man broke into the home of Joseph and Katherine Maggio. He killed them both with an axe found in the home."

"Oh my gosh."

"Two weeks later, he breaks into another home, killing another couple with an axe. Over the next year, he killed five more people."

"Wow. This is the first I have ever heard of this."

"It was in all the papers. The newspaper called him 'the Axeman.' The entire city was petrified. Everyone was afraid to sleep. Up until then, we never even thought about locking our doors."

"This sounds like a campfire story."

"No, it's all true."

"What does it have to do with jazz saving your life, though?"

"I am getting to that." Smiling, Camille remarks, "You young people these days have no patience."

"Yep, I would agree with you there."

"Well, in March 1919, the Axeman wrote a letter to the newspaper. He wrote that at a quarter past twelve the following night, he would strike again, but anyone with a jazz band playing in full swing in their home at the time mentioned would be spared. Those who did not jazz it on Tuesday night would get the axe."

"That's almost funny if it weren't sad for the people he killed."

"Well, everyone got a jazz band or played jazz music at parties in their homes. We were all nervous, but it was beautiful. You could hear jazz being played throughout the entire city. It was heaven to my ears and heart. It approached twelve fifteen; we were incredibly fearful as the time came and passed, but we kept playing all night. The next morning the city woke to find nothing bad had happened."

"Wow. That is amazing."

"Over the next year, the Axeman killed three more victims. I wasn't worried for myself anymore, though, after that night."

"Why? He or she was still killing."

"His letter and the keeping of his word told me he loved jazz, and I played it every night on my phonograph anyway, so I knew he would never bother me."

"What happened to him? Did they catch the person?"

"No. He disappeared and never attacked again. A local composer Joseph John Davilla wrote a piece called 'The Mysterious Axeman's Jazz.' And that is how jazz saved my life."

"That story can never be beaten. Wow."

Camille smiles the biggest smile ever, and Chloé reciprocates.

"Okay, so when does my great-grandfather come into your life?"

"That would be in late summer of 1919. His name was William Marlow. He was originally from England, a smooth talker, and much older than me. William had dark hair, a strong build, and irresistible brown eyes. He was in town for the summer and swept me off my feet. He was an actor-playwright, and I was an amateur actress with a local drama group. We went dancing every night. He was an incredible dancer… and a few other things." Camille winks at Chloé. "Well, the end of the summer came, and I found out I was pregnant. I told William, and then one morning, he was gone. I found a note he left me saying he could not stay and wished me the best with the baby."

"Wow. So he never married you?"

"No, never saw him again."

"Wow."

"I suppose he *couldn't* marry me. He wrote me a letter later again apologizing, and in that letter, he said he had returned to Arkansas to his wife and three kids."

"Wow! He had a family?"

"Yes. That came as a bit of a surprise, but it was nice to know I could let it go and not have to wait for him to return."

"That's amazing. So you were a single mom. Did you ever marry?"

"No, I never did, though I had lots trying to catch me." Again Camille winks.

"So you were an actress?"

"Yes. Not an exceptionally good one, but it was something I enjoyed. I got interested in it early on. When I was young, René would take our family to the French Opera House. It was called the Heart of New Orleans. They would have grand opera productions, concerts, and Mardi Gras balls. Evening concerts would sometimes last five hours. I remember a shop next to it out front that sold wigs and masks. Sadly, the opera house burned down in 1919. If you go where it stood, you can see the street is still wider where the carriages were meant to pull over to let out their passengers.

"All those nights, there was my inspiration. My acting group was called the Drawing Room Players. Louise Nixon was the founder of the group, and also our group's president. It seems like just yesterday. We started out meeting at the home of Mrs. Abe Goldberg. We all chipped in together to buy playbooks. In 1919 we moved into an apartment in the

French Quarter. We would all get together and act out the plays. Then in 1922 we moved into the Le Petit Theater du Vieux Carré. It is a Spanish-style building built in the 1700s, the oldest nonprofessional theater in the country. It is located on St. Peter. If you have time, you should go by there. You may even find an old photo of me hanging around."

"I will. I'm in awe of how well you remember names."

Camille winks and asks, "You mean, at my age?"

Chloé's face turns red and she quickly says, "I'm just amazed because I can't even remember my professors' names from a couple of years ago."

"That's what a nice reporter told me on my hundredth birthday."

"Reporter?"

"Yes. I was on television and in the paper. They just asked me a lot of stuff about turning one hundred and about the history of New Orleans. I've seen a lot of things."

"I bet you have. So I'm talking to a local celebrity."

Blushing, Camille waves her hand dismissively. "Oh, I would not say that. I was just an old lady telling a story. I suppose there are a lot of people out there who want their presence known... but I think most of us just want our absence felt."

"Why did you stop acting?"

"It was just too much for me to be a single mom and to find the time. In 1920 Adam René Laver was born—your grandfather. I wanted to honor Papa with his middle name."

"Where did the 'Adam' come from?"

"Oh, I was thinking of the Bible and the creation of man in the beginning, so I named him Adam because this was a new beginning for him and me. Adam grew up to be a good man and loved jazz almost as much as I do. After college, he fought bravely in World War II on the beaches of Normandy and, after the war, became a highly respected saxophonist, teaching music in schools. He married a schoolteacher, Pam —your grandmother—and they had a son, Henry Laver, your uncle, in 1945, and your mother, Monica, in 1950. Henry was in the army and was killed in Vietnam on November 8, 1965. I will never forget that day... It devastated everyone, but especially your mom. Four years later, your mother married Thomas Hall, your father. Tragedy continued to follow us, however. The day before your mom found out she was pregnant with you, Adam suffered a major heart attack and died. My baby boy was only fifty. Too young... Too young." Tears begin to fall down Camille's cheek. "He never got to see you. Then you were born in 1971, and life seemed new again; however, Pam was diagnosed with breast cancer later that year. She passed away in 1972."

At this point, she reaches out to hold Chloé's hand. "Your parents had moved up to Arkansas—Little Rock, to be exact. They were returning home from Pam's funeral in New Orleans with you in the car when an oncoming driver fell asleep and hit them head on. You survived the crash. Your mom and dad did not. Thomas's parents had passed away, and he had no siblings or living relatives. I was eighty and found myself alone in the world, except for you, all within six years." Both Camille and Chloé are now in tears. "How was an eighty-year-old woman going to raise a one-year-old? I knew I had to find a good home for you, so we did with the help of a local agency. Your adoptive parents, Richard and Sharon, attended medical school here, and Richard was doing his residency when they took you in."

"I wish I could have contacted you sooner," Chloé tells her. "I am so sorry for that. I struggled with it for almost a year, wondering what to do with the letter."

"I made your new parents promise not to tell you until I contacted them."

"I understand." With a sniff, Chloé changes the topic. "I got to see the French Quarter last night."

Camille nods. "Oh, the Quarter. It isn't what it once was. Back in the twenties, we had quite a bohemian ambiance happening. Some were calling it the Renaissance of the French Quarter. There were artists and writers everywhere. I joined other creative individuals and attempted to bring a Montmartre District to New Orleans. The French Quarter was going downhill fast, and we saved it. There was a melting pot of people at the time all around Jackson Square. A friend of mine named Lyle Saxon did much to encourage creatives to move to the area. I made several attempts at painting at the time of the Quarter's buildings but was never as good an artist as my mother. During this time, though, I included much of my pottery in a few galleries in the Quarter. We really had something special going on, before it became what it is today—a tourist destination. We had some wonderful artists here during this renaissance. One, for example, was one of my close friends and an aspiring young artist named William Spratling. You may not know his name, but you will his roommate's, William Faulkner."

"Yes, I definitely know of Faulkner."

"Another name you might recognize is Sherwood Anderson."

"I don't recognize that one."

"Well, my favorite book of his was *Dark Laughter*. It was about certain unnamed freedoms during the roaring twenties, if you know what I mean." Camille gives one of her characteristic winks. "Quite controversial. Well, I often attended parties thrown by him and his wife, Elizabeth. Let's just say during the time of Prohibition, they were good people to know. Sadly in 1941, Sherwood died from complications from swallowing, of all things, a toothpick."

"That's terrible."

"Sorry, I got sidetracked, back to the Quarter. We had something really special happening, but unforeseen to us, the popularity became a curse as the cost of living there pushed out the very people responsible for saving it. If that wasn't enough, what I feel was the final nail was the tourists, and by the thirties, our renaissance was over."

AFTER THEY TALK for a few more hours, it is beginning to get dark. Camille tells Chloé while pointing to the sky. "See that really bright star?"

"Yes."

"That is Arcturus. René told me when I was a little girl that that star was my mother. He said she would always be watching over me. Still to this day, I have the nurses take me out here some nights, and I talk to her. I told her last night all about you. One day I'll be up there with her watching over you."

"I hope that will still be a long time from now."

"I will not live forever, even though sometimes I feel like I will. Between you and me, I hope it will be a long time also. Well, I think it's probably time for me to get some rest, dear."

Chloé wheels Camille back to her room. "Before you leave, sweetheart, here is something I wanted you to have last time you were here, but I forgot. I do that sometimes, you know, forget." As they approach the bed, Camille reaches into the drawer of her nightstand and pulls out a key. Her hand trembles as she places it delicately with both hands in Chloé's palm. "This is the key to my house. I'm sorry, it may be a mess. I haven't had anyone clean it since I've been here."

"I'm sure it's fine."

"All the paintings throughout the home were done by my mama, Tessa, your great-great-grandmother. You can see some of my pottery also. On a shelf downstairs in the library, when you enter, you will find a stack of journals tied in a ribbon. These are Mama's journals. Please bring those with you next time."

"I will," Chloé says as she hugs Camille goodbye.

Returning to her hotel, Chloé is given a stack of messages left by Nick at the front desk. Still troubled by how fast her feelings for him have been deepening, plus his relation to René and the fortune teller's reading, she feels she needs more time to process it all before seeing him again.

Reflections

THE FOLLOWING MORNING, rather than taking a cab, Chloé catches a streetcar to Camille's house just as she told herself she would if given another opportunity. She gets on the green-colored St. Charles streetcar at the corner of Carondelet and Canal. As it is only half full of people, she has her choice of seat; she opts for a wooden bench on the right side of the streetcar toward the back.

During her ride, an old man wearing a tall black top hat, a black tuxedo vest over a red hibiscus flower Hawaiian shirt, tan shorts, and Birkenstock sandals enters the streetcar and sits on the bench across from her. He looks over at Chloé and says, "Hello, my name is Henry Beauregard LeBlanc the Third. Many say I step to the beat of a different drummer, but I say I skip to the strum of a different ukulele."

Laughing, she responds, "Hi, my name is Chloé."

"Chloé, what a great French name. You don't sound local. What brings you to New Orleans?"

"I'm from Seattle."

"Seattle. A great city."

"I'm in town to visit my great-grandmother. She is in a nursing home currently, but I'm on my way to check on her house in the Garden District for her."

"Great homes in Uptown. I've lived there for over sixty years myself. Is this your first time to ride the streetcars?"

"Yes."

"You picked a good time to ride. It's best to catch the streetcar early. It gets crowded fast. You might want to open your window—there is no air conditioning. When you need to stop, you can pull the cable. Also, when you exit, you leave out the back door. Sometimes you have to push it open with a little force."

Chloé smiles in gratitude for his tips. "So, Henry, what do you do for a living?"

"Well, I am a public speaker."

"That's awesome. Where have you spoken?"

"Well, here. Right now. I am speaking to you. This is public. Also, I am a part-time magician, comedian, and juggler. Not a cat juggler... anymore. Poor little kittens. Just a juggler. I also am an artist."

Laughing, Chloé asks, "What type of paintings do you do?"

"Oh, everything. I prefer painting dogs with human bodies doing human things the best. One of my favorites I sold for a little over twenty thousand dollars at auction. It was a Great Dane dressed in spandex doing aerobics. I called it 'Dane Fauna.' I also made a fortune in the stock market. I once was one of the richest people in New Orleans. Now my ex-wife is." He laughs. "Just joking. Actually, I have never been married. I'm sure you're thinking, as handsome as he is, how can that be? I hear that often."

Again laughing, Chloé asks, "Who is the flower for?"

"This flower? You really want to know?"

"Yes."

"Well, it sounds silly, but I met a woman fifty-seven years ago this past March on this streetcar. We talked and laughed. It was the best day of my life. Her name was Mary. The next day I got on carrying a flower to give to her, but she wasn't there. I have ridden this car the same time every day since with a flower to give to her when I see her again."

Chloé finds herself choked up but gets the words out, "That's a beautiful story. Hopefully, you will get a second chance. Well, Henry, this is my stop. It was nice speaking with you. I hope you find Mary again."

"Nice to meet you as well. Have a nice day, Chloé."

Chloé steps off the streetcar at the Washington Avenue stop and proceeds on foot to Camille's home. She is in awe of the charming houses and beautiful oak tree-lined streets along the walk.

Approaching the house, she notices details that escaped her on her first visit. She runs her hands across the exquisite rose motif ironwork of the fence. Before climbing the steps to the front door, she walks off to one side to see the striking grounds behind the home, featuring sprawling gardens full of crepe myrtles and azaleas surrounding a lush outcropping of roses and camellias. Beyond the fountain-graced courtyard, she observes a charming gazebo encircled by ornate ironwork and laced with English ivy, nestled in the shadow of an old magnolia tree. She looks up at the house and sees the spacious balcony shading the sidewalk underneath. This place, she feels, is truly paradise. Imagining the beauty that must wait inside, she delays no longer and hurries to the door.

Upon entering the house, she is in awe of the colors in the foyer cast by the stained glass windows above the door and the beams of sunlight projected onto the cypress ceiling. The smell of mothballs fills the air. To her right is a large living room with all the furniture covered with beige canvas cloths. Pottery is scattered everywhere throughout the house. Beautiful pieces, though some are broken and others unfinished.

Stepping to her left, she enters the library full of classics from wall to wall. Taking a deep breath in, she savors the smell of the old paper. The sensation speaks to her of an appreciation of books that is lost to many people these days. Glancing at the books, she sees a copy of *Le portrait de Dorian Gray* by Oscar Wilde. This is Chloé's favorite book. Delicately opening it, she lets out a gasp, seeing that it is a first edition. She carefully returns it to the shelf. Looking up, she sees the library's ceiling is painted with cherubs dancing through trailing vines. Looking to her right, Chloé sees the stack of journals right where Camille described. Besides the journals, she finds a glass jar full of tiny pieces of paper with a small card on the top. The card, which is written in French, isn't hard for Chloé to translate.

My dearest Tessa, on our second anniversary, here are 730 reasons I love you. One for each day we have been together.

Sitting on the floor, she pours out the jar and begins reading slips of paper.

How you are patient and understanding with me even when I do not deserve it

The way you lay your head on my chest

Your beautiful artistic ability

The wonderful, caring mother you are

Your gentle kisses

The way you always know what I am thinking

Your strength and independence

The glow of your naked body in the moonlight

Your incredible caring heart

The sound you make when I kiss the back of your neck

Your intelligence

The smell of your skin that I constantly long for

Your kindness

Your laugh and smile that light up a room

Your sensual intimacy

The sacrifices you make for Camille and me

How you complete me

The way you melt in my arms

Your dreams

How we can talk about everything or nothing as long as we are together

Your delicately sweet voice

How you make me wonder how I ever lived without you

How every moment away from you feels like an eternity
You showed me what love really is
The beauty you find in the simple moments of life
You are the true embodiment of beauty
Your love of poetry
How my passion for you defines me

Chloé doesn't make it through them all, but after reading many more, she returns the jar to the shelf and steps back into the foyer—when she is suddenly paralyzed by what she sees suspended on the wall before her. How could she have missed it when she entered?

Chloé is face to face with her own reflection. Not in a mirror, but in a painting. Hanging on the wall is a self-portrait of Tessa, her great-great-grandmother. She grips the railing at the foot of the stairs, stunned at the resemblance between herself and Tessa. Camille was right; they really are a mirror image of each other. No wonder Camille recognized her.

Once she recovers from her emotions, she continues up the stairs to explore each room. She finds one bedroom full of porcelain dolls and even more pottery. Strangely, she finds no closets in any of the rooms. "Extremely odd," she thinks.

Back downstairs, Chloé discovers a wine cabinet fully stocked. She uncorks a 1969 Chateau Margaux and pours a glass. She feels that, after all that's transpired over the last several days, including most recently finding the painting of Tessa, she may need the whole bottle. Chloé is mesmerized by all of Tessa's paintings as she walks again from room to room. Admiring each one, she notices how similar Tessa's brush strokes are to her own.

Chloé returns to the library and takes up the journals, untying the ribbon around them and opening the top one. Not surprisingly, like the slips of paper in the jar, it is written in French, but with her knowledge of the French language, she knows that will not be an issue. She notices how beautiful Tessa's handwriting was, strikingly elegant and like the paint strokes similar to her own. Even though she is highly tempted, she replaces the journal on the stack, deciding to wait and read them with Camille.

Needing to leave soon, she finishes her wine and collects the journals. Upon exiting the house, she takes her time walking back to the streetcar stop. Soaking in the beauty of the Garden District, her curiosity is aroused by wondering how far away Nick's home might be. She cannot keep him off her mind. One part of her says to run into his arms, while the other says to run away. She feels scared, confused, and overwhelmed.

Stepping onto the streetcar, she sees Henry still in the same seat as before. She sits down on the bench across from him, and he says, "Why hello again. Did you have a nice visit to your great-grandmother's home?"

"Yes, I did."

"Good. Good. Well, young lady, this is my stop. No luck today. It was really nice talking to you, though. Here, you can have my flower."

Taking it from Henry, Chloé says, "Thank you."

With his chin up and an unconvincing optimism, he says, "Maybe tomorrow. Yep, tomorrow."

As Henry exits the streetcar, a man dressed in a gray suit enters and sits on the bench in front of Chloé. He turns and asks her, "Did you get to meet Henry?"

"Yes, I did. Do you know him?"

"Yep, most of New Orleans does. At one time, he was considered one of the greatest artists around. He is quite the mystery, though. Rumor has it that his wife Mary, who he met on the streetcar when they were young, passed away several years ago. They say he rides every day, hoping to recapture the past and meet her again. Others say he never was married." The man shrugs his shoulders and, turning to face forward, says, "Who really knows?"

WHILE CHLOÉ IS CATCHING a streetcar back to her hotel, Nick, having left work early, visits his parent's graves at the St. Louis Cemetery Number Three, a historical cemetery dating back to 1854. Standing by their tomb, he says, "Hey, Mom and Dad. Sorry I haven't visited in a while. I've had a stack of files to work on and significantly little free time. Dad, I am sure you can appreciate that.

"I met a girl. She is so amazing. You both would really like her. There is something about her that calms my soul… She is like no one I have ever met. Mom, I wish you were here to offer me some advice about women. I really like this one. I don't want to mess it up like I always seem to do. If there is any way you could guide me, it would be greatly appreciated. I'm kind of running blind here." He laughs, looking down at the flower arrangement in his hands. "Oh yeah, I brought you some flowers." He places them in front of their tomb. "I guess I'll be going. I miss you both so much. *Vous êtes toujours dans mon coeur.* You will always be in my heart."

THE JOURNALS

LATER THAT AFTERNOON, Chloé returns to Meadowbrook with the journals in hand. Entering Camille's room, she finds her lying on her bed. She walks over and hugs her great-grandmother.

"Hello, my angel," Camille says excitedly. "Thank you for coming back today."

"You are very welcome. The only thing on my mind has been hearing more stories. I couldn't sleep last night, I was so anxious to come back."

The elderly woman smiles and sees what Chloé is holding. "Oh good, you brought the journals. Did you have any problems finding them?"

"No, they were right where you said they would be."

"Good, good. How did the house look?"

"It was beautiful."

"Thank you. Yes, it is."

Chloé places the journals on the nightstand. "I thought you were just being kind when you said I looked like Tessa."

"Oh no, dear, you both are identical and so beautiful. It is almost magical."

"The house is gorgeous, and so is your pottery and all of Tessa's paintings. I also found a French first edition of *The Portrait of Dorian Gray*. That is my favorite book."

"It was my mother's as well. That was her copy. I brought it to America when we came here. You are welcome to it."

"Really? Thank you. I have a question about the house that is baffling me."

"Yes, dear. What is it?"

"Why are there no closets? I know that is an odd question."

Camille chuckles. "No, not at all. Back when many of the houses around here were built, there was what many called a closet tax. You were taxed on the number of rooms you had, and closets counted as rooms. So many people decided to save money and use armoires instead of closets."

"Wow. That is fascinating. Oh, I also opened a bottle of wine. I hope that's okay."

"Which one?" Camille asks eagerly, as if she were about to drink a glass herself.

"The 1969 Chateau Margaux."

"Ooh, that's a good one."

"I'm sorry. Is it okay that I opened it?" Chloé asks, worried.

"Of course, dear. That is wonderful. I would have chosen that one myself. There should be a '72 there also. Maybe you can sneak it to me past the doctor and the nurses sometime." Camille winks at Chloé, and they both laugh. "Oh, how I miss my wine... and dancing."

"I have another question. Have you heard of a Henry LeBlanc?"

Camille leans her head back and replies, "You must have ridden the St. Charles streetcar."

"Yes, I did. So you have heard of him?"

"Yes, he is a wonderful artist. He must be at least eighty-five by now. Glad to hear he is still around. When Mary passed away, he took it really hard. I hope one day he will find peace." Chloé looks downward, feeling her heart break for Henry. Camille, sensing this, bursts forward with the energy of a child and says, "So you brought the journals. Excellent. Have you read them yet?" Before waiting for an answer, she says, "Of course you have not, silly me. They are in French. I will have to try and read them to you. I will warn you, though, my French is a little rusty these days. Can you hand me my reading glasses, dear, and I will give it a try?"

"I am actually fluent in French," Chloé tells her. "I can read them to you instead and translate as we go."

"That would be wonderful. I may have the figure of a twenty-year-old, but the vision of an old woman."

Laughing, Chloé reaches over to the nightstand, unties the ribbon of the first journal, and, after clearing her throat, begins to read. She reads entries from 1891 and 1892. Once into 1893, Camille says, "Alright, this was my favorite year of all the journals. This was probably Mother's happiest time of her short life. It makes me kind of melancholy to think some people only have one or two good years. I was extremely fortunate to have so many happy ones. Sure, there were some rough ones too, but all in all, definitely more good. I hope you will have even more than me, my dear. I tell you, though, I would have traded them all to have felt the kind of love René and Tessa experienced."

"I hope I find that one day. All of it, the happiness and the love."

"Me too," Camille says warmly. "Okay, keep reading. This is my favorite part."

9 June 1893

Today was my first day at the Moulin Rouge. I am so happy Monsieur Zidler gave me this opportunity. He scares me, but the other girls have been so lovely to me. I do not know what I would do if it were not for them helping me backstage with Camille. Oh, Camille, my little angel. I am glad to be away from the Elysee-Montmartre. A dreary place, much less elegant than the Moulin Rouge. I am also happy to get away from La Goulue and the rumors that were flying around about her and me. I do miss Jane, though. Jane Avril was always a good friend to me. She helped me get off the streets, and I owe her so much for that. I have always been so envious of her beautiful red hair. I may not be able to be as beautiful as her, but I think I will use her name. Jane. What about a last name? I cannot just dance under the name Jane. What about Jane Pierre? Yes, I like that. So, Jane Pierre it is. Hello world, get ready to meet Jane Pierre.

CHLOÉ SAYS, "I still can't get over that my great-great-grandmother danced at the Moulin Rouge. This is so amazing."

"That's just the tip of the iceberg. Keep reading."

"I'm just in awe."

12 JUNE 1893

I really like working here. Hopefully, I can start earning more soon. I need to find a better home for my little angel and me. Camille is my everything. I'm not sure I am feeling well today. Have you ever felt the universe is listening to you? I really feel like something good is going to happen very soon. I can just feel it.

15 JUNE 1893

I have caught a dreadful cold. I should not have danced tonight, but we need the money. I think Camille might be getting sick too. I must make enough tomorrow to take her to the doctor. As for me, I cannot let anyone know I am sick. If they find out, they may not let me dance. As they say, the show must go on, and so must I.

22 JUNE 1893

Camille is doing better. I feel like I should also be, in a day or two. Luckily I have not missed a day of work. Intuition keeps telling me that something amazing is going to happen very soon. Brighter days are ahead; I just know it. Something big is coming. It has to be. I just know it.

25 JUNE 1893

I am so excited. Today I was asked by Toulouse-Lautrec to model for him. We went long into the night. They were all beautiful posters he painted of me. It is exciting to think about posters of me being hung all over Paris. I wasn't paid much, but this may lead to something bigger. What if this is what I have been feeling is coming?

CHLOÉ STOPS READING. "She knew Toulouse-Lautrec? My college professors would be freaking out right now. I know I am!"

30 JUNE 1893

Tonight was a wonderfully special night. I met someone—and not just any someone. I met René Louis Nattier. He is so handsome and so polite. Men give us much attention, but this one is different. There is something familiar and exciting about him. He made my heart skip a beat. He asked me to join him in the garden, in the open area off from the bar. I love the garden, with those tiny lights strung from tree to tree. The note he sent backstage simply said, "Meet me by the elephant." There is a giant elephant statue with a room inside of it in the garden. I think there is a small stage inside it, but I have not been in there yet. I waited a few minutes, and then he arrived just like he said he would. I've discovered he is a wealthy banker; however, I've also discovered he is married. Not really surprising; most men who come here are wealthy and married. He asked if I would meet him at the Eiffel Tower tomorrow at ten. I said yes, hoping I can get one of the girls to watch Camille. Then I was called back onstage. I almost missed my number. That would have been really bad. He kissed my hand and bid me a good night. I am speechless. It sounds silly, but I think I might be in love.

1 July 1893

I met René today at the tower. We had such a good time. It is hard to believe that so many people do not appreciate the beauty of it. The lift was not working, so we climbed the stairs. It was well worth it for the view we had of the city. We both placed a secret wish on a small piece of paper, put it in a gas-filled balloon, and watched it float away from the top of the tower. I wonder what he wrote on his. It is said if you tell your wish, it will not come true, so I had better not write mine here, in case someone sees it.

4 July 1893

Yesterday someone was killed in a demonstration between students and backers of Senator René Berenger. Unfortunately, unrest here in Paris has always been and probably always will be. What will the world be like when Camille is older? I fear for her future.

12 July 1893

René and I have gone out several times now. We went for a picnic at the Parc de Vincennes today. Lake Daumesnil is so beautiful. On the Isle de Reuilly at the Temple of Love, René asked me not to tell him but to make a wish and see if he could guess it. I told him I was ready, and he began looking me up and down, not saying a word. Then out of the blue, he said he had it. He told me to close *my eyes, and he would tell me what my wish was. I closed my eyes, and suddenly his lips met mine. He kissed me; he kissed me, he kissed me. René Louis Nattier kissed me. I am most definitely in love.*

CHLOÉ LOOKS UP AND REPEATS, "He kissed her. That is so sweet. She sounds like a little schoolgirl."

15 JULY 1893

Today René took me just outside Paris to Neuilly. It was so beautiful there. He kissed me passionately while walking along the river. He is such a gentleman. All the other men I have known have expected to sleep with me the first night I met them, and unfortunately, too many did. René is so different. I have fallen so deeply in love with him. If he wanted me now, I would give all of myself to him. We stayed out until dark, and he took me home by carriage. As I was going in, he stopped me, kissed my hand, and told me, "Good night, my love. May you have sweet dreams, Tessa."

20 JULY 1893

Yesterday Gustave Eiffel invited René's father to dine in his apartment on the tower's third floor. He was not able to attend and asked René to go in his place. René asked me to join him. We had a marvelous time, but René's wife, Diana, was furious with him. She had other plans and could not go with him, but she wanted René to go alone or not at all.

CHLOÉ SAYS, "WOW! GUSTAVE EIFFEL."

· · ·

25 July 1893

I am so happy. My friend Jane Avril has joined us at the Moulin Rouge. I have missed her so much. I caught her up on my romance with René. She seemed extremely happy for me, but also worried. She reminded me of what I have been trying to block out: René is married. She does not want me to get hurt. It already hurts me, knowing he will never stay with me at night and he will always go home to her.

1 August 1893

Today René gave me the biggest surprise ever. René brought me to a beautiful new flat in the Plaine Monceau District. We stepped out of the carriage, and I asked him who lives here, and he said, "You and Camille do." I almost fainted. He said he wanted us out of where we lived and into somewhere nice. I hugged him and told him I did not know what to say. All I could say was thank you. I was so happy. Then he said, "Let us look inside." It is beautiful. It has enormous mirrors and carpeted floors. Yes, I said carpeted floors. Can you believe it? The bed in Camille's room, René says, once belonged to Marie Antoinette. Her room was already filled with dolls of all shapes and sizes. We went to the master bedroom, which has a beautifully carved mahogany bed. He looked at me and said, "I need to tell you something, Tessa." Then he told me he loved me. My balloon wish came true. That is when I knew I had to have him right then. The moment was right, and we made love for hours. He was so gentle and caring, yet still rigid and strong.

CHLOÉ SAYS, "Holy wow! You slept in a bed that belonged to Marie Antoinette?"

"Yep."

"Wow!"

"Keep reading."

. . .

4 August 1893

   Today René asked me to leave the Moulin Rouge. He promised he would provide for Camille and me. He said he wanted me to be a lady with class and not a lady of the night. I no longer have to perform. Tonight was my last night. Monsieur Zidler was furious when I first told him, but he wished me good luck at the end of the night. I will miss dancing and the girls I danced with, but I will not miss being away from Camille.

"I STILL CAN'T BELIEVE she danced at the Moulin Rouge," Chloé says. "And that you were being babysat backstage."

10 August 1893

   Today René asked me about Camille's father. I told him everything about him being a playwright originally from Norway. How, like René, he swept me off my feet. We would spend our time at the opera house, where we brushed shoulders with society's elite. He was a handsome man with a silky mustache who always kept a lit cigar even though smoking in front of women was frowned upon. He was, like René, married. Most like him would not divorce their wives, out of a strange kindness. Divorced women are considered social outcasts, and he said he could not do that to his wife. He always kept his hair parted and laid flat. He loved the Russian ballet. The night we met, he gave me the flower from his button-hole, telling me I was the most beautiful woman he had ever seen. He was a great poet and playwright but an even better liar. He said he wanted to be with me forever. When I found out I was pregnant with Camille, he refused to see me again. Every time I went to see him, I was turned away by his servants. Last I heard, he had returned to Norway. After telling René all of this, he was dearly consoling. He promised me he would never refuse me. Something about René makes me believe him. There is nothing I love more than being in love with René, except Camille.

15 August 1893

René's father was in a duel today on the Isle La Grande Jatte. He is a highly reactionary man. I am so glad René does not carry his traits. The contest was with a local newspaper publisher. He was upset with the newspaper for unfavorable remarks. I understand they had nervous men standing next to them holding parasols since it was raining so hard. That's not a job I would want to have. The publisher's gun accidentally discharged, shooting a bullet into his own foot. The doctor on hand determined it was a wound and called the duel. René's father was so upset with the decision he wanted to duel with the doctor. They all finally calmed down. Luckily no one died. Men. I just do not understand some of them.

19 August 1893

I spent the day with René at the Luxembourg Gardens. I love the statues and the fountains. In the springtime, the flowers there are gorgeous. Some call it the most romantic park in Paris. I would have to say it is an incredibly close second to the Parc de Vincennes. The garden was created in 1612 by Queen Marie de Medicis, who wanted to capture the beauty of her native Florence. I would have to say she did just that with its exceptional beauty. René and I sat and talked and kissed. Every time I begin to talk about the future, René always cuts me off, saying, "Shh... let us live for the moment; the past is gone, and the future will be there tomorrow. Today belongs to today as this moment belongs to us."

21 August 1893

I have spent the entire day painting. Camille went to bed early. I am sitting here with paint all over my hands and now on this page as well. I have not heard from René today. Days like these are the hardest. I miss him so terribly. Almost time for bed, but first a glass of wine and a few favorite poems from Baudelaire.

13 OCTOBER 1893

I have done a terrible job remembering to write in my journal these past few months. There was a time when I never missed a day. Now I miss weeks instead of days. I spent all day painting. I just finished one of Camille holding one of her dolls. I planned on starting one of René, but I am running low on paint. I will have to buy more tomorrow.

22 OCTOBER 1893

René brought me to the Cafe Anglais for dinner. We dined in the Grand Seize on the second floor. The Grand Seize is a private dining room reserved usually for royalty, which René's family is treated as. It was a gorgeous room decorated in white, gold, and red. René locked the door after we ate, and we made love on the sofa in the alcove. Magical evening.

1 November 1893

While dining at Voisin's, René and I ran into Duke d'Aumale and Léonide LeBlanc, my favorite actress. The duke invited us to the Castle Chantilly for a holiday. Can you believe it? Our nanny will keep Camille. It will be difficult to leave her, but I know she will be in good hands. This is going to be such an exciting trip. I wonder what wonderful people we will meet. I cannot wait to go.

. . .

10 November 1893

After a short train ride, we arrived at the train station and were picked up by a private coach to take us to the Castle Chantilly. The duke is a famous war hero, but I did not realize he was a book connoisseur until I saw his enormous collections of books in his library. Chantilly is so beautiful. It is truly a fairy-tale castle with its gorgeous gardens, lakes, parks, and surrounding woods. Other guests were there, and we all gathered before the dinner party. I met Duchess d'Uzés, a woman I have always admired. She is the president of the Union of Women Painters and Sculptors. We had lots to talk about as the men escaped to the smoking room. We spent some time with the Duke d'Aumale and his mistress, Léonide LeBlanc. Also there was Count Boniface de Castellane. He is highly handsome and is referred to by many as quite a ladies' man. Famous playwright Georges Feydeau was speaking with René when I walked up as René was talking about me. He said I was not only an enchanting, gorgeous creature and intelligent, but clever and seductive as well. In a world surrounded by beautiful women, René makes me feel like the only one there. We were in the company of wealthy aristocrats, crown heads, and noblemen, many with irresistible charm. However, René has a way of making me feel so comfortable in an environment that still seems so strange to me.

12 November 1893

Today I read Madame Brandon's publication she wrote this past summer on her return to Paris following her American trip. She said she almost did not return to France because of how well women were treated there compared to in Paris. I recommend to every Parisian woman to read Impressions d'une Parisienne a Chicago. *I wonder if I will ever visit America. I could not imagine living there, though. I love Paris too much.*

. . .

27 November 1893

   Our short holiday to the French Alps was amazing. I left my journal home by mistake. René taught me how to ski. He said I was a clumsy natural, whatever that means. I loved to ski but did not care much for the falling. The only falling I like is falling in love. I am doing more and more each day with René. I so missed Camille, though.

1 DECEMBER 1893

   I have been in a shopping mood ever since I woke up this morning. René was sweet today, telling me I could go pick out anything I wanted. I opened the Echo de Paris newspaper today, not for the political editorials but for the shopping advertisements describing the latest dresses, jewelry, and furs. I probably spent more than I should have, but René did tell me there was no limit. The proudest purchase of the day was matching dresses for Camille and me.

10 DECEMBER 1893

   Another anarchist exploded a bomb in the National Assembly yesterday. Almost fifty people were hurt. I so worry about René. I hope he is careful.

14 DECEMBER 1893

   Attended a meeting of the Union of Women Painters and Sculptors. It was so inspiring. I could listen to Duchess d'Uzes speak all day and almost did. It was a particularly long meeting, but so empowering. Camille was so happy to see me when I returned home.

17 DECEMBER 1893

I am becoming increasingly angered by the way Diana treats René. She does not want to be around him, but she also does not want him around anyone else. Recently she scolded him for coming to see me, so he told her, "Fine, I will stay by your side." It only took four hours for her to tell him to go away.

21 December 1893

René is extremely upset with me. Jules Chéret asked me to pose for a series of posters that will hang all over Paris. I met him at his studio yesterday, and I went back today to finish. René is upset because I did not speak to him first about it and secondly because he is right; I should be painting posters and not posing for them. Who will ever view me as a serious artist if I keep posing and not creating? Some of them were incredibly difficult poses. One had me dancing in a dress, holding a glass of wine. It was impossible not to spill wine everywhere, which I did, including on my dress. For another, I had to hold a cat in my lap. It is amazing how hard it is to keep a cat still that long. I have several claw marks to show for proof. I also sat fanning myself. I posed dancing with a little person who was dressed as a jester. I had to keep lighting a lamp and another one riding a bicycle. I rode around the room in circles for what seemed an eternity. And finally, the most scandalous one of all—I smoked a cigarette. One would never see a woman doing that in public.

6 January 1894

I love the world of parasol stands, Tiffany glass, drawing rooms and dinner parties, white gloves in flutes, men with monocles, canes, and their polished silk hats. The dancing from learning the American Consuelo to the Napoleonic Quadrilles. All the intellectuals and their fascinating conversations, classical music to baritone singers. I love this world. But most of all, I love René.

. . .

27 January 1894

I spent the day painting, drinking wine, and reading a fantastic book by an author named Oscar Wilde. It is titled The Picture of Dorian Gray. *Just to think, what if one of my self-portraits I could cause to age instead of me? I could stay young and beautiful forever, and the painting of me could wrinkle and wither away.*

Chloé tells Camille, "You were right; she did like *The Picture of Dorian Gray.*"

"I told you."

5 February 1894

I love going to Maxim's. Not a prominent place, but I love the shaded lamps, gleaming tablecloths, and the people. It is perfect for eating, drinking, laughing, and dancing. René is taking me there tonight. I knew Maxime Gailurd, the owner, back when he was only a waiter. The place is a stunning example of Art Nouveau. I am so proud of Maxime. A true rags-to-riches story. I still remember when it was an Italian ice cream shop before Maxime took it over. Now it is a haven for beautiful women and delicious lobster.

11 February 1894

This evening René and I sat at the Cafe Terminus drinking and having a gay old time. It was more crowded than normal, but I must add they are always busy, just much busier tonight. Many new faces here we have never seen before. When René escorted me home in a carriage, Camille was already fast asleep. I sent the nanny home, and before leaving, René kissed Camille good night on her cheek, being careful not to wake her.

13 FEBRUARY 1894

A terrible thing happened yesterday. A person described by the paper as a twenty-something-year-old man with an unkempt beard was at the Cafe Terminus drinking a beer and smoking a cigar when he lit a bomb he concealed under his coat with that same cigar. At least one person was killed and many more injured. That is so dreadful. To think that René and I were just there two days ago. It easily could have been us there. Oh wait, here it gives the man's name Emile Henry. These anarchist types need to realize hurting innocent people is not a way to further one's cause.

20 FEBRUARY 1894

René finally got me outside today. Over the last few days since the Cafe Terminus bombing, I have been too afraid to go out. René said, "You cannot live your life in a shell. You cannot be afraid to live life to the fullest. Otherwise, the anarchists win. Fear is a powerful weapon, and it is up to us to disarm it." I know he is right.

1 MARCH 1894

Maxim's was incredible last night. And also surprisingly engaging. A gentleman stood up with a bundle of vegetables and began conducting the orchestra. Oddly, he actually did a better job than the actual conductor. There were quite a few men from Poland filling up the restaurant who got into a plate juggling contest with a group of bohemian little people. The juggling little people won, and people started tossing gold coins at them. This just seemed to encourage even more bad behavior, eventually leading to women jumping on tables and dancing seductively. A very interesting night *out. A typical night at Maxim's, however. We all had a great laugh. During all of it, all I could think about was looking forward to René's kiss good night.*

5 MARCH 1894

René and I spent lunch today at the Cafe Cuillier, sipping freshly roasted coffee. We continued to laugh hysterically about the excitement we witnessed nights before at Maxim's. Our laughter was so loud, I thought they were going to ask us to leave.

16 MARCH 1894

Another anarchist set off another bomb yesterday. This one was in the church of La Madeleine. It is becoming extremely scary to go anywhere. These anarchist bombers look like the rest of us. There would be no way for someone to pick one of them out of a crowd. On a brighter note, René took me to see the opening of Jules Massenet's opera Thaïs *tonight at the Opera Garnier. Exceptionally good, but definitely not for the modest. One might describe it as theologically sensual.*

AFTER MANY MORE JOURNAL ENTRIES, it is time for Camille to get some rest. Deep down, neither wants to stop as the stories of Tessa's life are played out before them. Chloé thinks to herself how amazing it is to be sitting with Camille, who played as a child backstage at the Moulin Rouge during its heyday.

But before departing, Chloé has something to share. "I want to tell you about a man I met."

"A man? Yes, tell me more, dear. After what we just read, love is in the air," her great-grandmother exclaims, throwing her hands up.

"I do not really know what to do. I have never fallen for someone so quickly."

"Sounds serious." Camille winks at her. "So, does he know how you feel about him?"

"Yeah, there is no way I can hide it."

"Does he feel the same about you?"

"Yeah, that's pretty obvious also."

"Then what could possibly be wrong, dear?"

"Things are going just way too fast. I have been dodging his calls for a couple of days now."

"Why would you go and do a silly thing like that?"

"I'm scared and confused."

"What in the world of? It sounds perfect."

"I guess that's just it. It's just too perfect that he's too perfect. That there's something purely magical about him, about the whole situation, about us."

"I say the moment you leave here, you call him. Sweetheart, love has no time frame. Just as it can be eternal, it can also happen instantly. There is no rule saying it has to be two seconds, two weeks, or two years before it can be called love. Sometimes for whatever reason, the stars line up perfectly, whether it is a greater power, fate, or destiny. Whatever it might be, you will never know if you don't give it a chance. And unlike how love can last forever, our opportunities to find it can pass by so quickly if we don't take that chance."

Chloé takes a deep breath. "There is something about him I think you should know."

"What would that be, dear?"

"His name is Nick Nattier."

"Nattier?"

"Yes. He is René's great-great-grandson."

Shocked, Camille asks, "How do you know he is related to René? There are other Nattiers in New Orleans."

"I verified it with him. He is René's great-great-grandson."

Camille leans back. "Well, is that not something?"

"Yeah, tell me about it."

"How did you two meet?

"We met by accident."

"By accident."

"Yes. The night I arrived here in New Orleans, the hotel recommended Arnaud's for dinner."

"Oh, I used to love eating there."

"They were busy and had no tables available. I was about to leave when a nice young gentleman offered to let me join him. That young gentleman turned out to be Nick Nattier, René's great-great-grandson."

"And I guess you could say the rest is history… I'm sorry, sweetie. I do not mean to make light of it."

"It is just like you said—it must be either a higher power, or destiny, or fate. Whichever it is, it seems meant to be. I don't know if I am ready for meant to be."

"You won't ever know if you don't try. Call him, talk to him, tell him about all of this."

"What if that scares him away, or what if it doesn't? Both options scare me."

"Talk to him," Camille urges. "Next time you return, I want you to bring him with you, sweetheart. I want to see him."

"You would really like him. He loves jazz almost as much as you. Also, Tennessee Williams."

"Oh, good. I like him already. I was friends with Tennessee Williams. Thomas, I called him. That was his real name. Thomas Lanier Williams the Third."

"Oh my gosh. Nick would love to hear about that."

"We would often have lunch together at the Pontchartrain Hotel. Lovely gentleman. Nick sounds like one as well… Talk to him."

"Okay, I will," Chloé replies. "Thank you for listening."

"Anytime, sweetie, anytime."

WHEN SHE ARRIVES BACK at her hotel, waiting for Chloé are more messages from Nick—plus a dozen red roses with a note attached: "Miss you, Nick." She contemplates calling him immediately but decides to wait for the morning. She spends the evening planning how and what exactly to tell him.

FACE FROM
THE PAST

THE NEXT MORNING, after having dodged Nick for the last couple of days, Chloé calls him at his home.

"Go ahead, caller. You are on the air."

"Nick?"

"Nick speaking."

"This is Chloé."

"Chloé! Where have you been? I must have dialed your hotel twenty times."

"Twenty-two, to be exact. I just needed some time to think. By the way, thank you for the flowers. They are beautiful."

"You are most certainly welcome. I missed you."

"I missed you too."

"Was it that fortune teller? I told you not to let them get in your head. They prey on people."

"It was just a lot of things. So much is happening so fast around me. I just needed a little space to figure things out. So where can we go for a great breakfast?"

"I know the perfect place," Nick tells her.

"Can you pick me up?"

"I'm on my way."

HE PULLS UP in front of the Ambassador Hotel, where Chloé is waiting on the sidewalk, in his Porsche with the top down. Parking in the street, he jumps out and opens the car door for her, saying, "Your chariot awaits, my lady."

She takes the seat. "Thank you, my good sir."

Making a U-turn, he drives away quickly, tires screaming. "You are going to love this place."

Loudly over the sound of the wind and the engine, she says, "You always say that."

"Have I been wrong yet?"

"No, I can't say you have."

Rounding a corner fast, he responds, "Well, there you go then."

Trying to keep her hair out of her eyes, she yells at the top of her lungs, "Do you always drive this fast?"

"Only when I'm trying to impress a beautiful lady."

Surprisingly she responds, smiling at him, "Well, just to let you know, it's working."

"We're here."

"Wow, that was fast. I think we could have just walked."

He parks and escorts her the rest of the way to Café du Monde. As they approach, besides a delicious smell of fried dough and powdered sugar in the air, she notices the charming green-and-white-striped awnings that beckon from a block away.

Chloé feels this is the best time to tell Nick about Camille and to ask if he would go with her today to Meadowbrook.

At the counter she asks him, "Will you please order for me? I have no idea what to get."

"No problem." He turns to order. "Can we have two plates of the sugar-dusted beignets and two cafe au lait?" He then looks at Chloé, who has a look on her face of *What did you just order?*, and tells her, "We each have three French-style doughnuts lavishly covered in powdered sugar, along with coffee and milk, on the way."

"Wow. That sounds delicious."

Relaxed at their table, they are engrossed in the sound of a nearby group of street musicians. Chloé, working up the courage to tell him about Camille, is just about to speak when Nick stands up from their table, walks over to the musicians, and drops some cash in their open guitar case on the ground.

As he rejoins Chloé at their table, she leans into him and says, "I have a story for you."

"Excellent. I like stories."

"I think you'll really like this one." She smiles and begins, "Once upon a time, there was a gypsy princess in Paris who lost her prince..." And she proceeds to tell him all about Tessa, René, and Camille.

"Wow. I'm speechless," says Nick when she's done. "That is an incredible story. I don't know what else to say. Just wow."

"I pretty much had the same reaction."

"Who would have thought two strangers' families would be so connected when we met at Arnaud's."

"Yeah, tell me about it."

"I mean, what are the chances."

"Right. I've asked myself the same question."

"I would love to meet Camille."

"Great, she wants to meet you as well."

"When?"

Chloé says with a laugh, "Today. Like, now."

"Today? Now?... Well, today it is. Strange, no one in my family ever mentioned her. She sounds amazing, and I would love to hear more about my family... *our* families, that is."

THEY CLIMB into his car and head to Meadowbrook. Once there, they wait in the lobby. As the orderly wheels Camille around the corner and Nick comes into view, Camille's heart skips a beat. Surprising everyone without saying a word, she rises from her wheelchair on her own for the first time in months and, with little help from the orderly, walks up to Nick and hugs him, starting to cry.

Suddenly she breaks the silence—"Oh Papa, I have missed you." Then she realizes what she has just said and that everyone is staring at her. "I am so sorry. Nick, I believe it is. I do apologize."

Smiling, he says, "No worries."

"You just look so much like your great-great-grandfather. He raised me."

"Yes, I know, Chloé told me the story. An amazing story, actually. And here we are. It is so wonderful to meet you, Camille. I am truly sorry about how my family neglected you when René passed away."

"That was long ago."

"So I hear you are a jazz fan," Nick says.

"Yes, one might say that," Camille responds, and smiles. "I hear you are also."

"You might say that as well. So what is your favorite song?"

"'Pretty Baby.'"

"Oh yes. Tony Jackson."

Camille smiles again, impressed with his knowledge. "I understand you also like Tennessee Williams. I knew him as Thomas."

"Oh wow, you knew Tennessee Williams?"

"Yes, we would have lunch at the Pontchartrain Hotel together. He was always writing. He never showed interest in women romantically, but one day my friend Blanche joined us for lunch, and he seemed intrigued with her. Not in a romantic way, of course. He did not like the ladies that way. He was interested in her chaotic personal life, which she too often shared."

"Wait. Wait. You had a friend named Blanche with whom he was intrigued. Did she inspire...?" Camille smiles. "Wait,

wait, wait— Don't tell me. I would rather just imagine the possibilities."

"You do that." She smiles once more and says, "Let's go outside and enjoy this day."

They all go out to the courtyard, and the topic stays primarily on jazz. Camille tells them, "Back in the spring of 1931, I got to meet Louis Armstrong for the first time at the train station. He was returning to New Orleans, and it seemed everyone in the city was there to greet him, and I was right in the front."

Chloé sits back and listens. It's like watching two old friends catching up; Nick and Camille get along like two seasoned soldiers returning from war. Nick learns more about his family and lots about Camille—her life with René, school at Newcomb, her pottery, and her career as a nurse.

After several hours of sharing life stories as if they were battle wounds and medals, it was time for Camille to get some rest. She rises from her wheelchair, giving Nick a huge hug and whispers in his ear, "Please take care of my baby girl."

"I promise," he replies.

THE MISSING
PAGE

THE NEXT DAY Chloé returns to see Camille with the journals and an umbrella in hand. Walking into her room, Camille's face lights up with a smile and the words, "My angel has returned to see me."

"Yes, even this New Orleans rain couldn't keep me away. Anyway, I'm from Seattle. We get lots of rain."

"This, my dear, is nothing. You should have seen the Grand Isle hurricane of 1909. More than three hundred people were killed, and all the telegraph lines were downed. With no communication, people around the country were worried for us. Rumors began that the city was swept away. The flooding was terrible. Then there was the New Orleans hurricane of 1915. Over two hundred people were killed that late summer into early fall—roofs were blown off buildings. The roof of the Presbyterian church on Lafayette Square collapsed. The wind was worse than in 1909, but besides Lake Pontchartrain overflowing, the flooding was not. I also remember Hurricane Betsy back in '65. Of course, the one I remember the most for some reason was Hurricane Camille." She winks at Chloé.

Laughing, Chloé says, "I wonder why?"

"That one was in 1969. It was the largest one I ever went through. Highway 90 was over ten feet underwater. The wind was so strong."

"Not much wind out there today. Just a lot of rain."

"We sure could have used that rain in 1919 with the fire in the French Quarter. I remember I told you about the French Opera House on Bourbon and Toulouse Street when it was destroyed by fire. It was more than just an opera house. More than a beautiful concert hall. It was a special place to me."

"What is the earliest memory you have from here in New Orleans?"

"Oh gosh, that is a hard one. I would have to say it would be the moving of the Henry Clay statue. In around 1860, before my time, barely." She laughs. "The artist Joel T. Hart erected a statue of former senator and secretary of state Henry Clay in the median of Canal Street on the corner of St. Charles. By 1900 it became a hindrance to the streetcar lines, and around that time, I remember it being moved to Lafayette Square. If I remember right, I think someone got injured that day trying to move it. We all gathered in the street to watch. I remember sitting on Papa's shoulders. Then there were trips to the White City Amusement Park. We rode the rides and even attended an opera there. But my favorite amusement park was the Old Spanish Fort." Getting excited, she tells Chloé, "Oh my dear, we had so much fun there. I was older then but so loved that park."

"What was it like?"

"Oh my. There was everything. There were rides like the Scenic Railway. It was a roller coaster." A wink at Chloé. "I like roller coasters. Oh, that wind in my hair. During the summer, the breeze coming off the lake was magical. We did not have these air conditioners your generation is used to. There was a casino, restaurants, a hotel, and even an alligator pond. Oh, and also a dancing pavilion. I danced, danced, and danced to Paoletti's Orchestra. It was called the Coney Island of the South. For good jazz music, I used to catch the streetcar and ride it there to enjoy Piron's New Orleans Orchestra and Johnny Miller's New Orleans Frolicers. Oh, those were good times. So many memories there. I remember once a young gentleman named Mitchell Brenner proposed to me at a German restaurant there called The Rhine."

"What?"

"Yes. We had not gone out but a few times. He was such a sweet man. I broke his heart that night, but I was not ready to settle down. I told you men chased after me." Smirking, she adds, "I was quite a catch."

Laughing, Chloé asks, "Is the park still there?"

"Oh, no. In the late twenties, some land was reclaimed from Lake Pontchartrain, forming Pontchartrain Beach. That was what they called the new park. It was opened in 1928 by Harry J. Bart Sr., where the old fort stood. It was a nice park. There was a wooden roller coaster called the Zephyr." She puts her arms up in the air laughing. "Whee! They also had a carousel, Ferris wheel, and other common rides. There were swimming pools and bathhouses—lots of concerts. Your uncle Henry worked as a busboy for the Bali Ha'i Tiki restaurant that was there when he was in high school. If you go out on Bayou near Robert E. Lee Boulevard, you can still see some brick ruins from the fort, and the Milneburg Lighthouse still stands. Everything else now is just a memory."

"I love hearing your stories. Are you ready to hear more of Tessa's?"

"Oh yes."

"I'm glad I marked the page we left off on."

24 June 1894

What a terrible evening. We just attended a banquet in Lyon at the Chamber of Commerce for President Carnot. He delivered a fantastic speech stating sadly he would not seek reelection. Afterward, a little after 9 p.m., outside an art exhibit at an exposition we were attending, a man charged the presidential carriage beside us and fatally stabbed the president. Why would anyone do such a thing? Why could they not just wait? He was leaving office anyway.

27 JUNE 1894

We visited Arcachon in the Landes forest of Southwestern France. We soaked our cares away in the baths, then walked along the beach collecting shells. The setting sun was glorious over the horizon. The sky was dancing on fire with the most brilliant of colors. While there, we visited the small village of Brassempouy to lay eyes upon a recently discovered ivory statue of a woman. We were able to speak to archaeologist Édouard Piette about the discovery. He let me hold the head in my hands. Monsieur Piette said he thought it was approximately twenty-five thousand years old, making it the oldest statue of a human face ever. Its name is the Venus of Brassempouy. I was in awe of it as well. We also went to the Dune du Pilat, Europe's largest sand dune at one hundred meters tall. I got to sled down it twice. It is amazing. I would like to bring Camille here someday and let her slide on the dunes.

CAMILLE SPEAKS UP, "I visited France in 1967 to see Mama's grave. Do you know what I did?"

Chloé answers excitedly, "You did not!"

"I did! Can you picture this seventy-five-year-old woman sliding one hundred feet down that sand? That was a sight, I tell you. I doubt I could pull that off today. I was a youngster back then. Even though I thoroughly enjoyed it, I mainly did it for Mama."

"I cannot wait to see it one day."

"You must! It is your heritage. Also, you need to pass all of this on to your children—once you find the right man, of course. Maybe you already have, huh?" She winks at Chloé.

"I am definitely not rushing that." They both laugh, and Chloé continues reading.

29 JUNE 1894

I wrote a poem today sitting on a bench by a small pond in the Parc de Vincennes.

"Down by the water in the moonlight
I sit staring at a water lily
It beckons for me to paint it
The reflections of the stars on the water frame the lily
The stars, like sprinkled white seeds, appear to be dancing
Dancing with each ripple
Ripples caused by the slightest breeze
Oh, water lily, do I paint your bloom or pluck it
Now I have seen your bloom, will I ever forget you
Will you command all my thoughts if I do not have it?
Will I cry when your petals fall to the floor
Will I wish I never saw you?
Yes...Yes...
Like other beautiful things, your bloom, too, will leave
It will be gone
Gone
I should have painted you instead."

1 JULY 1894

Tonight was a much-needed relaxed evening. I put Camille to bed early while René and I sat in the study and sipped champagne while reading poetry from Charles Baudelaire's collection Les Fleurs du mal. *We take turns reading our favorites. I love when René reads poetry to me.*

. . .

2 JULY 1894

René commissioned a private railway coach that took us to Côte d'Azur (the French Riviera). We stayed in Nice and dined on delicious food and fine wines. We lived and played like royalty on our holiday. Last night we waltzed late into the evening with not a care in the world.

10 JULY 1894

We traveled this week to Biarritz, a city nestled on the Bay of Biscayne. The Atlantic coast is so beautiful. We are so close to Spain. It seems a waste not to go there also. We are staying in the Hotel du Palais. We walked this evening west of the main beach to a glorious view from the cliffs. Absolutely breathtaking. I so miss Camille. I look forward to her getting older and possibly traveling with us.

16 JULY 1894

Today we attended a glorious garden party. I usually despise garden parties, but I was treated like a real respectable upper-class lady today. We were taken there in a coach driven by a female cabbie. Times are changing. Soon we women will be wearing pants. Nah... I doubt that.

21 JULY 1894

We have just returned from Deauville. René has a house there, being the closest seaside resort to Paris. By the sea, it is truly gorgeous. I had my hair styled and scented with sandalwood and relaxed in glorious hydrotherapeutic baths there while René sampled much absinthe and cigars. In the evening, we walked on the promenade. I cannot wait to show this to Camille someday.

· · ·

22 July 1894

How exciting, Le Petit Journal hosted a competition today for horseless carriages. I am not exactly sure how these contraptions work, though we had the opportunity to see them up close yesterday at an exhibit. René called this a motor race. The participants were to ride these horseless carriages from Paris to Rouen. The person I thought won did not, because René said their vehicle needed something called a stoker, I believe; well, anyway, that disqualified them. René is calling these horseless carriages the transportation of the future, but I think they are just a novelty. They will never take the place of a good horse and a lovely carriage. I would much rather hear the hoofbeats of horses than these clanking things.

24 July 1894

I am worrying more and more about Camille. Her moods are ever changing like a kaleidoscope. She constantly asks for René. She thinks of him as a father, but she just cannot understand why he never spends the night with us. I knew this is hard on me, but I don't know why I never thought it affects her deeply as well.

27 July 1894

I have been so bad this year keeping up with my journal entries. Today at the Café Anglais, we dined on an exquisite meal prepared by the chef Adolphe Dugléré, who has been called the 'Mozart of French cooking.' I have never eaten so much in my entire life. I think Camille enjoyed the atmosphere as well. It is so cute the way she stares and studies each person. Then she smiles at all the men. She will someday be a heartbreaker. René is so good to us.

1 August 1894

I spent my day playing dolls with Camille and began working

*on another self-portrait. It has been two days now since I last saw
René. I caught myself this evening talking to one of my paintings
of him.*

4 August 1894

*We attended the Bayreuth Festival in Bayreuth, Germany. It
was a wonderful festival started by Richard Wagner and his close
friend Friedrich Nietzsche. In memory of his passing, we gave our
condolences to Cosima, Wagner's widow. I have always loved
Wagner's music. It is hauntingly beautiful. It borrows your
thoughts during the day and owns your dreams at night. Camille
would have loved playing in the grass with the other children there.
René bought me some bohemian glass, and we engrossed ourselves
in the music of Wagner in the Bayreuth Festspielhaus Theater. It is
such a beautiful opera house. The exterior seems quite ordinary,
but the wood interior leads to magnificent acoustics.*

14 August 1894

*René and I visited the Bois de Boulogne, where we strolled
through the beautiful rose garden in the Parc de Bagatelle. René
picked a rose and placed it on my hat. Why cannot more days be
like today?*

23 August 1894

*I spent the day with René and Camille at the Louvre. No
matter how many times I see it, I find the Winged Victory of
Samothrace. The most amazing sculpture I have ever laid eyes
upon. The detail, the drapery lines, and the marble's flawless grain
are breathtaking.*

. . .

27 August 1894

Today René took me on a romantic boat ride on the Lac Daumesnil. My parasol relieved me of the sun. Once the evening drew near, it was much more comfortable. It is hard to imagine in this heat that children will be skating on this lake in several months. I do look forward to cooler temperatures. No trip here would be complete without a kiss on the Isle de Reuilly. This is an extremely happy girl.

5 September 1894

Dining out at Maxim's tonight, René and I ran into the actor Sarah Bernhardt. Years ago, there were rumors of a short affair with René's father, so the two acknowledged each other, and René introduced me. She is so beautiful. She told us she is practicing for a Victorien Sardou play about fifteenth-century Athens due out later this year. She, as expected, will play the title role.

CHLOÉ SAYS, "That's so cool she got to meet such a famous French actor as Sarah Bernhardt. Did you know in the early 1900s she had her right leg amputated?"

"Yes, I remember reading about that," Camille replies. "Sometime around World War I. Maybe just before it."

"Today, that would be like meeting Meg Ryan or Julia Roberts."

"Who, dear?"

Laughing, Chloé says, "Never mind."

10 September 1894

René was attacked on the street today. He is okay, but I believe he is a little shaken still. And I am sure his pride is a little damaged. If it would have happened to me, I would be in shock, and probably afraid to walk out my door. The police told René the attack was called Le Coup de la Petite. I had to ask him what the 'trick of the little chair' means. René said the thief came up behind him and placed his knee in René's back, causing him to bend backward like sitting in a chair, while the thief grabbed his throat with one hand and reached around, stealing his pocket watch with his other. It reminds me of the world I grew up in.

15 September 1894

I finished a painting today. I titled it the 'Heart Pizzicato.' It is a nude figure crying with her head down alone, playing a cello with her bleeding fingers. The top half of the cello gives the appearance of a heart, while one of the strings is broken. Her soul is stripped away. Her heart has snapped like the string, having been plucked away by a lover.

21 September 1894

I have been finding myself drawn more and more into the world of Post-Impressionism lately. More precisely, Paul Gauguin. His work feels different to me than most Impressionism. I do not feel he is getting the notoriety he deserves. His colors are alive and daring. I would like to meet him someday.

25 September 1894

I waited all day for René. I miss him so much. The hours without him pass like years. Whenever Camille asks me where he is, it so breaks my heart. When? When will he ever be here forever? When will it ever be just the three of us? A real family. As I fall asleep tonight, please let me dream, dream about our family and our happiness. René, oh René, please, where you are, dream of us, please dream of us.

· · ·

27 September 1894

René sent over a dressmaker today. He said it was time I needed something new. We are attending a ball next week. Hopefully, Diana will not ruin this one. It seems she always tries to interfere with our plans.

3 OCTOBER 1894

René gets so much pressure from his father about how he should train me to be more like Diana. His father feels so threatened by enlightened women. Telling René, "Women need to be reminded of their place." He told René today, "Women need boundaries. They need to be reminded of their places, whether it's your wife raising your children and supervising your servants or your mistress as a whore.' René defended me, telling him I was no whore. He told his father how special I am. His father thinks he has gotten too close to me. That women like me are what is wrong with society. I am glad René does not share his father's beliefs. We women are not to be our men's servants to cook for them, press their clothes, and lie on our backs whenever they like. We have ambition, brains, and hearts. I am so thankful René agrees.

6 OCTOBER 1894

We dined at Maxim's again tonight. It was much less exciting than usual. No one jumped on any tables. Probably a good thing. It was Camille's first time there, and I would not want her to be scared to go back. We called it an early night as the coach dropped us at home. I kissed René good night and watched him ride off. I so wish he could spend just one night here with me.

· · ·

7 OCTOBER 1894

I am wishing for more and more one-on-one time with René. All these balls, horse shows, dinners, operas, and conversations with the other ladies about fashion and hair are wearing on me. I want to talk about art and poetry. So many of these so-called sophisticated ladies at these parties cannot name at least three artists or have ever opened a book of poetry. I so long for the quiet nights with René when we would look at the stars, kiss in the moonlight, take long walks, and share poetry.

10 OCTOBER 1894

Saw the most brilliant palette created by Alphonse Mucha today promoting Sarah Bernhardt's new play, "Gismonda." It is the one back in September she told René and me about. It will open at the Theatre de la Renaissance.

16 OCTOBER 1894

Oh, quite the scandal has erupted. Alfred Dreyfus, the French army officer, was arrested yesterday. They are saying he was arrested for spying. René knows him and said today he believes he is innocent. I overheard René mentioning something about corruption, though. René's father believes he is guilty.

AFTER MANY MORE JOURNAL ENTRIES, judging by the sparseness of the remaining pages, Chloé knows she is close to the end of the final book.

26 August 1895

We went to Trouville in the lower Normandy region of North-western France. It is so beautiful there. We strolled on the beaches and bathed in the waters, and the highlight of the trip was when René took me sailing. He showed me how, and I mastered it like a great ship captain. I loved it. I love René. I only wish Camille was with us.

28 August 1895

René told me today he and his family are leaving for a holiday in Scotland. Immediately I was heartbroken. Then he told me he wants me to go with him. He has already arranged a nanny to stay with Camille here in Paris. I am not sure if I can be away from her for so long, though. This would be the longest she and I have ever been apart.

31 August 1895

We arrived in Scotland yesterday. Diana knows I am here and is making it very difficult for me to find time alone with René. She followed him grouse shooting today, as if she was keeping up with his every move. René has arranged for me the most beautiful chateau. When he came to see me, I had tea prepared, but he refused to drink it, saying it was only for when you are sick. Tea just has not caught on in France as it has in Scotland. I miss Camille so much.

3 September 1895

Today out walking in the woods by a stream, René took me by the hand, spun me around, and placed his hands on my cheeks. I thought he might kiss me, but he quoted Keats out of the blue. "I almost wish we were butterflies and liv'd but three summer days— three such days with you I could fill with more delight than fifty common years could ever contain." Then he kissed me.

. . .

15 September 1895

Today after his hunt, René shed his outdoor attire, we made love, and then I joined him in a little more formal dress. We sat out on the terrace that was covered in vines in the shadow of the chestnut trees, and I finally got him to drink some tea. He actually enjoyed it. At least, he said he did.

22 September 1895

Autumn has arrived, and like most of the other wives here, Diana is staying in Scotland for the season, and like most of the husbands, René is returning to the city. I cannot wait to get back to Paris. I so miss Camille.

1 OCTOBER 1895

I am so in love with René. My love for him has breathed breath into each day I am beside him. Today we took a long walk through the rolling hills of Scotland. I could easily be persuaded to return here every year. We will be returning soon to Paris, and finally, René will be able to lay with me each night until Diana returns. I so look forward to feeling his strong arms around me as I sleep with my head on his chest.

10 OCTOBER 1895

Finally, back in Paris. I so missed Camille. In the weeks we have been gone, Camille has grown so much. It is good to be home. It is nice to have some time with René to myself, too. I know it will not be long, though, and Diana will be home from Scotland. Today we attended a garden party, and I was bored stiff. I used to enjoy these types of events. Women in all their female elegance, with their wide-brimmed hats, hoop skirts, and corsets squashed under their breasts, all to try and impress the superficial men and women who are as foolishly frivolous as they are. How did I ever see this as elegant?

11 OCTOBER 1895

Last night was the first time René stayed the night. We made love as if it were the first time as he held me. We made love again, and then I fell asleep in his arms. To wake up and see him sleeping beside me with his arms wrapped around me, draped across my breasts, was like the existence of some sort of divinity, purifying every part of my soul, as if God himself was pulling heaven down around me. Camille was so happy to have René here. She loved seeing him eating breakfast with us. This is the closest she and I have ever been to a truly normal family life. I want to hold onto this feeling forever.

13 OCTOBER 1895

I took Camille down to the Parc de Vincennes, where she played by the lake. I cannot help thinking about the first time René kissed me every time I am here. Camille and I played hide-and-seek following a lovely picnic. It was almost a perfect day. The only thing missing was René.

19 OCTOBER 1895

René brought Camille and me to a play tonight at the Palais Garnier. He picked us up in a coach with a private coachman. Inside the carriage, it was upholstered in red satin, extraordinarily elegant. We had a wonderful evening, and again, René stayed the night with us. It may seem cruel, but I hope Diana never returns from Scotland. I must go; René is coming in from smoking his cigar.

. . .

20 OCTOBER 1895

I have not picked up my paintbrush in days. That must change immediately. I saw breathtaking orchids today that I feel I must paint. I have been sucked too far into the life of these aristocrats. I caught myself today reading an article published in the Gil Blas *periodical about prize poodles, as well as the latest fashion. Yes, I need to start painting again before I am turned into some faux sophisticated, aristocratic snob.*

21 OCTOBER 1895

I was afraid she would do this. Diana decided to return home to Paris a month early. I am sure she cannot stand the thought of René sleeping with me. I do not understand why it should matter to her. She does not love him, she does not kiss or touch him, and they sleep separately. I do not think it would be far reaching to say she hates him; of course, it does seem she hates everyone.

AFTER MANY MORE ENTRIES, Chloé finally gets to the last page containing writing. "Wow. We have finally reached the end."

13 November 1895

Today Camille and I visited the tower. We went to the very top. I had her tie a wish to a gas-filled balloon and let it go. I told her never to tell anyone her wish, or it will not come true. We fed pigeons with some bread crumbs when we got back down to the bottom.

CHLOÉ LOOKS up at Camille and asks, "Do you remember what your wish was?"

"Why, of course. I am the one who wished it, but I never told anyone. It is one of my oldest memories."

"Can you tell me what it was?"

"Yes. I remember it because I spent my entire life regretting it."

"Why would you regret it?"

"Well, it came true. My wish was for René to be my father, and he became my father, but at the cost of losing my mother. I should have wished for the three of us to be a happy family and live together forever."

"It was not your fault."

"As I got older, I began to realize that. For a long time, though, I carried much regret. Go on, dear, keep reading."

15 November 1895

I am working on a painting I cannot wait to present to René. It is of our family—René, Camille, and me. I so wish he could hang it in his home, our home, but I know it will never see the light of day outside these walls. Walls that shelter Camille and me from the elements but do nothing to protect my heart from the pain it feels every day. Jane Avril warned me about getting too close, but René is my soul mate. It is so close to perfect. But I fear this lack of perfection will be my downfall. I must always keep Camille safe. At all costs.

Chloé turns the page to verify again it is the last page, hoping by some miracle she will find more pages, like a child searching under the tree at Christmas for just one more present; but what she finds surprises her even more. She can see the edges of where a page has been removed. She says, "It looks like there was one more page, but it has been torn out."

Camille reaches for Chloé's hand and places a folded-up piece of paper in her palm. "This needs to return to where it belongs."

Chloé unfolds it and, by the color and texture, can tell exactly where it belongs. She places the paper beside the book, and the torn edges match perfectly. She reads it aloud.

DEAR SWEET RENÉ,

Was it preordained that we not share this life as one? I know not how I survived all those wretched years I lived before you found me. Oh my lord, what have I done to deserve this torment bestowed upon me? I cannot go on living without you, René. Here I lay, breathing my last breaths, just a hapless casualty of love. Just a martyr of some tragic love story. I know you are leaving, and I know I will never see you again. The thought of this is the reality I must face. The choice I have is life without you or death without you. One, for me, is far more painless. I cannot bear for Camille to struggle as I have. Without you, I can never provide or protect her in this cruel world. I do this hoping she will have a better life and an opportunity I never had. Please embrace her and raise her as your own. Never let her forget me or my love for her. Please forgive me, my sweet darling. Please, I beg you not to think ill of me.

I recall the words by Keats you spoke to me: "I will be 'awake for ever in a sweet unrest, still, still to hear her tender-taken breath, and so live ever—or else swoon to death.'"

I will find you one day in another life, and we will be together again. Look for me, my love. I will be there.

"She dwells with Beauty—Beauty that must die." -Keats
Your beloved, Tessa

BY THE TIME Chloé is finished reading, tears are falling everywhere, even on the paper. "I'm so sorry I got tears on it."

"Oh, my child. No worries. Believe me, you are not the

first and possibly will not be the last to drench this page with tears."

Chloé realizes she is holding the last words Tessa ever wrote. She ensures it is placed back inside with more care than it was that evening it was torn out so many years ago.

TWO WEEKS PASS as Chloé continues her visits with Camille, learning more about her family's past, and as Nick shows her his New Orleans.

One day, he takes her to the Arthur Roger Gallery in the Art/Warehouse district, which is not far from her hotel. She loves the artwork, and Nick describes it as "New Orleans on canvas."

They stroll down Royal Street, visiting the antique stores and galleries and stopping to listen to street musicians on almost every corner. They also visit the Le Petit Theater, where Camille once performed, as well as the French Market off of North Peters Street. Stretching six blocks, it is the oldest city market, dating back to colonial days.

They grab a hot dog from Lucky Dogs wagon, followed by a "sno-ball" from Hansen's. Chloé first calls them snow cones but was quickly corrected. She has over 150 flavors to choose from, but she goes with Nick's choice: the nectar with cream.

He shows her Audubon Park, the four hundred-acre oak-filled park named after the ornithologist John James Audubon, who briefly called New Orleans home. Chloé falls in love with the Gumbel Memorial Fountain at the entrance; she even rolls up her jeans and splashes into the fountain with Nick. They begin a water fight that is soon joined by a dog belonging to a passerby.

Nick shows her the St. Louis Cathedral and its clock bell, which was cast in Paris and has tolled hourly since 1819. He also tells her about how it was built originally in a Spanish style and rebuilt in the 1850s to appear more French, and that it is the oldest Catholic cathedral in the United States.

Chloé loves Angelo Brocato's, a great coffee house that serves, in Nick's words, "the best homemade cannoli ever made."

After enjoying their cannolis, they go to one of Nick's favorite places to relax, Armstrong Park. Nick tells her it's named after "Louis Satchmo Armstrong." Armstrong Park features an emblazoned arch at the entrance bearing its name. "This is what I call hallowed jazz ground," Nick says. "The area around here was once called Storyville."

"Where did the name come from?" Chloé asks.

"A former city alderman, Sidney Story. Story felt prostitution could be controlled by designating a specific area for it. So Storyville was set aside as a legal red-light district, with saloons and high-class brothels. It was closed down in 1917 by the Navy department because they feared it was too tempting to sailors shipping out from New Orleans during World War I."

Listening to Nick relate this history, Chloé reflects back on the stories Camille shared, which allows her to draw a more complete picture of the city where the latter grew up.

At one point she remarks, "If being a lawyer doesn't work out, you would make a great tour guide," which makes Nick laugh.

Walking around the artificial lake in the park referred to as 'the lagoon,' Nick says, "So, tell me about your adoptive parents."

"Well, my father is a doctor."

"What is his specialty?"

"He's a heart surgeon."

"Cool. I had a friend in college who became a heart surgeon. Demanding work."

"Yes, he's always busy. My mom is a physical therapist and a massage therapist."

"I bet that was nice growing up."

"Yes, I have benefited from many massages."

"I can imagine."

"And they are both amazing artists and outdoorsy people."

"Did they influence you and your art?"

"They saw what they felt was a natural talent, and more than influence, I would say they helped to *nurture* that talent. I guess nurturing and support of my dream would be closer to it."

"Are they from Seattle?"

"No, they are both from Vancouver, Washington, about two and a half hours from Seattle. When I tell people Vancouver, most think I mean the one in British Columbia. But no, they're both born and raised in the United States."

Nick asks, "So how did Camille find them all the way up there?"

"She didn't. At the time, they lived here in New Orleans, since my father was doing his residency at Tulane. They were married and unable to have children, and were going through the agency that Camille had chosen. She met with them and knew they were perfect. The rest is history... What about yours? Unless it is still too painful to talk about."

"No, I don't mind. First off, my mom—until I met you—she was the most beautiful woman I had ever seen." Chloé blushes. "She was a schoolteacher."

"What did she teach?"

"English. She also had a job on the side with a publishing company as a book editor. She would pick up random editing jobs here and there. She was wonderful. An amazing mother who loved my father so much. I still remember the day my dad sat me down and told me she had cancer. She fought so hard and so bravely, but it was just too aggressive. Until you have experienced that last week with someone who is dying, sitting by their side, holding their hand, you just cannot imagine."

"I am so sorry. If this is too hard, you don't have to continue."

"No, it's fine. Her last words to me are as clear today as they were then. She said, 'Nick, look after your father. He's going to need you. And remember, one day you will fall in love. You will know when it is right, like your father and I did. Find that person who an arm's reach is too far away from, who forever isn't long enough with. Remember, I will always love you.' That was it." Nick's eyes are tearing up as Chloé places her arm around him. "Then I told you about my dad. He never recovered from losing her. Our relationship was strained after she passed, and it never really recovered. I was a teenager and said some pretty harsh things to him. I always thought there would be time to apologize. There was not. There were so many things I needed to say. We so often keep words to ourselves, thinking we have more time. Always say what you need to, because you never know when you may see someone the last time. So after he passed, I continued on to fulfill his dream of me becoming a lawyer. I guess in a way, I was making it up to him. And here I am."

As he finishes his story, Chloé sees an amazing man before her. One who has opened his soul to her like no one ever has.

THEY CONTINUE WALKING in Armstrong Park. Nick shows Chloé the bust of Sidney Bechet, his favorite musician and considered by many as the greatest clarinetist and soprano saxophone player of all time.

Then they head to Congo Square, where, Nick tells her,

"the slave owners were forbidden to work enslaved people on Sundays, in order to encourage them to become Christians. This small piece of freedom allowed them to retain more of their own heritage through song and dance. They would congregate here in Congo Square." Standing in the center of the square with his arms spread wide, Nick exclaims, "This is hallowed ground! This, where we are standing, is the birthplace of jazz!"

"So it all started right here?" Chloé beams.

"Yep."

Before leaving the park, as they stand by the statue of Armstrong, Nick looks at Chloé. He comes up close and says, "I once read somewhere that a woman can tell when a man wants to kiss her."

Chloé replies, closing her eyes, "Yes, we can." Nick slowly presses his lips to hers, and they kiss passionately.

THEY END their evening by going to dinner at the Napoleon House in the French Quarter. As they enter the restaurant, Chloé studies the decor. She finds the patina of the walls fascinating, as well as the way it's covered in timeworn paintings and numerous quotes from past patrons, from celebrities to regulars. They walk across the uniquely uneven wooden floor on the way to their table in the courtyard surrounded by palm trees. Once seated, Nick orders a Pimm's Cup for both of them.

Chloé raises her eyebrows. "What, might I ask, is a Pimm's Cup?"

"It's their signature drink. British gin, lemonade, a splash of lemon-lime soda, garnished with a cucumber. They have been serving it here since the late 1940s."

"Sounds divine. What do you recommend as an entree?"

"I recommend the Muffuletta, their signature sandwich."

Chloé looks around again. "So, how would you describe this place? I mean, is it French Creole, Italian, or what? I feel like I am in the islands, France, and Italy all at once."

"Well, the building itself is almost two hundred years old. The Muffuletta is served as a bit of nod, you know, respect for the Italian immigrants who originally opened up an Italian grocery store here. All in all, I can see the European ambiance you are talking about, but more so, I would call it distinctively quintessential New Orleans."

"You know your history."

Smiling, Nick says, "It is my city, after all, remember." He winks at her. "Besides, I know the owner."

"Of course you do." They both laugh.

"The Impastato family has always been close to mine."

"Of course they have." Again they laugh.

"Hey, it's always nice knowing the owners. You usually can get a little *lagniappe* that way."

"Lagni... What?"

Laughing, he says, "*Lagniappe* is a Creole term meaning 'a little something extra.'"

THE TWO ENJOY THEIR FOOD, and conversation of Camille owns the night. On the way out of the restaurant, Nick shows Chloé the bust of Napoleon behind the bar. "I've sat at this bar and confided to that statuette many nights. I'm glad I had much nicer company and a much more beautiful face to stare at tonight."

"Me too." Chloé smiles and takes Nick's hand, feeling more confident and complete than ever before.

She is discovering she is not just getting to know more about Nick and his city but also, more importantly, about herself.

All That
Glitters

Friday afternoon arrives, and Nick calls Chloé.

"Hello, beautiful," he says when she picks up. "How would you like to spend an incredible evening with a man who thinks you are amazing?"

"Now, which man who thinks I am amazing is this?" They both break into laughter.

"The one who kissed you yesterday."

"Which of the ones I kissed yesterday is this?" Again they both burst into laughter, and Chloé drops the charade. "I would love to."

"Great. Wear a nice dress, comfortable shoes, and get ready for an incredible evening."

Accepting his invitation, she comes to a realization that she is missing him more and more every moment they are apart. Chloé begins getting ready for the evening and starts clock-watching, longing to be near him.

When Nick arrives, he is stunned by her beauty. Chloé is wearing the same black dress she wore on their first date. His gaze glides over every curve of her body. Nick himself is dressed in a striped navy blue double-breasted suit. His shirt is white, and his tie is navy with a medium blue printed pattern that matches the color of his suit stripes.

They begin the evening at Antoine's. Originally a boarding house in 1840, the delicious food and atmosphere make it a world-renowned restaurant today. They are escorted to a private dining room on the second floor. The room is called the Roy Alciatore/Capital Dining Room.

Chloé asks, whispering to Nick, "Why does the room have such a long name, and who is Roy?"

He chuckles. "It was once only called the Capital Room because the wooden paneling of the walls was taken from the old capitol in Baton Rouge. Later they added the name Roy Alciatore to it because he managed the restaurant back around the Prohibition era. This is actually the oldest restaurant in New Orleans."

"I suppose you know the owners."

Nick just smiles and lowers his head, and Chloé laughs.

She looks around. The room has gorgeous red walls, gold drapes, green carpet, two black marble fireplaces, and an elegant chandelier. She can't help but notice the hardwood floors are so glossy, she can see her reflection in them. Glancing at her place setting, she straightens her fork. She tells Nick, "Your fork is out of place also."

Nick just laughs and tells her, "That is your seafood fork. It is a tradition here to have it placed at an angle."

"Oh. I suppose I have a lot to still learn about this city. Your city, that is." She laughs.

"Yes, there are lots of traditions, but you are doing fine. The coolest thing is, at a restaurant like this, a person can have the same dish they ordered thirty years ago, served by the same waiter they had thirty years earlier."

"That is really cool."

AFTER AN INCREDIBLE DINNER, Nick takes her to their next destination. They swing by 632 St. Peter Street, just a block from Jackson Square. Nick tells her, "Right here at this address, where we are standing, Tennessee Williams was inspired to write *A Streetcar Named Desire*." Chloé smiles, absorbing his excitement. "He sat right here in his apartment back in 1946 and '47, listening to the Desire streetcar line coming down Royal Street. This spot. This is what I am saving for. One day I will buy this location and turn it into my Belle Reve."

"Is it for sale?"

"Not really, but I've learned through my job that everything is for sale at a certain price. It isn't a huge space, but I have drawn the club's floor plan out many times, and I think it will be perfect. Also, my father's best friend growing up works for the zoning commission, so there shouldn't be any red tape to work around."

"I was just about to ask about zoning."

"It all should be fine. Now I just need to come up with the money for it. You know, my grandfather used to dine with Williams at Broussard's. They both had quite a passion for gin. It's amazing that Camille knew him as well. I wish I could have met him myself. He's always been my favorite writer."

Nick then glances at his watch. "Okay. Time for our next stop."

As SUNSET NEARS, they continue on foot to Jackson Square. Chloé is quite fond of the square, as it was the location of their first kiss. Just like on her and Nick's other trips there, artists display their work along the iron fence outside the park. On the flagstones around the square, tarot card readers, jazz musicians, and clowns entertain. There are people dancing with bottle caps and smashed cans attached to their shoes, leading to different jangling sounds every few steps.

Nick feigns sternness as he looks at Chloé. "No fortune readings today."

"No, not today," she replies, then gestures around. "I love the Spanish moss on the trees."

"You may hear people in New Orleans call it 'tree hair.'"

"Tree hair?"

"Yes, tree hair. It is funny how the French called it Spanish beard, and the Spanish called it French hair." Chloé laughs. "A lot of people don't realize, but Ford Motor Company used to use it to stuff car seats."

"That's funny. I never heard that before."

Pointing to the statue of Andrew Jackson, Nick tells her, "Did you know this statue by Clark Mills was the first equestrian statue built with two legs unsupported?"

"Wow. I need you with me the next time I play Trivial Pursuit."

Laughing, he replies, "Just tell me when and where, and I'll be there."

Nick leads Chloé across Jackson Square to Washington Artillery Park. In front of the park are mule-drawn carriages with the mules wearing straw hats. The park has a raised platform featuring a nineteenth-century Civil War cannon with excellent views of Jackson Square, the St. Louis Cathedral, and the Mississippi River. At the foot of the plaza is an open-air concrete auditorium facing Jackson Square.

"This view is beautiful," Chloé says.

"You haven't seen the best yet," Nick replies. "I saved it for last."

He leads her down a staircase on the river side of the platform. Immediately she feels the temperature cool down. Past the steps below her flows the Mississippi River in all its grandeur, with a beautiful walkway running along it lined with lampposts.

"Wow. This is amazing!" she exclaims.

Nick tells her, "Take off your shoes." He removes his and rolls up his pant legs. She follows suit, and they climb down the steps that lead from the walkway to the river. He goes first, and she follows. There they dangle their feet in the whisky-colored water, watching the river barges pass by. A lovely constant breeze blows as they watch the sun setting peacefully over the still waters.

"The water feels amazing."

"It's good to take off your shoes and rest your feet in water and on stones. It is purifying to the soul."

AFTER SEVERAL MINUTES they take their feet out of the water, place their shoes back on, and saunter off along the walkway.

"Why do they call this the Crescent City?" Chloé thinks to ask.

"There is a curve in the river at Algiers Point, in the shape of a crescent, that gives the city its name," Nick answers. "But I'd like to think it's because of the beautiful moon you can see from here at night." He points up at the clear sky under an illuminated moon. "By the way, this walkway is called the Moon Walk."

"So the view of the moon, that's why they call it the Moon Walk?"

"No," he replies. "That would be too easy. It's called that because Michael Jackson first moonwalked here." There is a short silence. Then he laughs.

"Hey, that's not funny. I almost believed you." She lightly punches his arm.

"It's actually named after the mayor at the time Maurice Landrieu. His nickname was 'Moon.' The Moon Walk is only a mile, but it is truly a beautiful mile."

They continue walking as they come upon the Spanish Plaza with its breathtaking fountain in the center. The fountain is surrounded by circular mosaic benches featuring the coat of arms or seals of provinces in Spain. Nick explains,

"The plaza here was dedicated in remembrance of the common historical past between New Orleans and Spain. I love spending time sitting here watching all the people and writing."

"Writing?"

"Yes, I've been writing poetry since I was sixteen. Nothing published. It's just therapy to me. Like jazz is."

"I would love to see it sometime."

"Let's make a deal then. I will show you my poetry when you show me your artwork."

"Oh wow, I'm so sorry. I totally forgot I promised you I would show you what I brought."

"No worries. Deal?"

"Deal."

AFTER A SHORT REST on the benches, they head back along the Moon Walk. Along the way are many solo street performers with open music cases for tips. Chloé can't help but notice with admiration that Nick is dropping money in each one. She can tell he has a great appreciation for their talents, and she does as well.

Nick suddenly stops under one of the street lamps and looks her in the eyes. He tells her, "Put out your hands, palms up, and close your eyes." Chloé looks at him slowly, a little hesitant, but follows his direction. "Trust me." As she does, he reaches into his pocket and places his surprise into her adjacent palms. "Now close your hands, keep your arms out in front of you, and your fists closed... and now... now open your eyes. Chloé, have you ever thought about the simple things in life? How they are overlooked, and what a release it would be to just be reckless, to just let go?" She looks down at her hands, no idea what she is clenching. "Now, with all your might, recklessly throw what is in your hands high in the air toward the light." She follows his command, and as she does, glitter flies through the night sky. The twinkling colors are breathtaking.

She screams in surprise and joy, "Nick!... This is beautiful!"

Looking at her, he says, "So are you, Chloé. Your eyes sparkle just like the glitter... I feel eternity has been waiting for this night, for this moment, for us to be together."

Then he leans in, places his hands on her cheeks, and kisses her slowly. As their lips part, looking into her eyes—eyes that seem to him more beautiful than the sparkling glitter—he says, "I love you, Chloé."

With her heart melting, she replies, "I love you too, Nick." Never before has she ever meant any words so much as those five.

Again they kiss.

HOLDING HANDS, they walk a little further before stopping to listen to a group of jazz musicians. Like with the others, he tosses some money into their cases on the ground.

Out of the blue, one asks, "Hey man, you want to join in?"

Shocking Chloé, Nick says, "Sure, why not?" Stepping behind the musicians, he opens up a case, pulls out a brass trumpet, and walks back to the front of the group. Turning back, he says, "Alright fellows, let's do 'I Could Write a Book' in C major. A-one and a-two and a—" Then the band begins to play, and he begins to sing the jazz classic by Lorenz Hart and Richard Rogers. He ends with a triumphant trumpet solo.

The whole time, Chloé stands there in pure amazement with her hands cupped over her mouth as if praying, hiding a huge smile, laughing, hopping, and clapping. At the end, Nick and the rest smile and take a bow.

Chloé uncovers her mouth. "I am speechless. Wow."

Nick grins. "What can I say... I love jazz." He then turns to the band, introducing each member. "Chloé, these are some friends of mine. This is Shorty Simmons on double bass, Eric 'Safe Sax' Rogers on sax, Silly Willy Jackson on trombone, Alex 'Crash' Thomas on drums, and Sammy Tyler on clarinet."

Chloé claps again for them. "You guys are incredible."

They all say either "Thanks, lady" or "Thanks, Chloé."

Nick throws some extra money down for them as he takes his trumpet and case, saying, "Thanks, fellows. See you soon."

He then walks away with Chloé. She stares at him. "Wow!" she repeats. "You failed to mention the whole 'I can sing like Harry Connick, Jr. and play the trumpet' part when we met."

"Speaking of, I also failed to mention I know Harry Connick, Jr. personally. Growing up hanging around him and his dad is what really got me into jazz."

"Wait, what? Okay, put a pin in what you just said, and we'll come back to it some other time. Back to the moment at hand. You only said you *liked* jazz."

"Yeah, I suppose I left the playing part out. I didn't want you to love me just for my musical talent." They both laugh. "I've been playing with these fellows for years, and I thought tonight would be a good chance to introduce you and let you know I can play a little."

"A little?" Again they laugh.

More serious, Nick says, "These are the guys I want playing with me in the Belle Reve."

Finally, back where they had first put their feet in the

river, Nick looks at Chloé and says, "Would you like to see my home? I can play some more music for you on my piano."

"Piano? So you play the piano too, huh?" She smiles. "I would love that."

He slowly kisses her.

AS THEY APPROACH Nick's house with her hair blowing in the night air, Chloé is mesmerized by the surrounding homes. She is bearing witness to what is truly the wealth of the Antebellum South. All she can do is admire the mansions and the towering oak trees.

Nick pulls up to a two-story home with an ornate facade, a truly sweeping structure. The first thing she notices is the nineteenth-century cast iron balcony on the second floor. On the side of the house is a grand two-story veranda that extends around to the back, guarded by stately iron railings. Leading up to it is a lacy iron spiral staircase.

As they step inside his home, Nick gives her a quick tour of the downstairs. Chloé says admiringly, "I can't help but notice all the beautiful stained glass throughout the house."

"Yes," Nick replies. "Thank you. It was all imported from Munich."

He escorts her to the living room, where sits an elegant grand piano. Chloé is stunned as she sees a painting hanging above his mantle. "Is that a Pollock?! Oh my gosh, it is!"

"Yep, a Jackson Pollock."

"Where did you get it?"

"It has been in my family for quite a while. My father picked it up at an auction in New York when he was around my age. When you mentioned Pollock, I thought you would be intrigued to actually see one up close."

"Yes… I'm speechless. Why didn't you tell me you had this?"

"I didn't want you to love me just for my painting."

Laughing, she asks, "Do you realize what this painting is worth?"

"Yeah, I have a pretty good idea. You can touch it if you like." Chloé reaches out, touching it and giggling. "You soak that in while I will make us some drinks."

He pours them both a glass of wine at a bar cart nearby and then tells her, "Come sit with me at the piano. I have a song I want to play for you. It was written in the 1940s by Lorenz Hart and composed by Richard Rogers. It's called 'Where or When.'"

"Wait, didn't Harry Connick, Jr. cover that for the movie *When Harry Met Sally?*"

"Yep, he sure did. It's always been my favorite song, since I was a child. It's about soul mates who know deep down they have loved before. They just don't know where or when."

His words convey a meaning that is not lost on Chloé. As he sits down at the piano, she lowers herself on the bench beside him and listens. He plays and sings, and when the song ends, he kisses her.

Chloé tells him, "That was beautiful. Do you think you could show me how to play 'Pretty Baby'?"

"I don't know…" He smiles apologetically. "Learning an instrument like the piano takes time."

Suddenly she looks at the sheet music in front of her and starts playing 'Where or When' flawlessly. This time it was Nick's turn to have his jaw drop.

"How…?" He is speechless.

"Ten years of piano lessons."

"So you failed to tell me about your musical talent too."

"I didn't want you to love me just for my musical talent." She smiles at him.

Nick smiles back. "That one is not in my songbook, so I

will have to play it by memory." He begins playing 'Pretty Baby' for her, making corrections as he goes. "Now it's your turn." They trade places, and she sits on the piano bench while he stands behind her. As she begins to play, he stops her. "Wait, wait, wait."

"What am I doing wrong? Is it the wrong key?"

"No, you have the right key, E-flat major. It's not that. It's your foot."

"My foot?" She looks at her feet.

"Yes. You aren't playing jazz if you're not tapping your foot." He sits down next to her. After several practices, with him coaching her, he stands again. This time she begins to play it solo. He leans over her shoulder to correct her on a transition from a dotted eighth to a sixteenth note, with his cheek pressed up against hers. She feels his warmth, and the vibration of his voice tingles her neck.

The scent of her hair and the heat of their closeness overtakes him as he gently kisses the back of her neck. She looks up from the keys, letting out a sigh while turning to face him as their lips unite. The tempo of their kisses becomes more passionate, deeper, and intense. He spins her around, lifting her up, and resting her on the keyboard without impeding their kiss. She rips open the buttons of his shirt and begins kissing his chest. He slips her dress up to her waist. Reaching down, unbuckling his belt, she grips his desire. His hand slides between her legs, feeling her warmth as his fingers caress the heat between her thighs in perfect cadence. He lifts her off the keys, penetrating her soul. She lets out another sigh. They maintain a perfect rhythm with fluid motion, producing loud striking notes on the piano keys, leading to a symphony of uninhibited tonality. Reaching a crescendo with each movement, pleasure rushes through her, reprised over and over. The measure of their hearts is playing perfectly in unison as she suddenly feels the swelling release of his soul inside her. His brief immortality melts away in her essence as they both collapse to the floor.

Lying on top of her and kissing her gently, Nick says, "*J'entend ton coeur.*"

Chloé softly translates, "I can hear your heart."

MORNING LIGHT

THE FOLLOWING morning Chloé wakes before Nick, lying beside him in his bed. She rolls over to rest her head on his chest. While lying there, she reflects on all that's happened between them. "How did I fall in love so quickly? Why does everything seem so familiar? He's only the second man I have ever slept with. Gosh, has it really been over a year? Well..." With a smile on her face as she looks up at Nick sleeping, she adds to herself, "It was well worth the wait."

She notices shadows entering the room cast by the decorative wrought iron railing from the balcony outside the bedroom. Climbing silently out of bed, she wraps a blanket around her naked body. Beckoned by the sunrise, she walks out the French doors leading from the bedroom to the balcony. Looking out, she admires the spreading branches of the oak trees and the path leading to the carriage house. Looking back into the bedroom, she sees the beautiful man that she has fallen so deeply in love with still sleeping. She wonders what he is dreaming of. Tiptoeing back through the French doors, she drops the blanket and climbs back under the covers. As soon as she does, he wraps his arms around her, kissing her gently, and they make love again.

ONCE OUT OF BED, they go downstairs. In the kitchen, Chloé is dressed in Nick's New Orleans Saints football jersey and a pair of his black boxers. He is wearing blue and white plaid pajama pants and a navy blue T-shirt.

"Okay," Nick says, rubbing his hands together, "I am

going to make you a homemade New Orleans breakfast. Will you be my assistant?"

"I would love to."

"First of all, we need wine."

"To cook with?"

"No, to drink while we cook." They both smile as he pours their glasses.

"First, we are going to make sweet potato pecan waffles topped with some Creole cream cheese. Also, a Creole omelet sprinkled with parsley, and shrimp and grits."

"Wow. That sounds delicious. Where do we start?"

"With the sweet potato pecan waffles. I'll chop the pecans if you beat four eggs lightly."

During the process of making breakfast, they begin a food fight that ends with them both covered in flour and making love again on the kitchen floor. They do eventually finish breakfast, albeit much later than planned, and minus the shrimp and grits.

AFTER BREAKFAST, they play more on the piano until Chloé has 'Pretty Baby' perfected—as well as a few other jazz masterpieces.

Taking her fingers off the keys, Chloé tells Nick, "Tomorrow is Camille's birthday. Will you please go to Meadowbrook with me? I want to give her an incredibly special day."

"I wouldn't miss it for the world."

"So when are you going to show me your office?"

"We should do that sometime this week, maybe. You'll really like Sean. He'll probably be more interested in your hair, nails, and shoes than in what you have to say, but he's a great guy."

Chloé laughs, but then notices Nick isn't joining in, so she stops. "You aren't kidding, are you?"

"Nope."

Smiling, she says, "I guess I'll have to get a manicure before I go up there, then."

Now Nick laughs. "Yeah, you might want to. Or better, ask him for one. He is not only a lawyer but a licensed cosmetologist and esthetician."

"Wow! Maybe a facial, too, huh? That might be the strangest career combination I have ever heard of. It sounds like he and I might have a lot to talk about. Maybe some stories of you."

"Yeah, probably so, but sometimes he can talk your head off. I really admire him, though, for knowing what he wants and doing it. Oh, by the way, just in case you ever meet his mom, don't mention the whole cosmetology-esthetician thing. She doesn't know about that."

"He sounds more interesting by the second."

"He is. I'm a few years older than him, but I've known him all his life. His mother was a cook for my parents before I was born. As kids, Sean would come over, and we would play together. He was there for me when I lost my mom and my dad. His mom took it hard when each of them died. She cared a lot about all of us. When Mom passed away, she stepped in and was like a mother to me. She still is. It meant the world to her when Sean got his law degree. As soon as he did, I talked Mr. Jones into hiring him even though he had no experience. Sean's a great guy. I would do anything in the world for him and his mom."

"Who else will I get to meet?"

"Well, there's also Eric. Eric is..." Nick gives a long pause. "Eric would best be described as a Human Resources nightmare."

"Oh, really."

"Yes, really. I still, to this day, do not know how he hasn't lost his job. Let me just apologize in advance for anything and everything he might say. As for any stories he might tell you about me, I plead the fifth."

"Oh yeah?"

"Yeah."

"Maybe I need to ask him a few questions about you."

"Believe me, you would find his stories about himself much more interesting. Now, how would you like to help me clean up the kitchen?"

Slightly blushing, rocking back and forth with her finger on her lips, she says, "I will if we can have as much fun as we did making the mess. Maybe a little *lagniappe?*" She runs toward the kitchen laughing and squealing as Nick chases after her.

SURPRISE

SUNDAY MORNING, Nick and Chloé arrive at Meadowbrook. Chloé places the cake on a table in the lobby, and Nick hangs balloons and streamers as they wait for Camille to be wheeled in. As a nurse pushes Camille around the corner into the lobby, they begin to sing happy birthday. Surprised, Camille places her hands on her smiling cheeks. She, as well as other residents and staff, join in singing. From her wheelchair, she swings her arms through the air as if conducting an orchestra.

After the song, Camille is pushed over to her cake at the table. With all her breath, she blows out the one candle on the cake and then says while smiling, "What, you couldn't get 101 of those on there? Must be because of the fire code." Everyone laughs. "Thank you all for this. You make an old lady feel special. And thank you, Nick, for coming and for taking such good care of my Chloé."

"Thank you, Camille," Nick says. "It is my pleasure."

Chloé tells her, "We have a present for you."

"Oh, sweetie, at my age, I need nothing."

Chloé smiles secretly in reply. Nick walks over to the lobby corner beside the dusty piano and takes his trumpet out of its case, and she follows to sit down on the bench. She begins to play "Pretty Baby," and Nick accompanies her on the trumpet and sings.

Camille's face lights up like never before. Nick approaches and sways around her wheelchair, serenading her. As he does, Camille begins to blush. At the end of the song, she stands up on her own from her wheelchair, clapping, and then hugs both Nick and Chloé. She yells out at the top of her lungs, "This is the best birthday ever!"

To even Chloé's surprise, Nick says, "Camille, I have one more thing for you. It is a little something I have been working on." He walks over and takes a seat beside Chloé at the piano. He tells Camille, "This is a song I wrote for you. It's called 'My Queen of New Orleans.'"

Camille's mouth drops open, and she begins to smile. Nick starts to play the piano in a fast tempo.

GETTING DOLLED up for the night with your best dress on
  And me in my suit humming a song
  Having just stepped out, the first man we see
  He looks at you, then at me

HE ASKS, who is that?
  She has a smile like I've never seen
  A glow that shines a hellacious beam
  He asks, what is the name of this lady in heels
  I call her Pretty Baby, but her name is Camille
  Better cool your jets, or I'll have to intervene
  For no one gets between
  Me and my queen of New Orleans

WE WERE on our way down to paint the town
  When we saw some trouble up ahead
  It was a group of fellows causing a ruckus
  Then three of them began to rush us

THEY ASK, who is that?

She has a smile like we've never seen
A glow that shines a hellacious beam
One says, man, your lady is unreal
I say, you must mean my Camille
Better tell your dogs to heel, or I'll have to intervene
For no one gets between
Me and my queen of New Orleans.

AT THE SONG'S END, he adds, "Happy birthday, Pretty Baby."

Camille, almost in tears, says, "Oh, Nick, it's so wonderful."

Chloé leans over to Nick, kissing him on the cheek and whispering in his ear, "Thank you."

Camille looks at the two of them smiling and blushing and tries to hide her stare.

It doesn't take long for the other residents to gather around the piano. Before they know what's happening, Chloé and Nick are taking requests. They play a few more songs. Their surprise performance makes so many people happy, Chloé is glad she learned to play more than one song the day before.

AFTER A WONDERFUL EVENING, Nick and Chloé say good night to Camille, and Nick walks Chloé to his car. On the way back to the Ambassador, with the top down and the wind blowing through their hair, Nick tells her, "Chloé, I would like you to stay with me." Chloé does not answer. "You can grab your things and check out tonight. I know this may sound sudden, but I do not want to wake up another day without seeing you beside me."

Chloé takes his hand. "Thank you for the offer. I promise

I will consider it. Just not yet... I'm sorry. I hope you understand."

"Of course I do. No pressure. It's just, I'm crazy about you."

"That's a good thing." They both smile.

"An extremely good thing."

After a moment of silence, Chloé says, "I will stay the night with you. If you are offering, that is."

"That would make me incredibly happy."

"I just need to drop by the hotel and grab a few things."

"Tomorrow, I would like you to come to my office and meet everyone."

"I'd like that a lot."

"There's one thing you need to know," he tells her.

"Yes, what is it?" she says with a slight bit of concern in her voice.

"I know I've told you about Eric and Sean, but I have failed to mention Lydia."

Now more concern in her tone. "Lydia?"

"Yes, Lydia was the fiancé that I told you about."

"So you're saying she works there also?"

"Yes, she's the owner's daughter and a lawyer there also. Believe me, there's nothing there."

As she places her hand on his, she responds in a comforting voice. "It's fine, I understand. I'm not the jealous type."

"I just wanted you to know. If we see her there, she can come off as quite bitter."

"No worries. I can't wait to see your office and meet Sean. He sounds like an awesome friend."

"He is. He really is."

. . .

AFTER STOPPING by her hotel to get her things, they arrive at Nick's. He helps her with her bags and notices a cardboard tube. "What is this?" he asks, holding it up.

As they enter his house, she responds, "That, my good sir, is my artwork I promised to show you."

"Finally."

"What do you mean, finally? You still haven't shown me your poetry yet."

"Okay, I'll give you that one. You're right."

After getting into their evening clothes, they sit in his den on his couch, enjoying mojitos while looking through Chloé's paintings.

"Wow! These are incredible."

"Thank you."

"Seriously, I really mean it. They should be displayed somewhere and not rolled up in a tube." He pulls out one from her stack and says, "This one. I want to buy this one from you and hang it right there," pointing to the wall.

"Thanks. You can have it. No need to pay for it. So, where is this poetry of yours?"

He steps over to his credenza and pulls out a stack of notebooks, setting them down in front of her. "Here you go."

Chloé opens them and begins reading. "Nick, these are really good."

"Are you serious or just being kind?"

"No, they really are."

"You're the only person I have ever shown those to."

"This one is dated last week." Smiling, she reads a poem entitled "How Soon Is Never."

Standing here with you
As strong as I feel inside
I am weak in your presence
Desiring to kiss you

I must step away
For if I stay another moment
My heart will never leave

Chloé smiles and asks, "Is this about me?"
"Yes."
"I'm glad you did not step away."
Nick says, "So am I," and kisses her.

Pursued by
the Past

Monday arrives, and Nick is back in the office. Sean is sitting on the chair opposite Nick's desk as the latter tells him, "I'm sorry I have not been much of a friend lately. I miss our Thursday night dinners at your mom's."

"No problem, my friend," Sean replies. "I know you still care. Besides, you're in love."

"I'm glad you understand. Chloé is just so incredible. She is coming up to see the office and meet you this afternoon."

"I cannot wait to meet this mysterious girl who has captured your heart."

"You're going to love her. She is truly perfect."

"Perfect is overrated. She doesn't have to be perfect. Never hold anyone to that regard. Always remember imperfections are good things, Mama would say. Take rubies and emeralds. It is their imperfections that make them beautiful. Otherwise, they would look like colored glass."

Nick smiles. "You are a wise man, my friend."

"Yes, it is hard having brains and beauty," his friend replies, making him laugh.

Unbeknownst to them, Lydia has stopped by Nick's office and is standing outside his door, out of sight in the hallway, listening intently.

"We had an incredible date Saturday," Nick says, and goes into detail about the Moon Walk.

"Wow. The glitter was a great idea."

"Thank you. Yes, it came to me first when I thought of her beautiful eyes, then again after meeting her great-grand-mother and feeling her excitement for life at her age. It made me feel there was that spirit trapped in Chloé that she had never released before. That she could just throw her inhibitions into the wind."

"And then the band," Sean points out. "That was genius also."

"We've never played together down on the river in the open like that before. It was incredible at night with an awesome breeze. We definitely need to play there again."

"Well done, sir. The whole evening sounded like a dripping chocolate chandelier of deliciousness."

"And you, sir, have an amazing way with words." They laugh together.

In the hallway, Lydia is fuming. She still loves Nick and is incredibly jealous—especially since he did nothing like that for her on any of their dates.

Nick says next, "I even let her read my poetry."

"Wow! I thought that was locked away like Fort Knox. You have never even let me see that."

"Yeah, and I probably never will." Laughing. "So, how is your mom doing?"

"Fine, as usual. She's just Mama. I think she said she's baking a casserole and making some gumbo to bring up here to us for lunch tomorrow."

"That sounds amazing. I don't know how you stay so thin with a mother who cooks as amazingly as yours."

"It's not easy. Like I always say—I have to watch my figure, or no one else will." A burst of light laughter follows.

At that moment, Lydia steps into the doorway.

Nick, surprised, says, "Hello, Lydia. Can I help you with something?"

Sean speaks up. "I will talk to you later, my friend." As Lydia takes his chair, he walks out of Nick's office, turning to hold his hands up like cat claws behind her head.

Lydia gets to the point. "So, the word going around is you've gotten pretty serious with someone."

"Yes, I have." There is silence as she looks down. Nick says in a low voice, "Lydia, it's been a year. We just were not meant for each other. We didn't have the right chemistry, and we never will. You have to let go."

In a hostile tone, she shoots back, "You're just lucky my father didn't fire you."

Nick lets out a sigh, shaking his head. "Lydia, why are you here?"

"I was just dropping off these new foreclosures." She stands up and drops a stack of folders on his desk roughly. "Well, I wish you luck with this new girl. Maybe you won't break her heart like you did mine." She slams his door shut as she walks out.

LATER THAT AFTERNOON, Chloé shows up at the office, and Nick gives her a grand tour. They end up at Sean's office door, and Nick leans through it to introduce them.

"Sean, this is Chloé. Chloé, Sean."

Sean walks up to her, and she puts out her hand to shake his. He immediately compliments her nails. "Oh girl, your nails are so pretty. No, ma'am. Here we hug." He hugs her, and then, stepping back, adds, "Oh child, I have heard so much about you."

"And I you."

"You are much more beautiful than Nick described. Oh, I love those shoes."

"Thank you."

"You are just too cute."

"Thanks again," she says, feeling a bit overwhelmed.

Nick says, "Hey, let's all get together at my place for a crawfish boil this weekend."

"That sounds like fun," Chloé says.

"That does sound amazing," Sean replies, "but I have to be out by seven. I have a drag show at ten Saturday night."

Nick complains, "That's three hours."

"It takes time to transform this beautiful face."

"Okay, I will have you out of there by seven. Let's start at two on Saturday, then."

"Sounds good. Should we invite Eric?"

"I don't know, we'll see."

Then Nick directs Chloé next door and introduces her to Eric, not knowing what to expect. Eric immediately looks her up and down and says with his long Southern drawl, "Damn, she is hot. Good job, son. You got yourself a hot little filly. All those women all these years. I would have to say, out of all of them, this one is a keeper."

Chloé is taken aback and immediately understands what Nick meant by "Human Resources nightmare." Nick, placing his face in his hand in embarrassment, grasps for a distraction from the moment. Luckily, just then, Lydia passes them in the hall.

Out of respect, Nick tries to introduce her to Chloé. "Lydia, this is Chloé, the girl I told you about." But Lydia ignores the gesture and continues down the hallway. Nick looks at Chloé.

"So that's her," Chloé says.

"Yep. That's her."

Then they step into his office. Chloé says, "So, this is it? The office that steals your time from me?"

"Yes. This is that same office that denies me the ability to kiss you around the clock." They both laugh. "So what do you say we skip out of here, go home, change, and head to Preservation Hall?"

"That sounds amazing. Camille spoke so much about it."

Quickly straightening all the paperwork on his desk,

Nick replies, "Yes, it is a pretty amazing place, and no one should ever come to New Orleans without spending at least one evening there. One thing though—we absolutely have to be there before eight o'clock."

"Why eight?" Chloé asks as they leave his office.

Nick locks his door and slips his blazer on with Chloé's help in the hall. "Let's get out of here before I get stopped. We have to be there by eight because that's when the music starts."

A LITTLE AFTER SEVEN, they arrive in the heart of the French Quarter. Standing in the street outside Preservation Hall, Chloé says, "It feels so strange standing here just like Camille did years ago."

"Yeah, I loved the stories she told us about this place."

Immediately she recognizes the age and character of the building by its facade. If she didn't know it was there, though, she might think it's just an old small warehouse or maybe an abandoned workshop. Two worn instrument cases featuring brass letters hang over the wrought iron entrance spelling out its name, Preservation Hall. Stepping inside, Chloé first notices the rugged wooden benches topped with cushions, just as Camille described. Her eyes turn to the old paintings of musicians hanging on the walls, which are casting a gold hue all around the room. "The peeling paint," she thinks, "gives the place character." The dusty wooden floors are showing their wear. It is much smaller inside than she imagined; the benches are filling up fast as a line forms out the door. The lack of air conditioning does not seem to deter the locals and tourists who are here to enjoy the music. Taking a seat on a bench next to Nick, she cannot help but feel she is experiencing a piece of history, a real slice of Americana. The two of them sit there to wait, rehashing some of the stories Camille had told them about the venue.

By eight o'clock, all the benches are full and people are standing anywhere and everywhere they can find a space. A man walks out, welcomes everyone, and announces the first act of the evening. "If everyone will put their hands together for one of our regular bands... Please welcome Nick Nattier and the Barrelhouse Rhythm Section!"

Everyone claps as Nick stands up, leaning down to kiss a surprised Chloé. He speaks loudly in her ear over the clamor of the audience. "This is why I needed to be here by eight." Leaping onstage, he takes his trumpet from the case as the rest of the band gets in place. Nick says into the microphone, "With this heat we are having, I think we will begin with a little Coltrane. This is 'Summertime.'" The crowd snaps and claps.

He and his band follow with a little Sidney Bechet classic, "Nobody Knows You When You're Down and Out." Next, a Harry Nilsson hit, "As Time Goes By." Then Nick tells the crowd, "Here's a new one to our set. This is Louis Armstrong's 'Chloé.'" Chloé looks up at Nick, smiling. After the song ends, he says, "Let's do a little more Bechet. Here's 'Lazy River.'" Following, Nick introduces the band members each by name and says, "Okay, this next song is something a little different for us. It's a modern song, but it has every bit of the emotion that so many of the others we play have. We have only practiced it a couple of times, but we think you will enjoy it. This is dedicated to someone very special in the audience, and it's by a band named INXS. You may have heard of them. The song is called 'Never Tear Us Apart.'" Chloé's mouth drops open.

After the INXS cover, Nick and the band play several songs by artists such as Duke Ellington, Thelonious Monk, and Jelly Roll Morton, as well as more from Coltrane,

Bechet, and Armstrong. Nick steps up and says, "Now we want to play one more new one. It's about a special lady named Camille Laver. Some of you may know her. She couldn't be here tonight, but she spent many years in this audience enjoying this beautiful music we have been blessed with. This song is called 'My Queen of New Orleans.'" Finally, they close out with the Charlie Parker classic "Cool Blues."

All in all, Nick and his band performed for an hour before he rejoins Chloé.

Chloé grabs his hand. "Oh my gosh, you guys were amazing up there. You sounded just like Michael Hutchence on 'Never Tear Us Apart.' But every single song was just incredible."

"Thanks. It is a good way sometimes to work off a little steam after work. The last couple of weeks have been tricky finding time to practice to surprise you."

"How much do they pay you?" Chloé asks.

"I have no idea. I let the band take whatever they offer us. I do it for the pure love of the music. I have all I need right here." He kisses her.

For the rest of the evening, they sit and enjoy others' music.

WALKING BACK to his car while holding hands, Chloé asks Nick, "So what exactly did Eric mean today with his comment about 'all those women'?"

"Yeah, about that..."

"I mean, I can totally tell how vulgar he tends to be, but what did he mean about the other girls? I mean, how many others have there been? Not that I expect you to be a saint or something. I'm just curious." Nick, obviously feeling a little uncomfortable, doesn't speak. "You know, it actually is none of my business. I really shouldn't pry."

"No, it's fine." A little reluctantly, he responds, "A lot?... I guess. I don't know. I never counted."

"Okay... Not the answer I was expecting, but don't get me wrong, I'm not judging."

"No worries."

"So what was it all about? Was it a challenge? Like, was it a 'notches in your belt' sort of thing, or did you really feel something for them?" Again Nick is slow to answer. "Gosh, I am coming off sounding totally judgmental, aren't I?"

"No, not at all... I guess it began when I first started college." He stops walking and turns to her, saying, "Early on, I thought it might be about a challenge, but later in retrospect, I discovered it was all about trying to make them feel special. Which, turns out, is just as bad as treating them as conquests. I mean, who the hell was I to sweep in like some knight on a white horse trying to make them feel special for a brief moment in time? Who was I to do so, knowing it would crash and burn, leaving them hurt? A hurt that far outweighed that brief moment of happiness I felt I was giving them. I really didn't want to hurt anybody. I just wanted them to feel special. I think deep down, we all want that. I just thought in some way I could do that for them."

Chloé looks at him with a kind of admiration. She thinks to herself how profoundly honest that answer seemed. "So what about Lydia?" she asks now.

"What about her?"

"What was different about her from the other girls? Why were things more serious with her?"

"I guess with Lydia, it started like the others. Everything just moved really fast. Her father was my boss. She kept talking about how someday it would be the Jones and Nattier Law Firm, that we were meant to be. I got kind of caught up in all that. Then one day, I realized I wasn't in the relationship for *me*. I was just in it for her. I was only there to make her feel special. We had no chemistry. All we had in common was our occupation. An occupation I never wanted to be in anyway. Plus, she despised jazz." He laughs. "How can anyone from New Orleans not like jazz? I was not in love and was not happy. I didn't want to hurt her, but I knew it would end sooner or later. A relationship can never last when only one person is in love. So I ended it."

"We've moved fast. You and I. So tell me, how do I know you really love me? How do I know you're not just trying to make me feel special?"

Nick looks into her eyes. "Chloé, no one has to try and make you feel special. You already are. You don't need me or anyone else to show you that. I have never really known love. Not until now." He places his hands on each side of her face and kisses her.

UPON RETURNING that night to her hotel, Chloé writes in her journal.

Nick has shown me so many wonderful places, from the slow-moving romance of the streetcars to the ambiance of the French Quarter. I feel so at home here. I feel I am finding my place in his city.

Today I got to see his office and meet all his friends and coworkers, even Lydia—sort of. She is extremely beautiful. It may be wrong, but I was hoping she would be much less beautiful.

Tonight we went to Preservation Hall. Nick and his band performed a fantastic concert. He sang "Never Tear Us Apart" and dedicated it to me. Later in the night, we kissed in the peaceful little courtyard behind the building as the sound of jazz filled my soul. Tonight—just as it happened to Camille so long ago—tonight, I fell in love with jazz.

Walking back to the car tonight, I asked Nick about his past relationships. I really feel like he opened up his soul to me. I hope I'm not being naive. I'm genuinely falling even deeper in love with him. I didn't think that was possible. Please let him feel the same. Please don't let me be just "special."

TILL THE NEXT
GOODBYE

THE NEXT MORNING Chloé calls Nick. He answers, "Hello, beautiful."

"Hi, Nick," Chloé says. "Now hear me out. I haven't asked Camille or her doctor, but if the doctor approves, would you mind inviting her to the crawfish boil?"

"No, not at all. I wish I had thought of it. Do you think they'll let her go?"

"I'm not sure. Hopefully, I can get an answer today. I guess it has to do with how she feels as much as the doctor approving it."

"Yeah, lots of factors there. I have to run to the court-house, but keep me posted."

"I will."

THAT AFTERNOON, Chloé visits Camille. Before going to her room, Chloé asks to speak to her doctor. Luckily, he's there making patient rounds and soon is able to meet her in the lobby.

"Hello, I'm Dr. Stewart," he says, walking up to Chloé. "I look after Ms. Camille. I understand you have some ques-tions for me."

Chloé replies, "Yes. I'm her great-granddaughter. I was wondering how you would feel if she went to a family-type gathering Saturday afternoon for just a few hours?"

Dr. Stewart pauses in thought, then says, "Well, she has shown much improvement since you arrived in town. In fact, you are all she talks about when I see her. You know, at her age, how could I say no? That may not be what some would say is a medical answer, but when you are 101 years old, I think you should live what time you have left to the fullest. I would, however, say not too much excitement, and only for a few hours. Also, don't let her do any dancing." They both laugh.

"That sounds great. I didn't want to ask her until I had cleared it with you."

"I'll leave a note in her file, and you can sign her out when you're ready. Have a good day."

"Thank you. You too."

Chloé goes straight to Camille's room. She knocks, and Camille says, "Come in." Seeing it is Chloé, she says, "Hello, my angel."

"How are you feeling?"

"Surprisingly, better than I have in a long time."

"Good. How would you like to go with me to Nick's on Saturday for a crawfish boil?"

Camille's eyes get big and she whispers excitedly, "Are you sneaking me out?"

"No need to. I got Dr. Stewart to sign off on it."

"Oh sweetie, that sounds perfect. It will be so good to get out of this place, even if for just a day."

"Maybe after this, they will keep letting me take you, and we can go all over New Orleans together. You can show me all the places you've talked about."

"I would love that. Can you do me a favor?"

"Yes."

"Will you run by my house and grab my sparkling red dress from my armoire? I have to look good for the party. I certainly cannot wear this gown."

Laughing, Chloé says, "Will do."

. . .

Saturday arrives, and Camille has the staff help her get dolled up in her red dress. Chloé signs her out, and Nick folds up her wheelchair and places it in his car. Chloé rides in the backseat of Nick's Porsche, allowing Camille to sit up front. In her sparkling red dress, Camille gets a huge smile on her face when Nick tells her, "Hold on."

With the top down, Camille holds her arms up in the air, catching the wind in her hands like she is sledding down the dunes in France again, yelling, "Wheee!"—except now she calls out, "I feel so alive!"

Pulling up to Nick's home, Camille says, "Oh, Nick. Your house is so beautiful."

"Thank you," he replies. "It was originally my parents' and was passed down to me."

"Wait until you see the inside," Chloé remarks.

"I can't wait!"

Nick unloads the wheelchair and helps Camille out of the car. Chloé gives her a tour of the house as Nick heads out back to set up the crawfish boil.

Chloé notices Nick has already framed and hung her painting. Also seeing it, Camille says, "That painting there reminds me of one of my mother's. Do you happen to know who the artist is? I can't see as good as I used to."

"Actually, it's mine," Chloé tells her. "I painted it last year."

Camille looks up at her beaming. "That makes sense. You and Tessa share the same talent. It is wonderful."

About a half hour later, Chloé and Camille enter the backyard. The first thing they hear is jazz being played through Nick's outside speakers. Camille puts her arms in the air and starts dancing in her wheelchair. Nick says to her, "I thought you would like that."

Chloé looks over at two ice chests full of crawfish. "So that's what crawfish look like."

Camille speaks up. "We always called them mudbugs."

"They remind me of scorpions."

Nick, laughing, tells her, "I'm not sure what kind of scorpions look like that. Maybe you're thinking of lobsters. But speaking of scorpions, if you think about it, crawfish must seem like mermaids to scorpions." Everyone laughs.

Camille asks, "Nick, how did you get all of these this late in the year?"

"I picked them up from Kyle LeBlanc's," Nick replies. "One of the few places you can find live ones after June. They are a little harder to peel this time of year, but still delicious. These I got are already cleaned and purged. I also have some crawfish étouffée cooking inside."

Nick preps his cooker, and Chloé helps him bring out everything from the kitchen. Camille asks as they approach, "What all do we have to cook with the crawfish?"

Nick takes stock. "Let's see, we've got garlic, small red potatoes, lemon slices, orange slices, bell peppers, ears of corn, hot sauce, bay leaves, celery, smoked sausage, onions, mushrooms, crab boil, and cayenne pepper. Along with a little beer."

Camille immediately grabs Chloé's arm. "What did the doc say about alcohol?"

Chloé leans toward her. "I didn't ask."

Camille, smiling, says, "Good girl."

"Actually, I have a surprise for you," Chloé tells her, and then goes inside. She returns holding a bottle of wine and two wine glasses.

Camille is smiling. "Is that what I think it is?"

"Yep, a 1972 Chateau Margaux from your home."

"Yes!"

Chloé pours them both a glass just as Sean arrives. He

walks around the house into the backyard, calling out, "Hey, betches, y'all ready for some crawfish?" Camille, from her wheelchair, turns her head and makes immediate eye contact with him. Embarrassed, he says, "Oh snap. I'm sorry. Hello, my name is Sean. I work with Nick." He reaches out his hand to greet Camille. "I really wasn't calling you that. I don't even know what that means. I'm so sorry. I didn't know anyone else was coming."

Nick and Chloé are laughing. Nick says, "Sean, this is Camille, Chloé's great-grandmother."

Sean tells Camille, "Oh, child. Now I know where Chloé gets her good looks from."

Camille smiles and says to the others, "I like him."

Sean asks Nick, "Did you invite Eric?"

"Yeah," Nick replies. "I'll probably regret it, but I did. His wife couldn't come with him. She had some Bible study thing."

"That man should be going with her. Lord knows he needs some Jesus in his life." Sean leans over and asks Camille, "Sweetie, would you like me to braid your hair?"

"Go for it," Camille replies.

Sean stands behind her and gets to work on her hair. "Girl, you are looking fly in that red dress."

Camille, confused, asks, "Looking like a fly?"

Sean laughs. "No, baby. Looking fly means looking fine. Looking good. Looking sexy."

Camille turns her neck toward him, laughing. "Are you flirting with me?"

"Oh, child. I think we both know we fish in the same bayou."

Suddenly they hear Eric call out from the side of the house, "Where are the beer and the strippers?"

Nick looks at Sean. "Yep, I already regret this decision."

Camille turns toward the newcomer and says, "Oh boy. This one should come with a warning label."

Eric walks up and, looking at Camille, says, "And who might this be?"

"This is Camille, Chloé's great-grandmother," Nick responds.

After picking up a beer from the ice chest and opening it, Eric walks over to Camille. Leaning close as if she is senile and hard of hearing, he says loudly, "Hello, Camille. I'm Eric." Camille cocks her head and just stares at him. Eric looks at Chloé and asks, "Is she deaf?" Chloé is speechless. Eric continues, "Guess so." Even closer to her ear now, he yells, " Nice to meet you."

Camille looks over at Nick. "Nick, does this one work with you too?"

"Yep."

She turns back to Eric, "Were you born this stupid, or did you take lessons? Son, look at these people here who work with you. Forget about firemen, police officers, soldiers; these people who tolerate you on a daily basis are the real heroes."

Everyone laughs except Eric.

"Oh, feisty, I see," he says, then calls out, "Hey Nick, let me go in and change this music over to some country!" Looking around, slinging his arm in the air and hopping like a roping cowboy, he yells, "Let's hear some damn George Strait!"

After taking a sip of wine, Camille tells him, "Hey sap, touch it and die."

Eric stops in his tracks. He asks her, "You don't like country music?"

"Listen, chump," Camille responds, "you change that from jazz to country music, and you will be listening to chin music. Ya follow?"

Everyone but Eric and Camille bust out laughing.

Sean and Nick have never seen Eric look this humble in all the time they have known him. Sean tells Nick, "I like her. She's done put that boy in his place. I almost feel sad for him. Almost."

Clutching his beer, Eric walks over to Nick and whispers, "Damn son, that old lady has quite the yapper on her."

Camille sips her wine. "Hey palooka, this yappy old deaf lady can still hear you!"

"You might want to stay a bottle's throw away from that one," Nick advises Eric.

"Hell, she could probably still hit me from across town."

Again Camille calls out, "That's right. Now you're catching on." She leans over to Chloé, who is sitting next to her, and whispers, "I'm just giving him a hard time. I promise I won't hurt him." Both women laugh.

It takes approximately thirty minutes to get the pot boiling before Nick adds the crawfish. He stirs them with a wooden paddle. After around five minutes, he adds the potatoes and covers the pot with a lid. Five minutes later, lifting the lid, he adds everything except the corn and replaces the top. He then grabs a beer and sits down with the others. Twenty minutes later, he cuts the flame. He waits another five minutes and then adds the corn, stirring with the wooden paddle every five minutes for the next fifteen minutes.

Chloé asks him, "How do you know when they are done?"

"When they sink, you know they're ready."

"Looks like they're ready," she remarks, peering inside the pot.

"Yep. Hey Eric, come give me a hand." The two men lift the basket out of the pot and let it drain onto the ground. Then they dump the basket onto a folding table covered in newspaper. Nick calls out, "*Laissez les bons temps rouler!*"

They all gather round. Chloé fills a plate for Camille and then asks Nick, "So how do you eat these?"

"Pay close attention." Picking up a crawfish, he narrates his next actions. "You twist the head, pinch the tail, suck the head."

Chloé makes a face. "Oh my gosh, the last part, that is disgusting."

"Disgusting? That's coming from someone who eats sushi."

"With sushi, it's all prepared nicely. There is no head sucking. Gross."

Camille speaks up. "The head is where the 'fat' is. It's not real fat; that's just what we call the flavor. You don't have to suck it. You can just dig it out with your pinky."

"That's okay," Chloé tells them quickly. "I will leave the 'fat' for you all."

"Down here, we call sushi bait," Nick jokes.

"What the hell is sushi?" Eric asks. "Sounds Chinese."

Camille can't resist taking a dig at him. "If ignorance is bliss, you must be the happiest person on the planet."

"You are quite the firecracker, aren't you?" Eric says. "Ms. Camille, I'm sorry you and I got off on the wrong foot."

"Well, you pour me another glass of wine, and I'll forgive you."

Even though Chloé finds the freshly boiled crawfish somewhat repulsive, she does, however, enjoy the crawfish étouffée Nick made, finding it much more pleasant to eat. Sean is the first to have to leave. Shortly after, Eric looks at his watch and says, "Hey, I better be going too. I need to get home before the wife does. I told her I was feeling sick to get out of going to her church thing with her." He walks over to Camille and says, "Ms. Camille, it was mighty fine meeting you."

"Well, Eric," she replies, "I would say it was nice meeting

you, but let me say instead, someday you'll go far. I just hope you stay there." She winks at him.

Eric laughs with her and admits, "That's a good one."

ONCE THE OTHERS HAVE LEFT, Camille tells Chloé and Nick, "Thank you so much for inviting me today. I've had so much fun."

Chloé says happily, "It wouldn't have been the same without you."

"I'm sorry about Eric," Nick chimes in.

"No worries. He is a special kind of something."

"That's putting it lightly."

Camille nods. "I tell you, I believed in evolution until I met that sap." She turns to Chloé and asks, "Sweetie, before you take me back, can we stop by my house?"

"Of course," Chloé replies. "Let me help Nick clean up, and we will get on our way."

"Thank you. It has been so long since I've seen it."

WHEN THEY ARRIVE at Camille's home and turn into the driveway, Nick comments, "Wow, this is really a nice home."

"Why, thank you."

They park the car and Nick helps Camille into her wheelchair. Looking at the front yard, she says, "It needs a good mowing." Excitedly she adds, "Oh, look how big my camellias have grown."

With no ramp up to the front door, Nick picks Camille up into his arms and ascends the porch steps while Chloé follows with the wheelchair. Camille, cupped in Nick's arms, giggles a little.

Placing her back into her chair, Nick says, "You are as light as a feather."

Camille, smiling, tells him while reaching out and grabbing Chloé's arm, "You need to carry this one across the threshold someday."

Blushing, Chloé says quickly, "Let's just get inside for now."

Entering the house, Camille takes a deep breath. "Oh, I missed that smell. The smell of home."

"I'm going to take a look at this massive backyard," says Nick, excusing himself. "I think I saw a gazebo back there I want to check out."

Camille points to her left, and Chloé wheels her into the library. Camille tells her, "I told myself one day I would get around to reading all these books." She pauses. "I never made it. It seems many of us who purchase books are actually purchasing hours, days, and weeks that we hope or dream one day we will have to read them." Again she pauses. "Not enough time." Just then, Camille hears the passing streetcar. "Oh, I have missed that sound."

Chloé wheels her over to the window, saying, "You have a wonderful view of it from here."

As they make their way through the living room, kitchen, and finally back to the foyer, Camille asks Chloé, "Will you help me stand, sweetheart?" Rising from her wheelchair, Camille grips the carved pineapple staircase finial at the bottom of the stairs with her right hand while Chloé holds her left. Camille looks around and speaks with great emotion.

"The soul of this space that I call home is pieced together with all the laughter and joy, all the heartache and tears of so many decades. All the love that was behind its purchase René made for me can still be felt. This space contains so many memories. I raised my baby here. I watched him grow. I could show you every place in this home where he fell down or wrote on the walls. I could show you his bedroom where I tucked him in at bedtime. I could show you exactly which step on the stairs he used to step on during the night that would alert me he was out of bed. This home has been a vessel for my memories, which now are pouring out all around me. I've said goodbye to so many loved ones in my hundred and one years. No matter how many times, you are never ready for them to leave. Like those, this goodbye takes a part of me with it. There aren't many parts left. This space is just as alive as they were. Now, letting go... well, letting go is just as hard."

Chloé tells her, "You shouldn't talk like you will never be here again. The doctor allowed you to come out today. I bet tomorrow we can come here again."

"Oh sweetie, at my age, you no longer plan for tomorrow. You live each day as if it were a gift." Looking around, she says, "I have so many pottery pieces here I haven't finished." Almost in tears, she takes a deep breath. "Thank you for bringing me, but I shouldn't have come. This isn't how I want to remember it. This sad, lonely, dark, dusty place isn't the home I lived in. I want to remember it the way it was: full of color, the sun pouring in the windows, a laughing child, and jazz blaring from the record player as I danced around the room. That's how I will remember it. Not like this." With the help of Chloé, she sits back down in her wheelchair.

Nick rejoins them at that moment, saying, "Wow, this home is truly amazing." He can immediately sense the sadness in the room, though, and doesn't say anything else.

Camille says, "I suppose I should get back." On the way out, she taps her hand to her lips and, reaching out, touches the door.

Keep Me in
Your Heart

Monday morning, Chloé decides to call the front desk downstairs to see if her parents or Teresa have left any messages for her. The hotel receptionist answers, "Yes, Ms. Taylor, you have one new message. Meadowbrook Nursing Center called stating due to a medical emergency, a Ms. Camille has been transported to Charity Hospital on Tulane Avenue."

Chloé replies with her voice cracking, "Thank you." Since she arrived in the city and met Camille, she has been so afraid of the day she would get this call. She calls Nick's office, leaves a message for him, and calls for a cab.

Arriving at the hospital, she is escorted to Camille's room. Before going in, the nurse tells her, "The doctor would like to speak to you before you see her. He will be right with you."

Before long, the doctor walks up to Chloé and introduces himself. "Hello, I'm Dr. Nakhla. I've spoken with Dr. Stewart."

"I'm Chloé Taylor, her great-granddaughter. How is she?"

"I'll be honest with you, Ms. Taylor. She is not responding well. Her body is giving out sadly way before her mind. She is alert, but I feel it is not a matter of days or weeks but possibly hours for her."

Tears begin to fall down Chloé's cheeks. She asks, "Would this have anything to do with her having a field trip Saturday?"

"No, not at all. I understand she was doing amazing yesterday. Everyone has their time to leave us. Hers... I feel it is today. I'll give you some time alone with her. Please let the nurse know if you need anything."

"Thank you, doctor."

Trying to dry her tears, Chloé walks into Camille's room. Camille recognizes her immediately. In a noticeably weak voice, she says, "Hello, precious."

"Hello. How do you feel?"

"I've felt much better, sweetheart. Did the doctor talk to you?"

"Yes."

"Did he tell you what he told me?" Camille asks, holding her hand. "That the end is near?"

"Yes, but you're stronger than that. I know you are."

"I'm not as strong as I used to be, my dear. Which reminds me of what I used to always say—I am not as young as I used to be." She tries to laugh but does not have the energy to do so. "My old body is tired. I am tired. I know rest is coming soon." Tears start up again in Chloé's eyes as well as Camille's. "Now, now dear, do not cry, or you will get me crying too. It's okay. I am old. They would have shot me long ago if I were a horse."

Chloé can tell Camille is getting weaker and is having trouble speaking. She says brokenly, "I only just found you. I don't want to lose you."

Speaking softly and slowly, squeezing Chloé's hand, Camille responds, "We all go sooner or later, dear. I suppose this is the moment when I am supposed to give you some great advice about life. Some old cliché, like not blinking. How one day you're a little girl skipping rope, and the next you are 101 and in a hospital. However true that might be, there is nothing you can do to slow it down or capture a moment as it passes. That's just the way life happens. If I could offer you one thing, just one thing, it would be to love as much as you can every minute of that life. Love with all of your heart. Love like there is no tomorrow, for there will not be one day. I will tell you this: I have had several relationships in my life, but I suppose I didn't settle down because I had seen what love really is by growing up listening to René talking about my mother. That is the kind of love I was searching for but never found. You, Chloé, you have found it. I can feel the magic between you and Nick. You have what Tessa and René had. When the two of you are in the same room with me, I feel like I am in their presence. I may be old, but I am wise. Don't ever let a love like that slip away. Hold onto it."

"I will. I promise."

"For the rest about life, you will figure it out on your own. We all do. Life is about changing. Nothing ever stays the same. The sooner you accept that, the more you will enjoy the journey. Also, I made out my will several years ago. I included in it for you to get the house. Cherish it as much as I have since the moment René gave it to me. Like I said before, I never expected to live this long, so the house is all I have left to pass down to you. Take care of it for me."

"I will... I will. You're going to be fine, though."

"I love you, my precious angel... It's time." Camille lifts her hand with all her strength and places it on Chloé's chest. Chloé lays her hand over Camille's. Camille says, "Don't fret, my love. We will always be together when we love with our hearts and not just our minds."

The next moment, Camille lets out a whimpering cry and grips Chloé's hand tightly as the machines around her start beeping in unison.

Breaking out in tears, Chloé screams, "No! No! Please don't go. Please. No. Not yet. Please." Three nurses rush into the room, followed by the doctor. In a gasp of desperation, Chloé pleads, "Please help her."

One of the nurses escorts Chloé out while another pulls close the circular privacy curtain around Camille's bed. Down the hallway, Chloé spots Nick walking up to the nurses' station. She runs from the nurse's side and into Nick's arms. Immediately he knows what is wrong.

Minutes pass like hours until finally the doctor comes out and walks up to Chloé and Nick. He says heavily, "I am sorry, Ms. Taylor, but Ms. Laver has passed away."

Chloé bursts into tears, turns to Nick, and buries her head into his chest.

"We did all we could do for her, but like I said earlier, sooner or later, our bodies give out... even when we are not ready for them to."

LEAVING THE HOSPITAL, Nick drives Chloé to the Ambassador, and they put all her things in his car.

"Nick, thank you for letting me stay with you. I really don't think I could be alone right now."

"I want you to make yourself at home. Let me know if you need anything."

"Thank you, Nick. I love you so much."

"I love you too, beautiful."

ONCE AT HIS HOUSE, he walks Chloé to the door and then returns to his car to unload her belongings. After getting settled in, Chloé takes a walk in the backyard while he is in his home office, finishing up on some paperwork. She gazes up at the night sky, and what she sees makes her cry—and, at the same time, brings her comfort.

Nick joins her quietly. "How are you doing?"

"I was just thinking. See the Big Dipper? Follow the curve of the handle. Just past the end of the handle, that bright star is Arcturus. René, your great-great-grandfather, told Camille when she was little that Arcturus is where she could always find her mother. Camille told me one day she would join her there. So tonight, when I looked up at Arcturus, it is definitely shining brilliantly. Brighter than it had appeared before. They are together again. I can only imagine the stories she has for Tessa."

THE NEXT SEVERAL days are clouded with sadness and confusion for Chloé. She doesn't know what she would do without Nick. This kind of planning is profoundly hard for a twenty-two-year-old to go through, not to mention dealing with the loss of someone so dear to her.

On Saturday, the day before the funeral, Nick leads Chloé outside. "Climb into the car. There's something I want you to see."

"I'm feeling exhausted today, Nick." Having spent the entire day crying, she has no energy. "Is it something that could wait?"

"No, you need this."

They arrive at the New Orleans Museum of Art. Chloé sighs. "Nick, I love art more than anything, but my heart is just not into it at this moment."

"This is something you will want to see. I promise."

Reluctantly, she enters at Nick's side. He leads her quickly through the building, and she begins to realize they are there for a specific reason, not just to look at art. They walk up to an exhibit area, and she knows why they are there as soon as she reads the sign. All around her is pottery from Newcomb College.

They walk up to a vase with water lilies on it, and Nick says, "I thought you would want to see this."

The piece before her, as many of the others nearby, is labeled "Camille Laver." In fact, there is Louisiana flora and fauna-themed pottery all around them.

Chloé looks at Nick and says simply, "Thank you." She hugs him.

After studying each piece, Chloé stops and speaks to the curator about Camille's pottery collection and some of Tessa's paintings. Before leaving, she sees a painting of an orchid that gets her attention.

"That painting is so beautiful," she whispers.

"What is it that you like about it?" Nick asks.

"Besides the beautiful soft blue hue… orchids are my favorite flower. There is just something irresistible about them. Like their flowers, for example—they're bilaterally symmetric. They are two equal parts. Just like two identical souls that become one. One flower, or one heart."

LAY DOWN YOUR
WEARY TUNE

THE DAY of the funeral arrives. Camille has had a tomb picked out for years at the pristine St. Louis Cemetery Number Three. The funeral procession enters the majestic wrought iron gates. All around, one can see the well-maintained examples of New Orleans's unique crypts and funerary art. Approaching the grave site, Chloé notices a group of musicians all dressed in suits, with one carrying an umbrella.

She looks at Nick, confused. "Are they here for us?"

He nods. "I wanted this to be special for Camille. The man with the umbrella is the Grand Marshall. We'll follow him down to Camille's casket, which is awaiting us at her tomb."

They step out of the limousine, and Nick takes Chloé's hand, helping her to stand. He leads her behind the Grand Marshall and the musicians, known as the first line. The musicians begin playing soft and melodious funeral music. The mourners, also known as the second line—consisting of Chloé, Nick, Sean, Camille's neighbors the Wilsons, who are carrying their dog in their arms, and Ms. Margaret, escorted by several of the workers from Meadowbrook who had gotten close to Camille—follow them to the burial tomb. Standing over Camille's coffin is a priest.

As the music ceases, the priest begins to speak.

"God our Father, we beseech thee, O Lord, in thy mercy, to have pity on the soul of thy handmaid; do thou, who hast freed her from the perils of this mortal life, restore to her the portion of everlasting salvation. Lord, those who die still live in thy presence; their lives change but do not end. May they rejoice in thy kingdom. Through Christ our Lord, amen." He looks around. "Now Ms. Taylor would like to say a few words."

Chloé steps forward and speaks. "When I set out to write something for Camille, it ended up being more like a book. How can one summarize briefly the spirit of a woman whose life spanned over a century?

"She was a daughter, a mother, a grandmother, a great-grandmother, and, most importantly, my friend. I had little time with her, but those days were the best of my life. She was the wisest, kindest, funniest person I have ever known.

"The first time I saw her beautiful white hair, I marveled at how well she wore her wrinkles... like medals on a warrior's chest. Each line on her face told a story from a book. A book of mystery, comedy, tragedy, and romance that only she owned. And she owned it so well. I was given the gift of hearing all those wonderful stories. The greatest gift one can bestow on others is the gift of life—a life she shared with me.

"I will miss her smile and her laughter. I will miss her. I saw people walking down the street today. They were smiling. I thought to myself, how can anyone anywhere smile today? The world has no idea what they have lost. If they only knew, then today, the oceans would be unable to hold all the tears. Then I realized Camille would not want us to cry. She would want us to smile. To celebrate her life, not mourn her death.

"Her body may have left this earth, but she will live on, generation after generation for eternity, in her stories. We will miss you, 'Pretty Baby.' Now lay down your weary tune and rest. Your song may be over, but the music will never end."

· · ·

FOLLOWING CHLOÉ'S eulogy for Camille, the priest speaks again. "In sure and certain hope of the Resurrection to eternal life through our Lord Jesus Christ, we commend to Almighty God our sister Camille Marie Laver, and we commit her body to the ground; earth to earth, ashes to ashes, dust to dust. The Lord bless her and keep her; the Lord make his face to shine upon her and be gracious unto her; the Lord lift up his countenance upon her and give her peace. Amen."

As the final prayer is delivered, the priest performs the sign of the cross as a small amount of earth is ceremonially cast on Camille's coffin.

Suddenly a trombone with the pure spirit of jazz breaks the silence. Then all at once, in perfect accord, a trumpet, clarinet, and drums join in. All the musicians begin dancing rhythmically as if escorting the deceased to heaven themselves. The howling trumpet solo revels in celebration, beckoning back to the days of Congo Square. It is a celebration of a life well lived.

The Wilsons' dog begins barking as Chloé, with tears in her eyes, begins to laugh, thinking of Camille. Looking up at Nick, she says, "Thank you. From her and from me. Thank you."

A Blind
Betrayal

Nick spends the following week comforting Chloé and
helping her go through Camille's home. He returns to work
on Friday, and immediately Sean comes into his office to
find out how he and Chloé have been doing. They are just
discussing how the funeral went when the smell of cigar
smoke fills the air. It signals to them that Mr. Jones is coming
down the hall.

Fred Jones seldom comes to visit their wing of offices, so
they know this must be important. He is a large, balding man
who would never be without a cigar—if he could only find a
way to smoke in his sleep.

Unsure of his intentions, they are startled at his entrance
into Nick's office.

Sean immediately stands up and announces his presence
with, "Hello, Mr. Jones." Then he looks over to Nick
nervously and begins to prattle. "I need to get back to that
case about that thing in my office. You know that case
thingy? Okay, I'm going now... to my office. I'm going."

After Sean steps out, Mr. Jones says, "Strange bird that
one, but a good lawyer." This is only one of a handful of
times he has spoken to Nick since Nick broke off his engage-
ment to Lydia a year earlier. Now he tells Nick, "Son, I need
you to escalate a filing for me. We need to complete a
transfer of ownership on a house that just came available."
He drops the folder on Nick's desk.

"Yes, sir." Nick opens the file and immediately recognizes
the address, and turns to the photos of the house to verify his
suspicion. "Wait, I know this property."

"The old lady that lived there just kicked the bucket, and

the property is tied up with the nursing home and Medicaid. She signed a lien when she went in to cover the expenses. Probably didn't even know what she was signing or figured Medicaid would end up covering the cost."

"You mean you want me to help set up an auction of the property for the nursing home?"

"No, son. Just take it."

Nick frowns in confusion. "I beg your pardon, sir, but that is what happens the house gets auctioned, the nursing home or Medicaid gets their money owed, and the rest, if there is anything left, goes to the family. But more importantly, the family is given the opportunity to pay what is owed upfront to avoid the auction altogether. Often the family sells the property themselves and pays at that point. What you're talking about is taking it outright."

Frustrated, Mr. Jones says, "Dammit to hell, I know the law, boy! I have some friends in the state Medicaid department, and the owners of many nursing homes in Louisiana, including this one, are essentially in my pocket. They owe me some favors, and I'm cashing in. I gave a call to an appraiser I know who also owes me. I got him to appraise the house at $250,000 and keep the appraisal private. The nursing home is allowing me to purchase it outright for $250,000 without notifying the public—and besides, there is no family."

"There is, sir. I personally know the former owner's great-granddaughter."

Mr. Jones is taken aback. He sits there blowing smoke and studying Nick's face. "Well, does this great-granddaughter have $75,000? Because that's what is owed." Nick is speechless. "Didn't think so... Boy, do you realize the value of this property? This is prime real estate. Hell, it might become our new office site."

"I'm sorry, sir; I'm just confused as to how any of this is legal, especially with there being a living relative."

Laughing and coughing, Mr. Jones responds, "Legal? You know all these signs you see around town that say 'J. and Company Property Partners'? Son, how do you think we get most of these old mansions? *I* get them because of the power given to me by the people *I* control. We are fortunate to have a Medicaid system that is one of the slowest for approvals in the country. Hell, most states have people approved within a month. Here in the great state of Louisiana, it can take a year or longer. I'm contacted whenever someone ancient enters one of my friends' nursing homes. Then I reach out to my friends with the state and have that person's application held up for up to a year and a half. It looks too evident if we hold it longer than that. Then as long as they die within that time span, I have it denied. By doing so, the family has to come up with the entire balance owed to the nursing home. Most of the time, they can't pay, and the property gets taken by the nursing home and sold to me at a deep discount. In return, I... well, let's just say, *thank graciously* the individuals that assist us in the process."

Nick cuts in. "So you're saying this Meadowbrook patient Camille Laver was denied her Medicaid claim thanks to you, and now her great-granddaughter owes for the entire time Ms. Laver was under their care?"

"Absolutely. Listen. This is what we'll do. You write up the sale acting on behalf of the nursing home, showing the purchase price of $250,000. Then write out a check for $175,000, the difference of what was owed to them, made out to this great-granddaughter of hers. After we close the deal, give her the check and tell her this was what was left after we deducted what her great-grandmother owed. It's worth at least seven to eight times that, but that should be enough to buy her off; when most people see a check that large, they don't complain. If she gives you any trouble, we'll disclose the appraisal, and with my other connections in the courts, we can squash any fight she might provide us with, if necessary. But no one ever fights us and wins."

Mr. Jones looks at Nick with a sharp eye. "I chose you to handle this one because you are the best damn lawyer we have and the best I have ever seen for your age. That, and with my property company being the purchaser, of course, it might be, let us say, *frowned upon* for me to do the closing as well. It's all just part of the job. Your daddy did a good job preparing you for this career. He was a hell of a good lawyer. He would be proud of you. I tell you, that man would take this bull by the horns and run with it. I hope you're ready to run. There is a nice bonus in this for you too, by the way. Fifteen percent of my purchase price. Fifteen percent, son," he repeats, looking for a reaction from Nick. "That would go a long way to starting that little restaurant business Lydia told me you want on the side. Just remember that."

Nick is still sitting there stunned as Mr. Jones turns to leave. He suddenly looks back at Nick with cigar smoke swirling in the air. Mr. Jones blows a perfect smoke ring that hangs over Nick's head like a halo. "Son, this is a case for a lawyer." Then he takes a deep breath and blows it away. "Not an angel. Listen, kid. I like you. I kept you on even after my daughter begged me to fire your ass. Hell, to tell the truth, I wouldn't have married her either. She's too much like her mother. I think you're a good kid, a smart kid. Don't screw this up."

At that moment, as Mr. Jones leaves his office, Nick's phone rings. It's Chloé. "Nick speaking."

"Can you pick me up so we can go down to the River Walk and talk?" she says. "I really need you right now."

"Yes. Let me finish up a couple of things, and I'll be right over."

"Thank you. I love you, Nick."

"I love you too, Chloé. See you shortly." As he hangs up, he says aloud, "I have to tell her."

Sean runs in from his office across the hall. "What the hell are you going to do?" Nick looks dazed. "Oh, I heard every-thing. Ev...er...y...thing!"

"I have no idea," Nick replies.

NICK PICKS up Chloé at his house, and they head to the waterfront. As they start walking with his arm around her, Nick speaks up. "I need—"

At the same time, Chloé says, "Nick, I want to stay here in New Orleans."

"I didn't know that was even in question."

"Not only do I mean stay here, but I also want to keep the house. I owe that to Camille. She asked me to take care of it. It's a part of her. It's part of my family, and I don't want to sell it. She said in her will that I get it. I want to make sure it stays in the family. I don't know the legality involved, but will you please help me process the will?"

"You know if you sold it, you could get a lot for it."

"I don't care about the money. Will you please help me?"

He knows he should tell her the truth about what is happening with the house, but is struggling. If he helps her, he knows he will lose his job. He is afraid to lose her if he tells her, but he knows he'll lose her for sure if he doesn't. He says, "There is something I need to tell you." Just then, a mime comes up and begins to perform for them. Nick rolls his eyes and waits.

When the mime finally leaves, she asks, "What were you going to tell me?" He pauses. "Nothing."

Again she asks, "Will you please help me?"

Not knowing what else to say, he says, "Yes, I will."

"Thank you, Nick, thank you. I love you." She hugs him tight.

"I'll get right on it," he promises while holding her, totally unsure about what he is going to do.

"I don't know what I would do without you. The entire will process is so foreign to me. She mentions in the will that she has ten thousand dollars in bonds in a safe in her house that will mature in 1996. She wants it donated to the New Orleans Botanical Gardens for a camellia garden so we can walk through it and remember her. Like anyone who knew her would ever be able to forget."

Hugging her again, he says, "I'll make sure it will be done. All of it. I promise." He's trying desperately to sound confident, though he's still not sure what to do.

BACK AT THE LAW FIRM, Sean is in Eric's office telling him about Nick's meeting with Mr. Jones.

Sean ends with, "I don't know what he's going to do. I mean, he has to tell her. If he doesn't, he will lose her for sure. If he does, he probably will still lose her."

Eric points out, "And if he doesn't do what he was told, he'll get canned. Wow. This is messed up."

"I know he truly loves her. He'll do what's right. I just think he doesn't know what right *is* in this situation."

"This is one of the few times I can truly say I'm glad I'm not him," Eric remarks. "Is she staying in the house right now?"

"No, she's been staying at Nick's." Looking at his watch, Sean says, "Hey, I've got to get back to the courthouse, but I'll let you know when I hear more."

As he leaves Eric's office, he sees Lydia standing in the hallway smiling. With a frozen look on his face, all Sean can say is, "Oh snap!" He puts his head down and walks away.

. . .

WHEN NICK RETURNS to his office, he sits at his desk, staring at the file that still lies in the same place Mr. Jones dropped it earlier that day.

Lydia walks in. "Hello, Nick."

Annoyed, Nick replies, "Hello, Lydia. What can I help you with?"

"I am just about to step out for the day, but when you have time, could you please offer some advice on a case I have that may involve the city?"

"Yeah, sure... Is that it?"

"Thank you. I'll be in touch."

"Have a nice evening."

Lydia saunters out of his office. "I'm sure I will."

CHLOÉ ARRIVES BACK at Nick's after having been at Camille's, picking out the pieces of pottery and paintings she wants to keep and donating the rest to the New Orleans Museum of Art. As she's getting settled in, she hears the doorbell ring and goes to answer it. Standing before her is Lydia.

Chloé is startled and concerned. Why would Lydia come to Nick's?

"Hello, you must be Chloé."

"Yes, and you are Lydia. Am I correct?"

Lydia walks past her into the house, looking around. "Yes, I am." She then spins to face Chloé. "Nick must have told you a lot about me."

"No, he hasn't really mentioned anything at all about you. I only know your name because you ignored me when Nick went to introduce us."

Lydia begins touching table tops and vases as if inspecting them for dust, saying, "Yes, well, I sometimes do that to people who try to take something that is mine."

"Yours? Give me a break. I'm sorry, but Nick isn't home right now. He's still at the office."

Lydia looks at Chloé. "Chloé, I'm actually not here to see Nick; I'm here to see you."

Chloé is only partially relieved by her statement. "I really do not see what we possibly need to speak about."

"Chloé, I am here as a friend, not an enemy."

"Thanks, but I have enough friends."

"I'm sure you do; however, I come to warn you about Nick before he breaks your heart like he broke mine."

"I really do not want to hear anything more from you. I'm sorry things didn't work out for you, but you need to move on. Nick is a caring, compassionate person, and I'm not worried at all about him hurting me."

"Did he tell you he's selling off your great-grandmother's house right behind your back? All for the money to start his little club thing."

Chloé is paralyzed with fear, anger, and disbelief. "I don't know what you're talking about."

"He's handling it for my father. The house is being sold to my dad unless you can come up with $75,000. Nick didn't want to tell you because he'll get quite a large piece of the settlement. He really does not care about you, just the money."

"That cannot be true."

"Ask him, if you don't believe me." Lydia gives her a pitying look. "Don't make the same mistake I did. You're just another girl to him. Just another notch in his belt."

Chloé is almost in tears now. What if Lydia is right? She tells her, "You need to leave. Now." Lydia walks out the door and turns back. Chloé, who is already starting to close the door, holds up a hand. "That's enough."

Lydia stops the door from closing with her foot and deals her final blow. "Oh, by the way, did he take you to the Moon

Walk and sing to you with his band, and did he give you glitter to throw and show you his poetry? Believe me, neither you nor I are the first or last girls he has done that with. You are just another girl to him."

Now crying, Chloé yells out, "Enough!" and slams the door, collapsing against it to the floor.

Calling out through the door, Lydia tells her, "I'm only telling you this because I don't want to see Nick hurt you like he hurt me." Then smiling, she walks back to her car, saying aloud, "Yes, a truly nice evening indeed."

CHLOÉ COLLECTS her thoughts and calls Nick's office. He answers, and she confronts him immediately.

"Nick, please tell me you aren't taking Camille's house. Please tell me it's a lie."

Chloé's hope that Nick would deny it is quickly diminished by silence.

Nick finally speaks. "I'm sorry, Chloé. I didn't know what else to do. I wanted to tell you today at the River Walk."

"You mean the River Walk where you once took Lydia on the same kind of date you and I had?"

"What? No... I never even went with her on a date to the River Walk. Where did you hear that? Was it Lydia? She will say or do anything to break us up."

"I hope you enjoy the money you'll get for taking Camille's house and tearing apart my heart. Maybe you can spend it on the next special girl."

"I am not trying to take Camille's house from you. I'm just stuck in the middle trying to do my job. Just know it never was and never will be about money."

"Nor will it be about honesty. How could you do this to me? To us? You said you would help me, and the entire time you were plotting against me."

"I never plotted against you! I wanted to tell you, I just didn't know how."

Crying, she replies, "Well, this isn't how it should've been done. You and Lydia deserve each other. I trusted you; I loved you." She hangs up.

If You See Her,
Say Hello

NICK RUSHES HOME, but by the time he arrives, he discovers
Chloé has already returned to the Ambassador. He tries
calling over and over again, but she is refusing to take any
calls from him. All he can think about are her last words: "I
loved you." In the past tense.

Nick starts trying to think of a way to get her to respond.
Then he begins calling around to nearly every florist in
town.

THE FOLLOWING DAY, a delivery is made to the Ambassador.
The front desk calls Chloé's room.

"Hello. Please, as I told you before, I am not taking any
calls."

"Yes, ma'am, I understand." The concierge begins to stam-
mer. "W-we have a delivery for you."

"Alright. You can bring it up."

Stammering again. "Ah... y-yes ma'am, right away then."

A few minutes later, Chloé hears a knock on her door.
She opens it and sees a hotel staff member holding a beautiful white orchid.

The sight takes her breath away, and she steps to the side,
holding onto the door handle. After a moment she says, "Just
set it over there by the desk." Suddenly another person walks
in, carrying two more. Again she says, "Over there." Then
they bring in two more. Then the first person goes out and
comes back in with two more. This goes on for quite a while.
Chloé begins laughing and crying as she watches more and
more orchids being placed in the room.

Finally, the last one is brought in. There is barely room to walk; she is now standing in a room with thirty orchids. One of them has a note attached.

CHLOÉ,

I am so sorry. I never meant to hurt you. I love you dearly.

With you, I am reminded of the words of Keats: "I cannot exist without you—I am forgetful of every thing but seeing you again—my Life seems to stop there—I see no further... My creed is Love and you are its only tenet."

Chloé, you and I have been part of each other forever. I cannot tell you why you should take a chance on a fool like me. I can only say I wish you would.

Just please, please just speak to me. I can explain everything. Nothing is as it seems.

I love you, Nick

AT HOME, Nick has just exited the shower, having spent the morning trying to reach Chloé by phone, when the doorbell rings. Putting on his robe, he answers the door. Standing before him is Lydia, holding a thick folder in her hand. Nick rolls his eyes. But the next second, his disappointment that it is not Chloé at his door changes over to anger over what Lydia has done.

"What are you doing here?!"

Smiling, Lydia says, "You said you would give me some advice on my case."

"How dare you come here after what you have done?"

"She would have found out sooner or later."

"It wasn't your place to tell her."

"You're right. It wasn't my place. It was yours. I just did what you should have done yourself. So are you going to help me or not? Please, pretty please. Are you going to invite me in? It is purely professional. I promise."

Nick throws up his hands. "Fine." He lets her in.

She steps inside. "Thank you."

"When I said I would help you, I didn't mean outside of work. Can this not wait until Monday?"

"No time is better than the present."

Reluctantly he responds, "Sure, whatever. Please excuse me. I'm going upstairs to throw on some clothes. Make yourself comfortable or whatever."

"I will," she replies, and walks over to the wet bar in his living room to make herself a martini.

Suddenly a cab pulls up in Nick's driveway, and stepping out is Chloé. She immediately notices a car parked behind Nick's Porsche. She asks the driver to please wait for her because she wants to speak to Nick alone, and it appears he may be entertaining company. If so, she will not stay but a moment.

Lydia sees Chloé out the window and says aloud, "This is going to be good." She quickly unbuttons her blouse all the way down, glancing at the stairs as she races to the door. She wants to answer it before Chloé can ring the doorbell, to prevent Nick from learning of her presence. She doesn't make it there before the bell sounds, though. As Lydia opens the door, she begins buttoning up her blouse, smiling. Startled, Chloé looks over Lydia's shoulder toward the stairs— where Nick is coming down in jeans, no shoes, and pulling his T-shirt on over his head.

Nick calls out, "Is there someone at the door?"

He makes eye contact with Chloé just as she yells out, "Nice to see you replaced me so quickly! I guess old habits die hard!"

Nick notices Lydia's blouse unbuttoned as Chloé runs back to the waiting taxi. He runs out after her, calling, "This is not how it appears. Nothing happened! Please, Chloé, come in and talk." All to no avail, as the cab drives away.

For a minute he stands in his driveway with his fingers interlocked on the top of his head, like a runner catching his breath. Then he looks back to his house. Lydia is standing on his porch with her blouse still halfway undone, head cocked at him. He tells her, "Lydia, get the hell out of here, and take your damn files with you." He steps inside, grabs her folder, and throws it out. Papers fly everywhere as he slams the front door behind him. Lydia kneels to gather her files with a smirk on her face.

LATER THAT EVENING, Nick mixes a Manhattan with a sweet vermouth at the wet bar in his home office. Walking over to his record collection, Nick pulls out one of his favorite albums, Bob Dylan's *Blood on the Tracks*. Slipping the record from its sleeve, he places the needle on the third song of side two: "If You See Her, Say Hello." Nick then sits down at his desk, trying to find a solution while wishing he could see Chloé's beautiful smile again, kiss her soft lips, and hold her. He knows he has a job to do, but nothing means more to him than her.

Nick reaches into his center desk drawer, removing a letter he often turns to when life gets complicated. It is a letter his father left for him about challenges Nick will face as a lawyer. Nick, however, notices far too often that it also applies to life. He has a pretty good hunch his dad intended it to. Unfolding it, he begins to read.

AS A LAWYER, *you will be faced with situations of uncertainty. Early on, you will call these "crises," but as you mature and look back, you will confidently call them mere situations. These situa-*

tions will challenge you just as life will. And just as in life, you are going to make mistakes, lots of them. The key is not to run from them. You must face your mistakes head on. To get through any situation, you must first understand what you are up against. It is easy to let ourselves be led by our emotions. Know all your facts, not all your feelings. Come up with a plan. Always have a plan.

A plan is a series of ideas that we control. They start as thoughts in our heads, and then we become braver and speak them aloud. Once spoken, we critique them until they break. Then we pull them back inside to reconstruct. Again they build as thoughts until we muster the courage to say them once more aloud. This time, they withstand all scrutiny.

But you can never get to a resolution, formulate an answer, or have a plan if you do not understand the story or the question being asked. In the practice of law and in life, we all have stories, from cases in law books to lessons in novels. This is where you will find your answers. Look to your library. This is where you will find what to do—written in these stories, in these books.

NICK BEGINS RECITING the words over and over. "Look to your library. This is where you will find what to do—written in these stories, in these books. Written in these stories, written in—" As he speaks, he looks at the walls of books surrounding him. Suddenly he stops scanning, his eyes locked on one particular book: *A Streetcar Named Desire* by Tennessee Williams. He says aloud, "Always stay true to yourself, and always tell the truth."

He has found his answer written in these stories.

HASTEN DOWN
THE WIND

AFTER SEVERAL DAYS of calling her hotel, Nick still hasn't heard from Chloé. On Friday morning, he shows up to work four hours late.

Helen, the receptionist, is surprised to see him. "Mr. Nattier, we were starting to worry about you."

"No need to worry. I just had some errands to run to set some things straight. Do I have any messages?"

She replies, "No." Nick is disappointed, as he is still hoping Chloé might reach out. "Mr. Jones was looking for you, though."

"Great. He is exactly who I need to see." Nick begins walking towards Mr. Jones' office.

Helen calls out, "Wait, Mr. Nattier, he is in an important meeting! He asked not to be disturbed."

Continuing to walk, Nick replies, "I guarantee what I have to say will be a little more important and definitely disturbing."

Nick walks straight into Mr. Jones' office to discover the man sitting at his desk with a young blonde on his lap. Mr. Jones shoves the young lady off his lap onto the floor and says, "How dare you enter my office without being announced."

"I think your meeting here is over. We need the room," Nick tells the young lady, who is now gathering her clothes.

After the woman walks out, Mr. Jones yells at Nick, "This had better be life and death! By the way, what you just saw never happened unless you never want to work in this town again."

"Believe me, what I have to say to you is far more worrisome than that dysfunctional intertwining you had going on there."

WHILE NICK IS with Mr. Jones, Chloé arrives at the office. She hands the receptionist a note, telling her, "Can you please give this to Nick Nattier for me? Tell him it's from Chloé."

"He's in a meeting," Helen responds. "He said, however, if you were to come by or call, he wanted to be told immediately." Standing up, she asks, "Would you like me to let him know you are here?"

"No, just give him the note. Thank you," Chloé says, then quickly exits the building and climbs into a cab.

BACK IN MR. JONES' office, Nick sits in front of the desk as Mr. Jones asks, "Well, what do you have to tell me that is so earth-shattering?"

Nick reaches onto the desk, takes Mr. Jones' lit cigar out of his ashtray, and drops it into a cup of coffee. Mr. Jones' mouth drops open. Nick says, "I always hated the smell of those things."

Mr. Jones tells him, "Boy, you either have some mighty big brass gonads, or you are as confused as a fart in a fan factory." Nick then hands him a letter. "What is this?"

"That is my resignation letter."

"Resignation?"

"Yes."

"After this stunt, you won't have to worry about resigning."

"And here..." Nick hands him a second page. "This is a list of all my demands."

Laughing, Mr. Jones responds, "Demands? Boy, if you

think you can stand up to me, I know of a tree stump in a swamp with a higher IQ than you."

"I will read it for you, but you will still need to sign the bottom." Leaning over the desk and pointing his finger, he says, "Right there. So first off, I want a $50,000 severance package. Next, you will break all ties you have with the nursing home industry and the state Medicaid office. You agree to never prey on the elderly again. You also agree not to retaliate against me, and I expect to never hear from you again. Finally, you will immediately resign, retire, crawl back into the swamp you came out of, or whatever you want to call it, and make Sean the lead attorney. So before you ask, yes, your daughter will be answering to him. I also want Sean to receive a 50 percent raise, and I want him to have complete job security while working here for however long as he wants. Am I understood?"

Laughing, Mr. Jones replies, "Oh, is that all? If brains were leather, you wouldn't have enough to saddle a June bug. And what if I don't go along with this nonsense?"

"If you don't, this folder I have here goes out to the feds with the information on all the victims you took advantage of. Then you can spend the rest of your golden years in federal prison."

"And you think they'll believe you."

"They won't have to. They will believe the documents I have." Nick opens the folder and places it in front of Mr. Jones. "Like a signed deposition from Larry Wardale, the owner of Meadowbrook Nursing Home, giving names and dates of all involved on a state and local level for the last twenty years. He provided me with the patients', or should I say victims', billing records involving you from all his nursing facilities. He practically wrote a book. I'm really surprised he knew so much about the operation with all the details and the others involved. You really should learn to compartmentalize your illegal activities. The fewer people in the know, the better. Speaking of others, I found it interesting how often you've been using Lydia, your own daughter, to process some of these. I suppose they would want to question her as well. I also discovered in my research three certain shady individuals, in—let's see how do I say it—an *organized family* that you owe a great deal of money to. I'm sure the feds would also have a field day with that. I found all of this in just a few days. Imagine what they could do with a warrant. There are also some really questionable financial reports in there. I'm sure the money laundering you do for your friends through your property purchases would pique the interest of the Treasury department. I found allowing yourself to be the third-party purchaser to avoid any links between your organized criminal friends and the property was pretty clever. All the financial stuff is in the back there. Oh, by the way, the folder is yours to keep. I made those copies for you. Something to remember me by. Let's call it a reminder of consequences going forward, should you break our agreement."

Nick stands to leave. Looking around, he says, "This is nice. I think Sean should get this office. Make that happen. Oh, and if anything happens to me, the originals go straight to the feds. So you had better hope I stay healthy. You probably should go ahead and extend my health insurance indefinitely. Alright then, good talk, Fred. Have a great day packing up your office. I know I will."

As Nick leaves Mr. Jones' office, Helen hands him a note. He asks, "What is this?"

The receptionist says, "A Ms. Chloé dropped it off."

Upset, Nick responds, "I told you days ago to come to get

me if she stopped by or called." Looking up at the ceiling, he asks, "How long ago was this?"

"A little over an hour ago. I'm sorry, but she insisted on not notifying you."

"I'm sorry I raised my voice. Thank you." Nick opens the letter.

NICK,

I'm so sorry things did not work out between us. I really did love you, and I loved your city. You captured my heart the night we met. Something no one else has ever done. The handsome gentleman who offered me a seat at his table. The one who made me feel special. You made Camille feel special too. Thank you for that.

I have never truly loved anyone before. I did not know how good it felt to have or how terrible it hurts to lose it. I want you to know I believe you and do not feel like you intended to hurt me, but you did. I know you were only doing your job, but I feel like I let Camille down by not being able to keep the house.

I have to leave, and I will not be returning. My flight to Seattle takes off this afternoon. I should already be in the air by the time you read this. I wish you the best in life. Thank you for showing me this beautiful city and what love really feels like, even if it was only for a short time.

Like the wind, memories will pass by of a boy who met a girl, and what might have been between them. The French say, 'Tu me manques,' 'You are missing from me,' and you will be forever.

Goodbye, Chloé

NICK RUNS out the door and jumps into his car. He knows he may only have one chance to stop her.

He drives straight to the airport, pulling up behind a long row of cabs unloading their passengers at the terminal. Nick, in his suit, bolts out of his Porsche, leaving his door open as cars behind him begin honking. Rain is pouring down as he runs from cab to cab, peering inside their windows. He sees a baggage handler unloading a poster tube from one, and runs up to the dark-haired woman under an umbrella. He says, "Chloé!" and places his hand on her shoulder. The woman turns. Out of breath, he pants, "Sorry, I thought you were someone else."

He places his hands on his head and turns in all directions, feeling dejected and deploring how he could have let her get away. Then suddenly, he sees Chloé walking with her luggage on her way into the terminal. He runs up to her in the pounding rain.

Seeing him approach, she stares and says, "It's too late! It's too late, Nick!"

"No, it's not!"

"What about Lydia?"

"What about her? She showed up at my house after I showered to go over a case. I went upstairs to get dressed, and she unbuttoned her blouse to fool you. Nothing happened. Nothing. I promise. I'm sorry I didn't tell you immediately what I was being forced to do with the house. I just wanted to wait until I had a plan before telling you. I shouldn't have waited."

"I don't know, Nick. It seems all the magpies in the world could not build a bridge to span the divide between us right now."

"No, but this is a start." He hands Chloé the deed to Camille's house. "I paid the $75,000 and lost my job in the process, but working for Fred Jones was not meant for me. What is meant for me, though, is you."

"What? Where? How did you get the money?"

"It was my savings for the Belle Reve."

"Oh, Nick. But your dream."

"The house is free and clear. No one can touch it, Chloé. No one. It is all yours... and so am I, if you still want me."

"Nick. I don't know what to say. What about your beautiful dream?"

"My beautiful dream is right here. I am holding her. Say you will stay in New Orleans and that you will give me a chance to make this up to you."

Chloé pauses and looks into his eyes. "I will, Nick."

"Even if I still say the Stones?"

With a combination of laughter and tears she responds, "Even if you still pick the Stones. Listen, there is something I want to do. It's something I wanted to tell you but didn't have the chance to. I want to turn Camille's house into the Belle Reve."

Taken aback, Nick asks, "What? What do you mean?"

"I know you've had a spot picked out, but Camille would love knowing that her house would have jazz playing every night. It came to me when I was there going through the pottery. It is the perfect size for a restaurant and bar with a small stage. We could use the lot space on the sides for parking. Out back, we could string up lights and have an entire garden entertaining area. With your connection, zoning shouldn't be a problem. The best part is the perfect location with the streetcar line running out front. I would imagine even Tennessee Williams himself would love the serendipity."

"Are you sure?"

"Yes. But promise me one thing."

"What?"

"The last song played each night—I want it to be 'Pretty Baby' in honor of Camille."

"Of course," Nick says.

"But, before all of that, I want to take a trip to France."

"France?"

"Yes, there's something I need to do. You don't happen to own a sled, do you?"

He replies, laughing, "No. Wouldn't get much use around here."

"No worries."

Nick takes her hands. "Hey, do you remember you once told me an incredible love story about a gypsy princess?"

"Yes."

"Well, now I have a story for you."

Laughing, quoting him from earlier, she says, "Excellent. I like stories."

"Well, twice upon a time, a gypsy princess came searching for love, and both times found her prince." Then they kiss in the magical New Orleans rain.

Da Capo al Fine

Chloé, October 1993. The Dune du Pilat, France.

ABOUT THE AUTHOR

Michael Combs is an author and licensed massage therapist. Raised in Arkansas, he attended the University of Arkansas at Little Rock. He began writing at sixteen and has received numerous awards for his poetry. Now Combs has turned his primary focus to fiction and has been named a finalist in the *Arkansas Times* for best author of 2022.

Whether it involves months of research or traveling to the locations he writes about, Combs embeds himself into his writing. Unlike many authors who require silence when writing, he writes to music and has a soundtrack for each book, which imbues his work with a unique flow. When asked about his writing, Combs likes to describe himself as a storyteller, having lived a remarkable life that has given him abundant writing material.

Besides *Twice Upon a Time*, Michael's writings include *Lost Boy, Arcturus, Lost Boy: Brace Yourself,* and *The Long Road Home*.

Lost Boy tells the story of Mike, a massage therapist in Burbank, who, through his daily struggles, masks his sorrow with humor, women, and alcohol. While searching for love, he and his best friend Keith traverse many hilarious relationship faux pas. Then he meets Gabi and must decide if he can open his heart or stay lost forever.

Arcturus is a love story of two people who refuse to give up and the tale of a family on a cross-country journey learning to heal. Arcturus awakens the soul, gripping readers' hearts and leaving them questioning what truly matters.

Lost Boy: Brace Yourself continues the *Lost Boy Series* as Mike faces more challenges finding his place in the world. Just like the title says, brace yourself. For along with his friend Keith the laughter is non-stop, and so is his love for Gabi.

The Long Road Home is a story of returning home, dealing with loss, and finding true love. A woman discovering her heart and an outlaw biker who must decide how far he will go to heal his own.

www.lostboypublishing.com

Facebook.com/lostboypublishing
twitter.com/LostBoyPublish
instagram.com/lostboypublishing

ALSO AVAILABLE NOW BY MICHAEL COMBS

The Long Road Home

(Hardback, Paperback, eBook, and Audiobook)

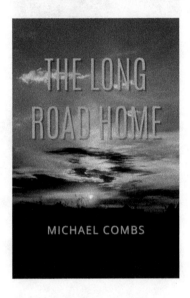

ARCTURUS

(Hardback, Paperback, eBook, and Audiobook)

Lost Boy

(Paperback, and eBook)

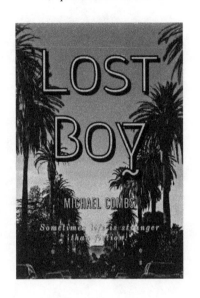

Lost Boy: Brace Yourself

(Paperback, and eBook)

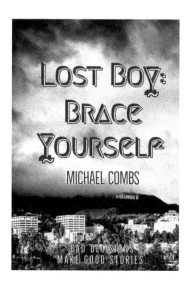

NEW BOOKS COMING SOON

New books coming soon by Michael Combs...

Twice Upon a Time (Audiobook)
Lost Boy: Leaving Neverland

Look for the next book from Lost Boy Publishing.

Lost Boy: Leaving Neverland

By Michael Combs

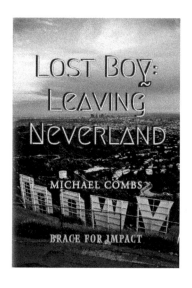

The Following Is a Preview of

The Long Road Home

And I heard, as it were the noise of thunder, one of the four beasts saying, "Come and see." And I saw, and behold, a black horse... And I heard a voice in the midst of the four beasts... And I looked, and behold, a pale horse. And its rider's name was Death, and Hell followed with him.

-Revelation 6:1-8

AS IT WAS IN THE BEGINNING

In Las Cruces, New Mexico, on a late summer day, a black Cadillac Escalade towing a flatbed trailer makes its way to the Doña Ana County Correctional Facility. Strapped on the trailer is a Dyna Wide Glide Harley Davidson motorcycle. Making a wide turn into the parking lot, the vehicle stops near the entrance. Behind the wheel is Mike White, a tall, slender man, only thirty-two, but balding prematurely. He is wearing a white dress shirt with the sleeves rolled up and a loosened black tie.

The door to the detention center opens, accompanied by a loud buzzer. Stepping out is Jacob McGuire. Twenty-six years old and handsome, Jacob stands tall at six feet and has a muscular build, brown eyes, a trimmed beard, and shoulder-length wavy black hair. He has just been released after serving eighteen months of a three-year sentence on third-degree felony charges for aggravated battery with a deadly weapon.

Mike climbs out of his SUV holding a leather vest—or cut, as it is referred to in the motorcycle culture—and walks over to Jacob, calling out, "There he is!" The two men hug each other and Mike speaks into Jacob's ear, saying, "I love you, brother. I'm so sorry. I'm so sorry we all failed you, and Maria."

Still holding Mike, Jacob replies, "I love you too, brother."

They release their embrace and Mike hands Jacob his cut. "We need you back, brother."

Jacob pauses for a moment as he looks down at the leather cut, then takes it. "Thanks."

"As your brother and your attorney," Mike continues, "I don't think you should go home today. I think... all of us think you should sleep at the castle tonight. Just don't go home yet."

Looking him in the eyes, Jacob says, "You know I can't do that."

"Yeah, I know. Just don't do anything crazy on your own. I know you've had a lot of time to think. We're still trying to find who did this."

Jacob jerks his chin in the direction of the Escalade. "Are you going to just stand there, or are you going to help me get my bike down off the trailer?"

The two men roll the bike down the ramp and Jacob slides his arms through his New Kings cut. As he starts his bike, Mike tells him over the sound of the engine, "Wolf and Hammer made sure she was serviced and ready to ride."

"Purrs like a lion. I'll come by the castle later."

"Good. We're having court at seven thirty."

As Jacob rides away, he calls back, "I'll be there."

Jacob pulls out into traffic on Copper Loop as Mike says out loud to himself, "And the Crow flies again." Then he looks down at his dress shirt, notes the appearance of several grease stains, and says, "Shit!"

Jacob arrives in the New Mexico town of Lost Valley. It is a small town of fewer than five hundred people, an hour northwest of Las Cruces off New Mexico Highway 152. His first stop is the Sand Lake Cemetery, a historical location with graves dating back to the Indian Wars. Walking across the lawn, he stops by a gravesite with fresh flowers on top of the tombstone. He looks around before picking up the flowers. As he is about to walk away, he notices the words on the gravestone: "beloved wife." Jacob looks down at the flowers, removes one, and places the rest back on the stone. Following the directions he was given by his biker brother Lee Tanner, who grew up with him and has always been his closest friend, he locates Maria's grave. As he steps before her tombstone, the physical reality of her death brings him to his knees.

He speaks, kneeling over her grave as tears began rolling down his cheeks. "Maria, I am so sorry... I am sorry I wasn't there to protect you. I should have been there... I don't know how to do this without you." After several moments of silence, suddenly as a light switch, Jacob stops crying and stands as his strength overtakes his grief. He places the lone flower on her tombstone as he kisses his hand and taps the top of the monument.

Leaving the cemetery, Jacob rides his Harley to his house in Lost Valley. Once his childhood home, it passed to him when he was only eighteen following his father's death. Bob McGuire spent his entire adult life as the ranch foreman at the Campbell Ranch. The position allowed Bob to provide a modest life for himself and his family, though they were not wealthy.

Entering the house immediately, Jacob smells the familiar scent of candles that Maria kept throughout their home. He walks down the hall to their bedroom, where he can see bleach stains on the carpet. His heart sinks as the realization hits him that the bleach was most likely used to clean up the crime scene. He takes a seat in front of Maria's vanity. Staring into the mirror, his mind drifts back to the days he would walk by the bedroom door and see her sitting at the mirror in her nightgown brushing her long dark hair. He can never forget the smile she would flash at him when she caught him staring at her from the doorway.

Jacob's memories of Maria are interrupted by his half-brother Thomas McGuire's voice coming from down the hall. Thomas is much shorter than Jacob, standing only five foot seven. He has light brown curly hair with freckles on his face.

Thomas walks in, seeing Jacob at the vanity. Jacob stands up, and Thomas hugs him saying, "I heard you were getting out today. I figured you would have called me by now."

"I've had a lot on my plate. It's good to see you."

"I am so sorry about Maria, and—"

Jacob interrupts him, "Yeah, thanks."

"So are you going to be staying here?"

"No, not right now. I think I'll stay at the castle for a few days." He looks around the room at some of Thomas's things. "Looks like you have been staying here, though."

"Yeah, I crash here every now and then. I hope that's okay." Jacob doesn't answer as he begins going through his closet. Thomas asks, "You know the people who broke in took Dad's gold coins?"

"Yeah, I know. I knew I should have put all of them into the safety deposit box." Jacob opens a secret compartment in the closet ceiling, pulls out a Beretta 92FS 9mm handgun, and places it in the waistline in the back of his jeans.

"You mean there were more?"

"Yeah," Jacob tells him as he pulls a shoulder harness holster out of one of his dresser drawers. He takes off his cut and puts it on underneath.

"Well, that's good, right? They didn't get them all."

Jacob angrily responds, "No, Thomas, there is nothing good about any of this."

"I'm sorry, bro. I didn't mean it like that."

Calmer, Jacob says, "Yeah, I know."

Thomas looks at his watch. "Hey, I need to get going. Call me later, bro. Maybe we can grab a bite at the cafe and catch up."

Jacob grabs some clothes from the house, placing them in a black duffle bag, and gets back on his Harley.

Arriving at the metal warehouse that the club calls their castle a little before seven thirty, he is greeted by all eleven of his charter's brothers, plus their prospect Rob Walker. Each of his brothers—Mike "Yale" White, Lee "Ranger" Tanner, Robert "Prez" Pierce, Jimmy "Smitty" or "VP" Smith, Bobby "Doc" Rush, Eddie "Circus" Reed, Eric "Smokey" Thompson, Jeff "Hammer" McGhee, Phil "Snake" Peterson, Henry "Wolf" Wolfe, and Joe "Joeronimo" Solomon—hug him.

Lee is the first to greet him. "I missed you, brother."

Prez chimes in next. "Son, it is good to have you back. I know after everything that happened, it wasn't an easy decision. I wasn't sure you would return. You have sacrificed much for this club. I know we let you down, but we will make it as right as we can. Love you, son."

Jacob shakes his head. "Thanks. I wasn't sure I would return until Yale offered me my cut."

"We will find the bastards who did this to you," Smitty says.

"We will find them before the cops do," Hammer adds. "I promise you, brother."

"Come on inside," Doc says, "and we will catch you up with all the club business you missed."

Lee puts his arm around Jacob as they walk inside. "Let's go to court, brother."

Entering the building, which inside resembles a typical downtown dive bar, they are met by a large group of girlfriends, wives, and hang-arounds who are all gathered to greet Jacob. They start yelling, "Welcome home!"

Smiling, Jacob humbly lowers his head. "Thanks, guys."

"Welcome home, brother," Lee says. "I knew you wouldn't come if we didn't tell you we were having court."

The prospect begins pouring drinks for everyone. After a few shots of Jägermeister, Prez speaks up. "Bring out his present!"

Suddenly a stripper they all know from Las Cruces comes out in lingerie. Wolf announces, "It's Trixie!"

"Not a bad present, huh, brother?" Smokey adds.

Trixie, a tall, thin blonde, walks over to Jacob, kisses him on the lips, and says, "Welcome home, baby."

Keeping his smile, Jacob lowers his head, leans over, and whispers in her ear, "I am going to take you by the hand, lead you to my room in the back. There is a back door. I want you to go home to your kids, Trixie. Be with your family. I won't let anyone know. Cool?"

Trixie humbly nods her head yes, and Jacob takes her hand and leads her to the back while everyone is whistling and cheering him on.

Stepping out of his bedroom at the castle the next morning, Jacob is greeted by Lee asking, "So, how was it?"

"How was what?"

"Trixie."

Playing along, Jacob says, "Yeah, yeah, it was great."

"Trixie is always a nice treat."

The prospect walks up and nervously says to Jacob, "Hey, Crow. You have a phone call."

Jacob waits for him to continue. "Well, prospect, who the fuck is it?"

"Sorry, I'll ask."

Lee looks at Jacob, shrugging his shoulders. "He's a son of one of Wolf's friends. He's still learning."

After asking, the prospect comes back and says, "It's Henry Campbell."

"Okay, I'll take it." Jacob takes the phone from the prospect at the bar. "This is Jacob. How are you doing, Henry?"

Henry Campbell is the owner of the Campbell Ranch, which was started by his grandfather. It's a little over

156,000 acres just east of Lost Valley. Whenever asked, Henry will tell you the exact size: 156,214 acres. Since Jacob's father worked as Henry's foreman, Jacob spent most of his childhood there. Henry answers, "Doing well, son. I hear you just got out."

"Yes, sir."

"I have a job you might be interested in. My last foreman did not work out well, and I'm looking for someone to replace his position. Would you be interested?"

Excitedly Jacob responds, "Yes, yes sir, I would."

"Good. Your father was an excellent foreman, and I know you worked a lot with him. You probably know this ranch better than anyone still around except me. I was thinking, if you'd like, you could move in here. This house has eight bedrooms, and I'm the only one here these days. Or you could stay in the guesthouse if you felt uncomfortable being in the big house." Henry chuckles. "I guess the term 'big house' is not your favorite phrase to hear these days, is it?"

Jacob laughs back. "No sir, it isn't."

"Whatever you want to do, son. I just need you to start tomorrow."

Even though he needs to get some answers about Maria's death, he also needs some steady work. "Yes, sir," Jacob says. "I will be there in the morning."

"Okay, good. See you at 5:00 a.m."

Rolling his eyes about the start time, he responds, "Okay, see you then." He hangs up and looks over to Lee. "I need to get with you guys about Maria's case."

"I'll try and gather what we found and get it to you, brother," Lee says. "It's not much."

Jacob hugs Lee, saying anxiously, "Anything is a start. Thanks, brother."

THE LEAVERS

A week later, Faith Campbell is entering 4 Times Square, formerly known as the Condé Nast Building. It is a forty-eight-story high-rise located on Broadway, between West Forty-Second and West Forty-Third Street, in the Theater District of Midtown Manhattan. Faith is a twenty-eight-year-old senior fashion editor for *High Style/My Style Magazine*. Originally from New Mexico, she attended New Mexico State in Las Cruces, earning her degree in journalism and mass communications with a minor in marketing. After she lost her mother to ovarian cancer at the age of twelve, she was raised solely by her father on the family ranch, which is one of the largest in New Mexico. Escaping the slow pace of her Southwest nest, she grew her wings and landed in the heart of New York. Faith worked her way to the top, mainly due to her career-driven attitude and the hard work ethic she learned from her father. With her long blonde hair and blue eyes, she could have easily gone into modeling if it weren't for her height of only five feet four inches.

Greeting her in the lobby is her best friend and assistant editor, Erica Thomas. Towering over Faith at six feet, Erica was a fashion model before transitioning over to the industry's corporate side. Like her friend, she has blonde hair and blue eyes, but she is a year younger at twenty-seven.

"Morning," Erica says to Faith. "Did you get my email? They want us to sign off on the new fall line."

"Yes, I did."

"Well?"

"It isn't there yet. I just don't feel like it is complete. I feel there's something we're still missing."

"What is it?"

"I don't know. If I did, it would be ready to present. Give Perry a call and see where we're at."

The two women step onto the elevator and head up to the twenty-second floor. "Do you want to go to dinner tonight?" Erica asks.

"I would, but I already have plans."

"Hot date with Steven?"

Faith laughs at her as they walk out onto their floor in different directions. She calls over her shoulder, "I'll let you know what I come up with."

While walking to her office, Faith is stopped by Cynthia, her secretary. Cynthia hands her two messages. "Your father called again, and Steven called to confirm dinner with you tonight at seven."

"Thank you."

Steven Rice is Faith's boyfriend, with whom she has become quite serious. Dedicating herself solely to her career has left her with little time for a social life and even less time for romance, however. Entering her office, Faith hangs her jacket on the coat rack and gazes out her window, which overlooks Times Square. She turns to her desk, where she picks up her phone and dials her father's number.

"Hello," Henry says.

"Hey, Daddy." Faith sits down. "I heard you had called."

"Yes, sweetheart."

"How are you doing?"

"Well, some days I feel like the truck, and some days I feel like the roadkill. Today the roadkill takes the prize."

"I'm sorry, Daddy."

"Oh, don't feel bad for me. You're the reason I called. I haven't heard from you for a few days and was starting to worry."

"I'm okay."

"Like I always said, you have to be careful there in the big city."

Faith smiles. "Okay, Dad, why did you really call? Let me

guess. You want me to find a guy, settle down, and give you some grandchildren?"

"Well, I'm not getting any younger, and neither are you."

"Daddy, when the time and the person are right, it will happen. Don't worry. One day you will have grandchildren. I promise."

"Okay, I was just worried since I haven't heard from you. You be careful there. I love you, sweetheart."

"I love you too, Daddy." Faith says as she hangs up the phone. Her father calls and tells her once a week to settle down, but Faith knows that right now in her life she has too much to accomplish to be able to give the necessary attention to having a family.

That evening, Steven picks her up in a cab at her Manhattan apartment. They head to the restaurant One if by Land, Two if by Sea for dinner. Called the most romantic restaurant in the city, the brick facade building has quite the history. More than an elegant place to eat with a baby grand piano, multiple fireplaces, chandeliers throughout, and a private garden, 17 Barrow Street was once a carriage house back in the 1790s belonging to the then-attorney general of the state of New York, Aaron Burr.

While waiting for their table, they enjoy a cocktail at the bar by the two fireplaces near the piano. Once they are seated in the Constitution Room, at the table closest to the fireplace, beside the bust of Washington, they both order the same entree they always do—beef wellington.

While waiting for their food, Steven looks into Faith's eyes from across the table and says, "Faith, I think you know how much I care for you. How much I love you." He removes a small box from his jacket and places it on the white tablecloth between them, beside the lit candle and her glass of wine. "I want you to know those things for the rest of our lives." A look of surprise shines brightly on Faith's face, changing quickly over to a look of fear and expectation. "Faith, will you marry me?"

For a moment, she is speechless as her mind processes the life-altering decision thrust at her without warning to make in only seconds. She finally responds softly, "Yes...." Then, smiling and much surer of her choice, she repeats, "Yes, yes, yes."

"Great," Steven says. "I already told my parents."

"You did? Aren't you supposed to ask my father before yours?"

"I didn't ask. I told them."

"What if I would have said no?"

Smiling, Steven says, "I knew what your answer would be." He holds out his glass of wine to meet hers. "To a beautiful marriage with lots of children."

Taken aback for a moment as their glasses clink together, she uncomfortably responds, "Yes... cheers."

The next morning at her office, she calls for Erica to come to see her. Entering her office, Erica says, "What's up? Did you finally decide on the fall lineup?"

"No, no. I had a lot more on my mind. Steven proposed to me last night."

"Oh my god! What did you say?"

Looking at Erica with a what-the-hell look, she says, "What do you mean? I said yes."

"I just know how career-minded you are," Erica says, sitting down, "and how your father keeps pushing you to settle down, and you always say you aren't ready yet."

"I know, but in life, you have to sometimes do things that scare you to grow."

Erica looks dubious. "Who are you, and what did you do with my friend?"

"What do you mean?"

"Remember, you're the person who has eaten the same thing for breakfast twenty years straight. You're the person who only walks the same path in Central Park each time. You're the person who won't walk over a sidewalk grid or manhole cover."

"Well," Faith says, tossing her head, "that is a matter of safety, an unnecessary risk."

Erica goes on, "You are—"

"Okay, enough. I get your point. I think it's time I start taking chances."

"*Chances* are odds gambling in Vegas, not deciding who you will spend the rest of your life with."

Faith hesitates. With a look of concern, she asks, "Do you think I made the wrong decision?"

"That's not for me to decide. Only you know the answer to that." Erica looks at her watch. "We have a nine o'clock meeting in the conference room, don't forget."

Faith checks the time too. "Crap, I almost forgot. I need to call my dad real quick and give him the news. He'll be quite happy, I'm sure."

"Okay, I need to grab my iPad and will see you there."

"Okay." Faith dials her phone to give her dad the good news. The phone rings several times before going to his answering machine. She hangs up and says out loud, "I will just have to try again after the meeting."

During the meeting in the conference room, Faith's presentation is interrupted by Cynthia, who pokes her head in to say, "Excuse me, Ms. Campbell, I have an important phone call for you."

With everyone's attention on her, Faith responds, "Cynthia, you know not to interrupt a meeting."

"I know, Ms. Campbell, but they said it was important."

Faith addresses the staff seated around the conference room table. "Everyone, I apologize. I need to take a call. I'll be right back. Erica, will you continue for me?"

Erica, taken off guard, stands up. "Yes."

"Thanks." Walking out of the room with Cynthia, Faith tells her, "Transfer it to my office." Once she is at her desk, she pushes the extension where the call is parked. "Hello, this is Faith."

The voice on the other end is unexpectedly familiar. "Faith, this is your Aunt Barbara. Sweetie, I have some bad news. Your father left us late last night."

"What do you mean, *left?*" Faith asks, even though she already knows the answer.

"He died in his sleep, sweetie. The doctors think it was a heart attack. I am so sorry."

Stunned, Faith stumbles out the words, "Me too, Aunt Barbara. Me too."

"The funeral home is picking up his body from the hospital this morning. I will let you know what I hear from them… Faith, are you still there?"

"Yes, Aunt Barbara. I'm still here… Yes, please get me the details, and I will get a flight out there as fast as I can. I will have to fly into El Paso since there are no direct flights to Las Cruces."

"Do you want me to pick you up there at the airport?"

"No, I'll rent a car. Thank you anyway."

"Again, I'm sorry, sweetie. I'll see you when you arrive."

"I'll call you when I get there. Bye, Aunt Barbara."

"Bye, baby."

Faith releases the call and starts to cry as she looks at a picture she keeps on her desk of herself as a little girl dressed in overalls with her dad on the ranch. It reminds her of the day she left to start her career in New York.

After graduating from New Mexico State, Faith secured an assistant position in the editorial department of *High Style/My Style Magazine* in New York. At twenty-one, she confidently felt she knew everything about life. Her father was loading her luggage into the back of his truck parked in front of their New Mexico ranch home. The day was especially hard for Henry. Not only was he sending his only child out into the world, across the country, but today also would have been his and his deceased wife's thirtieth wedding anniversary.

Walking back inside, he called out to Faith, "Sweetie, do you want me to make breakfast for you?" Henry had made breakfast for his daughter every morning since her mother first got sick.

"No, Daddy," Faith replied as she came downstairs, "not today. I want to get to the airport early." As she arrived in the kitchen, she could see the sadness in her father's eyes. Remembering that today would have been her parents' anniversary, she walked up to him and said, "Daddy, I think I will have that breakfast." A tear rolled down the cheek of a man she had seen cry only once before—the day her mother died.

After breakfast and a long drive to the airport, Henry said goodbye to his little girl.

Faith hugged him. "Daddy, I'll be back. Don't be sad. I'll come home every year, I promise."

"You do that. I'll make you breakfast." Faith laughed and received a smile from him. "Now, you be careful. New York City is a big place. Call me as soon as you get there."

"I will, Daddy. I love you."

"I love you too, sweetie."

"Bye, Daddy."

"Bye, my angel," Henry said as Faith made her way to her terminal.

Once in New York, life took over, and Faith did not make good on her promise; she made only two trips back home over the next seven years. Henry held up his end, however, by making her breakfast each time.

As she sits at her desk staring at the photograph, Faith now realizes that when we are young, we often rush life, even at the expense of cherished moments whose true value we understand only in later years.

Her memories are interrupted by Erica walking into her office, asking, "What the hell happened? I had to finish the rest of the presentation for you."

Despite an attempt to be her typical strong self—something she learned from Henry—Faith begins to cry anew. "My father died last night."

Erica runs behind Faith's desk and hugs her. "Oh Faith, I am so sorry."

"I need to get a flight."

Erica, trying to comfort her, says, "Of course. Let me take care of it. I'll let you know when it is booked."

Struggling to keep it together, Faith says, "Thank you. I need to tell Steven."

"I'm going to go get the flight. Will you be okay?"

"Yes. Thank you." As Erica leaves, Faith dials out to Cynthia's desk.

Cynthia answers, "Yes, ma'am?"

"Cynthia, please cancel all my appointments for the next week. I have to fly out to New Mexico. Erica will fill in for me while I am out. If you need to reach me, please use my cell and follow up with an email in case I don't have a signal." Faith hangs up with Cynthia and dials another number.

Steven answers, "Hello, beautiful."

Still trying to keep the tears at bay, she tells him, "My father died last night, and I need to fly back home."

"Oh Faith, I am so sorry. What can I do? Do you want me to fly out with you?"

"No, no, you don't have to. I know how busy you are. I'll let you know about the funeral plans, and you can come out then. I'll need to run home, grab some things, and go. I probably won't see you before I leave."

"Okay, baby. I love you."

"I love you too, goodbye."

Faith catches a flight from JFK to El Paso, Texas. Gazing out the airplane window, she reflects on the little time she had with her mother and the gratitude she feels for the years she has spent with her father. However, in the back of her mind, she wonders if this is simply her way of ignoring the guilt she has for what few trips she made back home.

Upon arriving in El Paso, Faith rents a car and drives the two hours to the ranch. Along the drive, she is captivated by the beauty of the red New Mexico sky at sunset, just now realizing how much she has missed the sight.

WHEN WORLDS COLLIDE

It is nightfall by the time Faith reaches the entrance to the Campbell Ranch. The ranch's land size is as impressive as always; however, since she flew away to New York, the activity has diminished much over the years, with now less than a thousand head of bison remaining.

She drives the ten miles down the winding, paved private driveway until she reaches the large ranch house. Much of the two-story adobe home exterior is glass, allowing gorgeous views of the surrounding mountains and hillsides.

The villa is dark as she parks by the fountain in the circle driveway outside the front doors, which are massive at thirteen feet tall. As she enters the house, the familiar smell of home delivers a rush of memories. Standing in the foyer, the realization takes hold of Faith that her father is no longer there to greet her.

Walking through the dark kitchen, passing by the refrigerator on her way to turn on the light, she walks directly into Jacob, who is in a black T-shirt and jeans. She screams, shoves her Louis Vuitton purse toward him, and says, "Here, you can have my purse! Take it!"

"No thanks," Jacob responds, "I think it might clash with my outfit."

"What do you want then? Please don't hurt me!"

"Just a beer from the fridge."

In confusion, Faith turns to the refrigerator behind her. "A beer?"

She steps out of the way as Jacob reaches past to open the fridge and grab a beer off the top shelf. He asks, "How are you holding up, Faith?"

"How do you know my name?"

"Your aunt told me you were on your way. Don't you remember me? We used to play together as kids. By the way, my condolences about your father. He was a really good man."

"Jacob?" She relaxes. "Oh my god, Jacob McGuire? You're all grown up."

"You should look in the mirror sometime. You are too."

"But what are you doing in the house?"

"I'm the ranch foreman now. I live in the guesthouse, but your Aunt Barbara thought it would be a good idea to stay here and keep it safe until you arrive since most of the state has heard about Henry's passing. Do you want a beer? I have plenty in the fridge."

"No, no, I don't want a beer. Where is your car? There wasn't one parked outside."

"I ride a bike. I don't have a car."

"You ride a bicycle?"

Laughing, Jacob answers, "No, my motorcycle."

Seeing all the tattoos on his arms, Faith asks in a superior tone, "So are you one of those biker people?"

Again laughing at her, he says, "Yeah, something like that. Are you always this friendly these days?"

Not sounding sincere, she responds, "I'm sorry. I just didn't expect to find a strange man in my home."

"Well, I can't be that strange. Your father offered me the opportunity to live in the house, but I chose the guesthouse. I've only been here a little over a week, but he really made me feel at home. He even made me breakfast every morning."

"Breakfast?"

"Yeah. Avocado toast. Strange, but pretty good. He insisted, and I didn't want to upset him."

Faith is taken aback. That is the same breakfast her father always made for her all these years. She wonders whether he was missing her so much that he made it for someone else, wishing they were her.

"As I said, I chose to live in the guesthouse, which is

where I need to head since you are here now." Reaching around her once more, Jacob says, "Excuse me." He opens the fridge and takes out the rest of his beers. "You sure you don't want one?"

Annoyed, she replies, "Yes, I'm sure."

"Well, good night then. If you need anything, I will be right next door." He exits through the back door and heads back to the guesthouse, an A-line structure with an upstairs loft approximately a hundred feet from the family home.

The following morning Faith walks into the kitchen in her nightgown that drifts down to her knees, rubbing her eyes. Seeing Jacob, she screams and covers herself with her hands, trying to be modest. "What are you doing in here!?"

Jacob turns to face her, smiling at her attempt to cover parts of her body already concealed by her gown. In his hands are plates for both of them with avocado and kiwi toast. "I thought you might want some breakfast." He places the plates on the wooden dining table.

Recognizing his effort and remembering the last person to fix her breakfast in this kitchen was her father, she feels a little guilty about yelling at him. Cautiously sitting down, she says, "Thank you."

Jacob sits down opposite her. "You weren't this nervous about being around me when we played cowboys and Indians as children, even that time when I tied you to the tree."

"It's just… I'm engaged, and I'm not sure how I feel being alone in my home with another man."

"Faith, believe me, you don't have to worry about that with me. That I can promise you."

"Why, are you gay?"

Jacob spits out his coffee. "No, I am not gay. Surely you aren't that arrogant."

"What do you mean?"

"Do you actually believe that every man you meet wants to have sex with you?"

"Well, it seems like it."

"I stand corrected. Maybe you are."

Faith sees a poster board on the counter filled to all four corners with a pinned map, addresses, lines, photos, and names. It reminds her of something from the television show *CSI*. "What is this?"

Jacob goes from friendly to defensive. "Nothing! Please stay away from it. I need to move it back out to the guesthouse."

Faith knows she has found something intriguing about Jacob. Something he is hiding. Her corporate instinct has taught her to look for things that give her leverage over someone else by knowing what pushes their buttons. She sees a certain name scrawled about everywhere and says, "So who is Maria? Someone you're stalking?"

Jacob rises, kicking his chair out from under him. He grabs his things, leaving his breakfast, and walks out, slamming the door behind him.

Faith sits there stunned, watching him stride toward the guesthouse, as her emotions go from curiosity to fear.

Following Jacob's blowup, Faith drives to the nearby town of Truth or Consequences to the funeral home where Henry's body is located. After making the remainder of the funeral arrangements, she calls Steven and Erica, notifying them of the services being held three days later, on Saturday. Erica lets her know she will be there Friday on the same flight as Steven.

Arriving back to the ranch while Jacob is out with the bison, Faith decides to try and find out more about his mysterious life. Entering the guesthouse, she first sees his leather cut, which is hanging up. Having a personal obsession with leather, no doubt received from growing up on a ranch, she cannot resist pressing it against her nose and inhaling its scent. Flipping it around, Faith admires the large patch on the back. At the top is what motorcycle clubs call a rocker—a patch with Jacob's club name, the New Kings. Below the top rocker is a skull wearing a crown. Underneath the skull are motorcycle handles that look more like the hilt of a claymore sword. The handle bars lead to the motorcycle's front, which is a medieval shield sporting the crest of a knight's helmet. At the bottom is another rocker; this one is the territory, New Mexico. Over the heart is a patch that reads *Crow*, and right above that is a diamond shape with *1%er* inside it. There are four other patches: one on the back, an *MC*, and three more on the front, the letters *F.E.A.R.*, the number *13*, and a Bible verse—Matthew 12:30.

Next, her attention is drawn to the poster board and map that earlier made him so angry. Faith's curiosity now is getting the best of her. She is determined to find out who this Maria is. Beside the map is a pair of black horn-rimmed reading glasses with one arm missing. Looking through some papers Jacob has lying around, she stumbles across his prison release and probation documents. Faith says aloud, "Holy shit… Just got released from prison for aggravated battery with a lethal weapon. Jesus."

She hears a farm truck pulling up outside, and she knows she needs to get out of there quickly. She rushes to place everything back the way it was. As she opens the door, Jacob is standing there staring at her.

"Can I help you find something?" he says.

"Yes. I mean, no. I mean, I was looking for you."

Entering the guesthouse, Jacob tells her, "Well, here I am." Looking her in the eye, he asks, "Well, what do you want?" before scanning the room to see what he left out.

Faith says, stumbling, "Well, I–I was hoping you could follow me to Truth or Consequences to return my rent-a-car." With an uncomfortable laugh, she adds, "Then I remembered you don't have a car, but then I thought you could drive one of the farm trucks."

"I do have a bike."

"Yes, I know, but I've never ridden on one."

"No better time than the present. Unless you're scared of them… or me."

"No, not at all," says Faith, avoiding his eyes. "If you don't mind, you can follow me, and I can ride back with you."

"I don't mind."

Walking out the door, she says, "Well, good then. I just need to grab my purse."

"Next time you want to know anything about me, Faith," he says after her, "just ask."

Faith looks back at him. "Well, we both have seen how that works out."

After dropping off the keys to her rental, she walks over to Jacob's bike. He asks, "So, you ready to ride?"

Feeling reluctant—after having already paid for an entire week on the rental and wishing she had made up a better lie for being caught in the guesthouse—she says, "I guess so."

Motioning with his head, he tells her, "Always get on and off the left-hand side." As she climbs on the Harley, he gives her his black dome-shaped Skid Lid helmet to wear. "Here, put this on."

"Are you sure *you* don't need this?"

"I'm sure. Hopefully, neither of us will need it." Jacob pulls his black neck gaiter up to just under his eyes. It sports the white image of a skull from the nose down. Sensing her anxiety, he tells her, "Don't be so nervous. You're safe with me. I've been riding a long time."

"I am more worried about the other cars on the road than you," says Faith.

Jacob starts his bike and says over the rumbling sound, "Good. You're already learning an important part about riding, and we haven't even left yet. Place your arms around my waist."

"What?"

"Place your arms around my waist." Thoughts of Steven pass through her mind as she cautiously places her arms around Jacob. "As you feel me lean, I want you to lean with me in the same direction. Don't lean on your own. Just follow my lead. Make sure you get comfortable. You can't be wiggling. Okay, hold on. Here we go."

Leaving the rent-a-car dealership, Faith's spirit is lifted by the New Mexico breeze blowing through her hair on her first motorcycle ride. Flying through the evening air makes her temporarily forget what has brought her home. The only experience that could even compare was racing her horse Cinder across the plains as a child.

When they arrive home that evening, Jacob parks his bike and walks off to the guesthouse. Watching him go, Faith calls out, "Hey, would you like to have a glass of wine or a beer on the patio?"

Jacob swings around and pauses before answering, knowing he has research to do but realizing it would be nice to have a break. "Sure, why not."

"Good. I really don't feel like being alone right now, sorry."

"Let me clean up, and I'll come over afterward."

"Cool. By the way, nice bike."

Jacob, surprised by her compliment, smiles at her. "I know."

A half-hour later, he joins Faith on the rock patio at the back of the house, with the mountains still visible in the setting sun's light. She has a glass of wine already poured for herself and an empty glass for him. As Jacob walks up to where she is seated, she says, "I wasn't sure if you wanted wine or not."

Jacob has a beer in his hand that he opens with a bottle opener as he sits down. "Not much of a wine drinker."

"I kind of figured that. You are still welcome to join me with some wine. God knows we have an entire cellar of it."

"What about this?" He pours some of his beer into the wine glass instead of drinking from the bottle. "How's that?"

"That'll work."

Jacob takes a drink and says, "Faith, your father was a good man. He took care of my father through some really hard years. Also, a little over a week ago, he gave me a second chance. I'm pretty sure you found out about that when you went through my stuff."

"About that… I'm really sorry."

"Really sorry you looked, or really sorry you got caught?"

"Both, I guess."

"I respect that answer. Honesty is a lost quality these days."

"So…" Faith looks into her glass. "What did you do to get locked up?"

"That is a complicated question with an even more complicated answer. If I told you, I would have to kill you." Faith's face shows the same fear it did when Jacob blew up at her earlier that morning. Then he smiles, making her feel comfortable again. "There's a smaller MC"—"

"An MC?"

"Motorcycle Club."

"Gotcha. Sorry, go ahead."

Jacob continues, "The MC I am speaking of is the War Wolves. Just seven ex-military guys in Las Cruces who, like us, love bikes. We, the New Kings, had been meeting with them about a patch over."

She asks, "A patch over?"

"Yes, a patch over is when one MC, let's say, incorporates another MC. Like in this situation, we were going to allow them to join our charter and become Kings. In the MC world, territory and numbers mean power."

"Sounds like the fashion world," Faith says.

Jacob chuckles. "Uh, yeah...Well, one of our rival clubs, the Desert Suns out of Las Cruces, got news of the patch over possibility. The Suns are originally from Mexico. They're only in Mexico, Southern California, New Mexico, and Arizona. Well, they showed up at the strip club ran by the Wolves. The Suns beat the Wolves president pretty bad. So bad he ended up losing sight in his right eye."

"Oh my god."

"Well, I was the only King available in town at the time when they called for help. When I arrived, there were only two Suns still there tearing up the place. I went in with my gun, and..."

She asks breathlessly, "Did you kill them?"

"No, no, I didn't kill them. You watch too much television. But I did shoot the toe off one of them and knocked the other one out cold with the grip of my gun. The toe thing was not intentional. I was firing a warning shot on the ground, and he stepped into it. Unfortunately for me, though, the Sheriff's Department arrived on the scene, and I, as well as the two Suns, was arrested. I got three years, but the Suns got five each for possession of narcotics with intent to sell as well as assault. We tried fighting it, saying it was self-defense, but the judge was determined to make an example of me. I served eighteen months." Jacob suddenly gets somber and stops short.

"So, what is it like being in prison?"

After a long pause, he replies, "For me, the hardest part was being away from and not being able to protect my family, and the lack of freedom. Being a King, I had protection on the inside, but the lack of freedom, the endless days and nights that give you too long to think, that was hard. I had a lot to think about." He pauses in reflection, staring at his beer. "Some guys in MCs who get locked up don't return to their clubs when they get out. I had plenty of reasons not to return, but the only family I have left is the club... and always will be."

After an uncomfortable stretch of silence, Faith asks, "Who is Maria?"

Jacob just sits there staring directly into her eyes, not blinking or saying a word. After a minute, he says, "Next question."

Faith respects his reluctance to answer the question, and without pressing him asks, "The patches on your vest, what do they mean?"

"It's called a cut. The vest is a cut."

"So on the cut, what does *F.E.A.R.* mean? Does it mean you are afraid of something, or I should fear you?"

"No, I am not afraid."

"You aren't afraid of anything?" she asks skeptically. "Surely something scares you."

"The only thing I am scared of these days, the only thing I think I am afraid of, is that nothing scares me anymore. *F.E.A.R.* stands for 'fuck everyone and ride.'"

"So it means I should fear you?"

"If that is what it means to you, then I guess so. Often what we think we fear in our hearts is only in our minds, though."

She smiles. "Interesting. What about *Matthew 12:30?*"

"It's from the Bible."

"I know that much. It has been a while, though, since I

picked one up."

"Me too… but I know Matthew 12:30. 'Whoever is not with me is against me.'"

"What about the *1%er* patch? There is one on the front and back."

"It means different things to different people. It depends on who you ask and whether or not they will answer. Some say it is because the AMA, American Motorcycle Association, said that 99 percent of the bikers out there are good God-fearing people, and the other 1 percent are hard-riding, hard-living people. Then law enforcement decided to add to that by convincing the public us 1%ers were all violent criminals."

"Well, what does it mean to you, though?"

He pauses before answering, "Next question."

"Really? That's your answer?"

"Listen, I am not a demon, and I am not a saint. I am just a man who lives only to ride his bike."

Faith takes that in for a minute. "And the *13* patch?"

"It's for the thirteenth letter of the alphabet, *M*."

"What does the *M* stand for?"

"Whatever you want it to."

"What does it stand for to you, though?" she challenges.

"Well, *motorcycle* starts with *M*."

"So do several thousand more words." Looking at his hand, she tells him, "I like your ring. What is it? I can't really tell in the low light."

"It's a skull wearing a crown. All New Kings wear one."

"Cool. So what about the name *Crow* on the front of your cut?"

"My mother was a full-blood Crow Indian, or Apsaalooke in her native Siouan language," Jacob tells her. "She was from Montana and had just moved here with her family when she met my father."

"Did she teach you the language?"

"No, she died during my birth. I never met her."

Faith says, "I am so sorry."

"My father told me right as she died she looked me in the eyes, smiled, and gripped my hand. I learned some of the language on my own."

"Will you say something in Crow?"

Jacob smiles and thinks for a moment before picking up his glass and toasting hers, saying, "*Íttaawaalichi.* 'All is good.' I actually speak to her often."

Faith raises her eyebrows at this. "I keep catching myself doing the same thing with my mother and now my father. Do you think they can hear us? Our loved ones who have left us?"

"My mind says no, but my spirit says yes."

"I never knew your mom had died. Wait then, who was Charlotte?"

"She was my stepmom. My dad remarried after my mom died. He and Charlotte were only married for about five years. She was a bad alcoholic. I don't know if you heard, but she's in jail now after killing somebody in a DWI accident."

"Oh my god, that's horrible. So Thomas is your half-brother then?"

"Yep."

After a moment of silence, Faith says, "God, I so miss my dad."

Somberly Jacob says, "I understand what you're going through. It isn't easy when we lose the ones we love. It's even harder when we're not with them to comfort them when they pass."

They both sit silently in reflection of these words, and then Faith asks, "So what is the most important to you in life? God, family…?"

"The club," he answers immediately. "The club comes before God, family, work, anything."

"Interesting. How many New Kings are there?"

"A little over five thousand."

"What!?"

"That's worldwide, over twenty countries."

"Worldwide?"

"Yeah, our club actually started in Scotland, back in the sixties."

"Wow. So how many are here?"

"Here in the Lost Valley area, our chapter has twelve and one prospect."

"A prospect?"

"Someone who wants to become a member but has to go through a process of earning the patch."

"Like an initiation?"

"Kind of, I suppose. There are also hang-arounds. Those are the ones who, just like the name says, like hanging around us."

"Like groupies?"

"Yeah, sure."

Faith then asks, "So tell me, why do guys join a motorcycle club anyway?"

"Honestly, if you have to ask that question, then you really would not understand the answer."

"Speaking of honesty, while I was…." She clears her throat. "Snooping in the guesthouse, I notice you do not have many belongings."

Jacob chuckles. "The only attachment I have is to my bike. That's all I need. I don't have personal items that I can't carry with me on my bike anywhere I go. Commitment is good, attachment is not. The problem with the world today is they have that backward. There's too much attachment and not enough commitment."

"Surely you have something besides your bike that you cherish. Like mine is the first Barbie I got as a child. It's what got me interested in the fashion world. I keep her in a glass case in my office."

"The only possessions I cherish like that besides my bike and my cut would be my dad's straight razor, pocket watch, and reading glasses."

"I noticed the watch."

"That watch has been around a long time. It originally belonged to my great-grandfather."

"Why don't you get it repaired?" she asks.

"No need to. That watch is never wrong."

"But it has no hands."

"That's right. The time is always now. Too many people these days live their lives by clocks instead of their circadian rhythms. Think about it. When you get tired, you go to sleep. When you wake naturally, you are rested. When you are hungry, you eat. You don't need a clock to tell you these things. You will actually feel more relaxed and less stressed, and you'll truly enjoy life more."

"I saw the glasses. They're in pretty rough shape too."

"Yeah, I know. My father always had an answer to everything. He was a hard worker but also a brilliant man. Whenever I get lost and cannot find an answer, I put them on so I can see through his lenses."

Faith stares at Jacob, her respect for him growing every minute. She tells him, "I wish I had something like that from my dad that I could connect with."

"Damn, Faith," he says, "look around you. Look at this ranch. What more do you need?" After a moment of silence, he asks, "So... you've asked me my life's modus operandi. What about yours? What is life like in the fashion world?"

Faith says, "Well, it sounds like our worlds are not that different—we both deal with cutthroats. When I went to college at New Mexico State, I knew I wanted a journalism and fashion career, but I didn't know the path to take. By the time I graduated, I knew New York was where I needed to be, and I knew I wanted to be a senior editor for a fashion magazine. Now I'm twenty-eight and the youngest ever at my company to hold my position. I made it with a lot of hard work and many sacrifices."

Jacob senses some regret in her tone. "But now you made it, you aren't happy. You aren't passionate anymore."

Feeling defensive, she responds, "Why do you say that? I am very happy. I am extremely passionate."

"No, you're not, Faith. Don't mix up happiness with ambition and passion with contentment."

Growing more indignant, she says, "What do you mean?"

"I mean, you were a little girl who had a big dream. That dream came true. You had the ambition to make it happen, but when it did, it didn't make you happy like you thought it would. The passion and desire that got you there has all turned to contentment. In life, contentment will always be the death of desire."

Faith sits there with her glass of wine, totally stunned and speechless. She realizes she has met her psychological match. Jacob just did to her what she has perfected over the years to gain a position of dominance over others in the corporate fashion world. "Wow... So just that quick, you think you know me."

"No, I am just telling you what you already know about yourself." After a moment of silence, trying to lighten the mood, Jacob changes the subject, asking her, "So, considering all these questions you have about the club... Tomorrow night we are having a party. You should come out with me, and I think a lot more of your questions will get answered."

"I don't know. I'm engaged. I can't see me going to a biker party, or any party, with another man."

"Jesus, Faith," he says, "I am not asking you to fucking marry me. Just hang around some pretty cool people who might change a lot of stereotypes of what you think you know."

She sits there tapping her glass, deep in thought. "Sure, what the hell? Why not?"

"Cool. We need to leave around seven tomorrow evening."

She looks at him. "You know, it's amazing… when we were kids, we were just that. Kids. We never asked questions about each other's life. All we wanted was to play."

"Yeah, I've learned more about you since you returned than I ever knew in all those years of playing cowboys and Indians."

She smiles. "So tell me about your tattoos."

"The ones you can see, or all of them?"

"You mean you have more than that?" she says, pointing at his arms.

"Yeah, I'm pretty much covered chest to ankle."

"Well, I definitely don't want you to strip down, so tell me about the visible ones, like that Indian."

Looking down toward his right arm Jacob says, "This is my grandfather. My mom's dad. We found a picture of him, and I had it done. They did a remarkable job. Then this one here is my McGuire family tartan."

"Scottish, nice."

"Yeah, Indians and clans. My family tree is very tribal." She laughs. He looks to his left arm. "This one you know, it's of the Kings just like on my cut. This one"—"

"Do you have any scars?" Leaning forward, she rests her elbow on the table, her palm supporting her chin.

He says, "Yeah, here," lifting his T-shirt and pointing to his right side. "This is where I got stabbed during a fight at a party."

Once she has recovered from the sight of the most perfect abs she has ever laid eyes on, she says, "At a party? Are you sure it's safe to go to this party tomorrow night?"

"Yeah, at this party we will be among friends."

Faith stands up. "You want to see mine?"

Laughing, he says, "Sure."

She lifts her shirt and slightly pulls down her pants, exposing the scar at the top of her left buttock. "This is from when I was a teenager. I was feeding one of the buffalos, and I got distracted. The buffalo moved his head to reach the bucket and gored me. Lucky it wasn't higher or would have gotten my kidneys."

Jacob is smiling. "Ouch!"

"Yeah, that's why from then on, Dad began cutting back their horns. He used to let them grow, he liked the natural look. But when I got hurt, that all changed."

"Ah, it's because of you, I have to risk my life cutting them back. Thanks a lot." He pauses and says, "I couldn't help but notice your little butterfly tattoo." She blushes somewhat. "So what is a high fashion magazine executive doing with a tramp stamp?"

"Hey, watch it. I like my butterfly. You actually should feel honored to have seen it. Very few men ever have."

"No, I definitely feel honored." Jacob looks at his watch and says, "Hey, it's later than I thought. I still need to do some work tonight and have to be up at five."

"Yeah, I need some rest too. Thank you for coming over and talking with me."

Laughing, he says, "Even though you may not have liked all that I said?"

She smiles back. "Yes, even if I didn't like it. It was honest —which, like you said, is something I don't see much of anymore."

They both go to stand simultaneously and collide with

each other, ending up face to face. They both feel the intense heat of attraction as their eyes lock, and their waiting lips rest only inches apart. Faith does not know or understand what has come over her. She feels a sudden desire that progresses from expecting a kiss to wanting, then needing.

Instead, Jacob pulls away, saying, "I need to go." He begins to turn away, then stops. Reaching into his back pocket, he pulls out an envelope. "Here, I almost forgot. This is a letter your aunt gave me to give to you. I believe it's from your dad."

Faith takes the letter slowly from his hands. As he turns to leave, she says to him, "This Maria, you really care for her, don't you?"

Jacob turns his head away, then back to Faith and says, "Yeah, yeah, I do." Then he walks away to the guesthouse.

Later that night, after calling Steven, Faith lies in her old bed with the open letter from her father on her stomach, looking up at the spinning ceiling fan. She is thinking of her father and when he would read to her as a child while watching the spinning blades.

Faith enjoyed getting to know Jacob again, and at the same time is troubled about the feelings that rushed over her earlier. Perhaps this confusion is why Steven kept asking her if she was okay during their phone call.

As Faith is struggling to fall asleep, Jacob is sitting at the table in the guesthouse under the dim light of a lamp, holding his father's reading glasses to his eyes. He is searching through endless police reports and newspaper articles about Maria's case. He lets out a scream of anger and frustration and swings his arm across the table, shoving it all onto the floor. Then he sits there with his elbows on the table and face buried in his hands.

9 781735 970387